Five Things
I Can't Live
Without

Five Things
I Can't Live
Without

Holly Shumas

NEW YORK BOSTON

5 Spot
Hachette Book Group USA
237 Park Avenue
New York, NY 10169

Visit our Web site at www.5-spot.com.

5 Spot is an imprint of Warner Books. The 5 Spot name and logo are trademarks of Warner Books.

Printed in the United States of America
First Edition: July 2007

10 9 8 7 6 5 4 3 2 1

Library of Congress Cataloging-in-Publication Data
    Shumas, Holly.
       Five things I can't live without / Holly Shumas. — 1st ed.
       p. cm.
       Summary: "The witty story of a woman approaching thirty who must abandon her penchant for overanalyzing her life and learn to trust her gut"—Provided by the publisher.
    ISBN: 978-0-446-69906-8
       I. Title.
    PS3619.H865F58 2007
    813'.6—dc22   2006030646

Book design and text composition by Ralph Fowler

Acknowledgments

Many thanks go to:

My parents, who've championed me in my writing and just about everything else. Every year I get more in touch with my sheer good fortune at having been raised by people like these.

My editor, Karen Kosztolnyik, for her enthusiasm and spot-on feedback. The book is much richer for her efforts.

My agent, Stephanie Kip Rostan, who knew when to be fun, when to be frank, and when to hold my hand. She made this process smoother than I ever dared hope.

My tremendous inner circle. It will forever include Alan, for innumerable acts of kindness and for always believing someday I'd arrive here. Avie, for knowing me so long and so well, and for being one of my first readers and supporters. Lisa and Jen, for their unwavering friendship and their great stories. Darla, for being my kindred spirit and confidante extraordinaire. And Tara—what role haven't you played to perfection for me this past year? Miss Y, you are nothing short of magnificent.

C.S. If only I got to write all my endings . . . Much gratitude for the ways you made my manuscript (and me) better.

My grandparents, those who are here and those who've gone. Especially Zayde, who, when I was seven, told me someday I'd write the great American novel. (Well, it's American, and it's a novel.) And to Pop-Pop, my favorite character ever.

Five Things
I Can't Live
Without

Chapter 1

NORA

Age:	29
Height:	5'6"
Weight:	130 lbs
Occupation:	Animal biographer
About me:	Under construction
About you:	Under construction
Last book I read:	*Can Love Last?: The Fate of Romance Over Time*
Biggest turn-on:	Under construction
Biggest turnoff:	Under construction
Five things I can't live without:	Under construction
Most embarrassing moment:	The window incident

Here's when I knew it had gone too far.

My kitchen window was stuck, and I was trying to open it. No mental gymnastics required, just simple physical action. There I was, starting to sweat with the effort, and the normal reaction would be, *Wow, this is harder to open than I thought*, possibly accompanied by some annoyance. Maybe the normal person would have been dimly aware that it smelled ever so faintly like cat turds because it was an unusually hot day and the litter box was sitting directly under the kitchen window—a spot that had been chosen because, in theory, that window opens while the living room "windows" are just floor-to-ceiling panes of glass. And the normal person might even go so far as to think what a glaring design flaw that is in an otherwise pretty decent apartment. What the normal person *wouldn't* do is what I did. Which was to think all those things, plus:

Why is everything always so hard? Why can't anything just open for me? Maybe this window is the symbol, and this is the key moment in my life. Maybe this is who I am and who I'll always be: some neurotic twenty-nine-year-old woman living with a roommate and her roommate's obese cat, not even having what it takes to commit to a cat of her own, or what it takes to open a window.

But that's not true. I won't always be twenty-nine. And in two weeks, I'll be living with Dan. Poor Dan. He doesn't deserve this crap, all the crap involved in living with me, living with me while I live in my head.

Oh, man! That's what this is! This is me, living in my head right now. Stop it! Sometimes a window is just a window. Stop it! Why can't I just perform a simple physical action without stepping outside of myself and wondering about it all?

Stop asking yourself questions!

All the while, as I careened from irritation to despair to rage, I was tugging at the window. It must have been the adrenaline from my anger that made the window suddenly yield. The cooling breeze rushed in and I thought, *Well, that should feel nice.*

I slumped to the kitchen floor just as the phone rang.

"Hey, you." It was Dan.

"Hey," I said, slightly dazed from the physical and mental exertion that had just taken place.

"You sound funny. What's going on?"

"I'd feel silly if I told you." I felt silly anyway. "What's going on with you?"

"I just got a lead on some moving boxes. This obsessive guy I work with actually breaks down and stores all his moving boxes in his garage, and he said he'll loan them to us." I noted how upbeat Dan sounded. He's one of those people who enjoys the little things, doesn't sweat the small stuff, etc.

"Meaning we have to return them?" I said. Yes, I generally do sweat the small stuff, sometimes quite literally. I wiped the back of my hand across my forehead.

"Yeah. And we can't write on them, either. You know how normally you write in Magic Marker, 'kitchen' or 'bedroom'? Well, we need to work with the existing writing. If it says 'bedroom' on it, that's where you're packing your socks."

"Okay," I said. "Cool!" I realized I was overcompensating; no one sounds that enthusiastic about used moving boxes. On loan.

"Nora, what's wrong?" Dan's voice was somehow warm and expressionless at once. He was remarkable that way. Even-keeled, that's what my mother had said when I first told her about him. She'd said it approvingly. She thought I needed someone like that "to balance me out," like my stepfather, Ed, does for her. It infuriated me because I suspected she was right.

"I went to open the window, and it wouldn't open, and while I was trying to open it, the whole time, I was thinking and thinking and thinking, analyzing and analyzing, and—" It all came out in one angsty, humiliating rush.

"Nora," he broke in firmly, "you're doing it again."

"It" meant leading my meta-life. Meta-life is the opposite of living in the moment. It's the syndrome of simultaneously having an experience and being an observer commenting on and questioning the experience. By observing something, you change it, sometimes for the better, but in my experience, usually for the worse. You know you're in the meta-life when you're critiquing an experience while you're having it ("This is fun but it would be more fun if . . ."), trying to talk yourself into happiness because you *should* feel it ("It's a beautiful day, and all I really need to be happy are fresh air and sunshine"), or worrying that you're not getting any closer to the Big Important Things ("Sure, this is a great date, but what are the odds this guy would ever marry someone like me?").

"I know," I responded miserably. "I *know* I'm doing it again. That's the worst part. I know, and I do it anyway."

"What could you possibly be thinking while opening a window except 'arghhh'?"

"Oh, you'd be amazed."

"Try me."

"No," I said, shoring my resolve. "I'm not going to talk about it. I'm going to get on with my day."

Dan gives me semiregular interventions, which are much appreciated. The only problem is, he thinks of me as having discreet episodes of meta-life, when, in fact, it's more like meta-life is the norm with discreet episodes of being fully, wonderfully, unthinkingly present. Maybe I should correct his perception, but I don't want to scare him off.

I completely adore Dan, but we've only been together six months, and I've been around long enough to know that you just never know. We're still in the flush of it all, though moving in together wasn't even a decision born of that flush. It was born of my roommate Fara asking me to move out so her boyfriend could move in. Dan and I had one of those "Well, you're over here so much anyway . . ." conversations, and after the decision was made, we were both lying there, looking up at the ceiling, trying not to let on to each other how freaked out we were at the prospect, and we sealed the deal with some perfunctory sex.

Speaking of my freak-outs, lately they're coming hard and fast. It's probably the stress of being only nine months from thirty. Now, I'm fairly certain that once I actually turn thirty, it'll be fine. But the approach—well, that's something else entirely. It lends a whole other level to my self-evaluation process, and believe me, what I don't need is another level.

It's worth noting that I'm not actually worried about my diminishing fertility, and I'm nowhere near ready for a husband or kids. But it's hard to resist feeling on edge when everyone takes it as a given that thirty will inspire panic, when well-meaning friends have started asking "how I'm doing with that whole turning thirty thing" and my friends who have rounded the corner pat my hand reassuringly and say, apropos of nothing, "Thirty is actually really great."

Okay, so it's not all cultural anxiety. I've got more than my share of personal anxiety. Turning thirty puts me in mind of something one of my ex-boyfriends once said while he was trying to pass a minivan illegally on a two-lane highway across a solid yellow line: "Life is about jockeying for position." Asshole context aside, it's true. Before I'm actually ready for marriage and kids, I need to get in position. Certain things need to be lined up: the great relationship, the satisfying career, the level of success that will allow me to, say, cut back to part-time while still maintaining the fantastic lifestyle to which I will have become accustomed. So on one hand, I've got the run-of-the-mill, pervasive, irrational, culturally driven backseat-borderline panic, and on the other, I've got the fact that for me, personally, turning thirty is about having a secure place in the world, the beginnings of a nest. Meta-life means all I see are a bunch of twigs.

. . . .

That night, I made a vow. I pledged to go a full twenty-four hours without self-investigation, starting first thing the following morning. I swore I'd be vigilant about not getting too much into my own head, and planned to internally yell "Stop!" every time I felt myself waxing self-referential. What this would accomplish, I wasn't yet sure, but it felt significant.

It definitely lent a pleasant clarity of purpose at the outset of my day. I read on the train, as always, but every time I found my mind wandering to a moment of self-congratulation about how well my plan was proceeding, I did my silent yell and returned to my place. I smiled at strangers instead of averting my eyes. I felt freer somehow.

When I arrived at work, it was 7:30 AM. I worked on Market Street, San Francisco's main drag. At one end, there's a farmers' market, the beautiful Ferry Building, picturesque views of the bay, and some of the world's greatest shopping. I worked at the other, nonprofit end, at an animal rescue shelter wedged between a furniture rental store and a fast-food joint.

My desk was right inside the door, since in addition to my other duties I got to play receptionist. My official job title, though, was coordinator. I could coordinate anything; really, you'd be amazed. I'd become a master of organization over the past two and a half years. The place ran nearly exclusively on donations, so there were fund-raisers to be coordinated and volunteer drives to be co-ordinated, and then once we had the volunteers, well, they had to be coordinated, too. I didn't coordinate the animals themselves, thankfully. I did observe them at the beginning of their tenure be-cause I wrote the descriptions of each animal that were posted weekly on our Web site to be viewed by potential owners. I also interviewed staff about the animals, particularly the dogs, to find out how they behaved on walks, interacted with children, responded to commands, etc. I'd saved all the dog and cat bios I'd ever written as clippings for the portfolio I meant to have someday.

As I was stowing my purse, Denise came toward me with Norman on a leash, about to go for their morning constitutional. Norman was one of our long-term residents. We were overrun with pit bulls, and unfortunately Norman—who had reportedly developed a rather sweet personality in his time with us—had a mean little face that rendered him pretty unadoptable. Our animal rescue actually did the bulk of its rescuing of dogs and cats from other shelters that were about to euthanize them. That meant we didn't always get the most appealing animals, and if they're not adopted, they're lifers with us.

"Hi, Nora!" Denise said brightly.

"Hi, Denise." I smiled at her, and down at Norman. I very rarely petted the dogs, or walked them, but I did smile down at them fairly regularly, especially when they're on the leash of someone I like as much as I like Denise.

Denise was twenty-three and started working at the shelter right out of college. She'd been with her boyfriend since they were both fourteen, and they lived happily together in a studio apartment with four miniature schnauzers named after members of the band Phish. She's earnest and guileless and sometimes just talking to her made me feel clean.

"What time did you get here?" I asked her.

"I came in at six." She absentmindedly scratched at her bare leg. She's a runner, and wore athletic shorts practically every day. "I've been worried about Norman. I wanted to get in some quality time with him." Norman yanked on the leash and she calmed him with a head tilt. She has a gift.

I, on the other hand, have no gift. Growing up we never had any pets, and I'm not all that comfortable with animals. That hadn't changed much by working at the animal rescue, since I tended to keep my distance. One Saturday a month, I had to get closer because every staff person took a turn at mobile outreach. Every weekend, our van parked in front of PetSmart and staff tried to entice people into taking home an animal in addition to the one they came to buy food for. So once a month, I was out there smiling at strangers and trying to talk up the charms of some dog whose mange we had just cured.

When I first got my coordinator job through a friend, I thought it would be just a few months before an opportunity materialized in publishing or journalism or advertising or some other writerly industry (i.e., someplace I might actually belong). Sometimes it was hard being at the shelter among the true believers. I worked with wonderful people who loved animals in that selfless way that we all wish another human would love us. They managed to love the ugliest, snarliest of mutts, and they didn't seem to mind being underpaid and overworked in the name of the cause in which they so fervently believed. They saw the good in every animal and so, incredibly enough, their sales pitch from that van came straight from the heart. About half the time I was around them, I felt like the worst person alive.

As Denise and I chatted, Estella sashayed by, looking far too hot for nonprofit work. She graced me with a smile. I said hi. *She must be a dancer*, I thought enviously for the tenth time since I'd met her.

Tricia was racing around, as usual. She got her smile at me out of the way, then said, "Maggie's looking for you."

"Do you know what she needs?" I asked.

"She just said to come by when you get a minute. By the way, do you have those flyers done?"

"Oh, yeah. They're on my desk. Let me just check in with Maggie, and then I'll get them for you." I excused myself and headed for Maggie's office.

Maggie was the director and cofounder of the rescue. She's about fifty and has the kind of soft, lineless face that makes you wonder why you know immediately that she's fifty. She's soft all over, and I don't think I've ever seen her in anything but a tunic and broomstick skirt.

"Hi, Maggie." I poked my head in her office. "Tricia said you wanted to talk to me."

"I do. Come in, and shut the door." Maggie generally radiates acceptance, and that made her facial expression confusing to me. On another person, it would clearly telegraph disapproval, but since it was Maggie, that seemed so impossible that I was suffering cognitive dissonance.

"Nora, I have something to ask you. It's not easy for me." And I could see that it wasn't. She wasn't used to having to do anything but praise her hardworking, committed staff.

I didn't feel worried; I just felt sorry that I had put her in that position. I nodded encouragingly.

"I have to ask you this. Nora, are you happy here?"

I paused. "Sometimes." I briefly gazed into the middle distance, then reiterated, "Yes, that would be the best answer. Sometimes."

Maggie nodded slowly. "That's comforting for me. Because I have to say that when I read one of the dog bios, I thought otherwise." She picked up a paper from her desk. "That dog bio is 'One-Eyed Frank.'" She locked her eyes with mine. "Do you remember writing this?"

"I think so. I just wrote it last week." I racked my brain, trying to think if there had been anything unusual about it. I couldn't come up with anything.

"So you remember it clearly?"

"Well, I wrote it pretty quickly. I was under deadline, I had other bios to finish—" I stopped. "I guess I don't remember it that clearly."

She began to read. " 'One-Eyed Frank, age eight, is not a treat for the eyes (no pun intended), but for the soul. He can be prickly, he can be ornery, he should not be in a home with children. But he has grit, he has fortitude, and he has a will to live that has taken him from the mean streets of Oakland to our very own hallowed halls, and I, for one, am glad we have him. You will be, too.' " She carefully replaced the paper on her desk. "Were you mocking One-Eyed Frank, Nora?"

I had been under deadline, that was true. It was late, I wanted to get home, I was scheduled to work the van that weekend, and somehow I just dashed off the sentences, uploaded to the Web site, and left. But Maggie was right. The bio dripped with contempt.

"No, no," I protested, stricken. "I wouldn't do that!" But I had.

Maggie, though, looked instantly relieved, her worldview mercifully unaltered. "I didn't think you would. But have you been getting enough sleep? Maybe we work you too hard."

"I'm fine," I said dejectedly. I knew that if I pushed just so, Maggie would lessen my workload, relieve me of some of my duties, perhaps even take them onto her already heaping plate, and after my behavior, that would feel absolutely seedy.

As I left Maggie's office, I thought how nothing stinks quite like realizing that the more beatific a setting, the less you belong there.

I found myself walking slowly past the animals' cages (the roomiest cages we could use and still warehouse so many animals). I looked in at them; I mean, *really* looked at them. It had been a long time since I'd done that. Unless they were making a serious racket or I was writing a bio, the animals hardly registered. That day, as I walked down the row, I met one particular dog's dull eyes. His name was Rudolph, and he was one of our pit bull mixes, the kind that just comes out wrong. He was never going to get out of there. He didn't even try anymore. Most of the dogs showed off when a potential owner walked in. They generally played to their strengths: the little ones yipped and pranced, the bigger, older ones held themselves with a certain watchful dignity, but Rudolph just didn't bother. He sat far back in his cage, often with his back to people walking by. I couldn't remember what Rudolph's good qualities were, I had written his copy so long ago, and he'd become so—well, so inanimate.

I couldn't tell you what shifted for me just then, because I followed my resolution and didn't analyze it. I can only say that in my gut, I simply knew, and I decided to honor that knowledge. I marched into Maggie's office.

"I quit!" I said loudly, filled with righteousness.

"Sit down, sit down," she said. "You can't say something like that standing in a doorway." She looked truly perturbed that I would even consider such a thing, not the quitting, but the doorway delivery.

Chastened, I sat. "I'm quitting," I said again, not as loud but just as forcefully.

"Shut the door, please," she directed in a low voice.

I did so obediently, then perched on the edge of the chair. "I think—" I began again. "No, I *feel* I need to leave."

"Nora, I hope I didn't upset you too much earlier. I didn't mean to come down so hard on you." Maggie looked genuinely distressed.

"No, no. It has nothing to do with that."

Maggie was quiet. "It's not easy work," she finally said, her face full of compassion. "It's hard to see all those animals suffering. We do our best, but still."

Did she think I was leaving because I couldn't take the suffering of the animals? On the contrary, I took it too easily. That was why I often felt so rotten.

"You're not like the other employees. I know that," she said.

She let it hang there, and I finally took the bait. "What do you mean?" As soon as I said it, I wished I hadn't.

"It's not your calling, so maybe you suffer more than the others who feel they have the power to heal."

What the hell?

"Maybe if you interacted more with the animals instead of just watching . . . it would probably enrich your bios. They'd be more personal."

"But I don't want to interact more with the animals," I said, frustrated that she was missing the point. Did she not see my determination? *This is not a negotiation*, I wanted to say. I knew myself well enough that if she got me thinking about the decision, I'd get too scared, or I'd want to please her, or both, and I'd stay. And I didn't want to think, I wanted to act. *I will not think. Whatever she pulls, don't think.*

"You're tentative. And you've been here awhile. It's harder to jump in, the longer you stand on the sidelines. But that doesn't mean it's too late. Tricia can help you. She's great at that."

"I don't think that'll help." *You don't think?* I mocked myself. *Say "it won't." Use forceful language. Blast your way out of here.*

"Maybe we could just try it. We could make some changes in your job duties, too, make sure you leave at a reasonable hour so you can sleep and replenish yourself."

My boss wanted to nurture me, and I wanted to throttle her. I decided it was time to put this conversation out of its misery. "It's not about my duties or my work hours. You said it yourself: it's not my calling. I don't want to work in a place where it's everyone's calling but mine." I looked at her kind face, and my annoyance dissipated. I suddenly felt touched that she was willing to fight for me when I felt like such a pariah. "Even if it is such an amazing place. You're tremendous, Maggie."

Maggie looked away. I hoped when I was fifty I'd be able to take a compliment, but in nearly every other way, it would be pretty cool to turn out like Maggie. "I'll accept your resignation," Maggie said. "Could you give me two weeks?"

Two weeks?!!! That's no time at all. You've got nothing lined up. Did you hear me? Nothing! You can't actually—

"Two weeks."

Chapter 2

FARA

Age:	29
Height:	5'7"
Weight:	Perfect!!
Occupation:	Fashion merchandising
About me:	I love Oakland!!! Who needs San Francisco anyway? (No offense to all my peeps who live there, of course!) I'm a vegetarian — seitan rocks! I'd let any of my friends borrow my shoes, and I'm the first to take care of you when you're sick.
About you:	Get on my e-mail list and come party!
Last book I read:	Anything by that woman who wrote *Sex and the City*
Biggest turn-on:	My boyfriend, of course!
Biggest turnoff:	Anyone else
Five things I can't live without:	My friends, my boyfriend, Goliath the Cat, my apartment, reality television
Most embarrassing moment:	I don't believe in those.

*I*t was ironic that I should have seen myself with such terrifying clarity while opening a window, since it was the only window to which I had access. I lived in a two-bedroom apartment, and Fara had the plum room facing the lake, with windows that opened, while I had no view and a sealed porthole.

A lot of people across the bridge in San Francisco don't know that Oakland has a lake. It's fetid and it smells, but yes, we do. It looks great at night, actually, because it has lights strung around its perimeter and people can take gondola rides along its putrid surface. It's kind of laughable, but sweet, like the peculiarities of so many fourth-tier metropolitan areas are. People jog around the lake, but not me. I'm afraid of West Nile virus from the bugs alighting on all that standing water. Also, I have a sensitive nose. And I've always hated exercise.

You must be thinking that I'm a real loser to have a roommate at almost thirty in Oakland. You're thinking, in San Francisco, in New York, in Boston—*maybe*. But *Oakland*?

First of all, Oakland has its charms. I've heard it called the Brooklyn of the West (once, but I did hear that). And like the trendy parts of Brooklyn, the safe parts of Oakland are anything but cheap. It's only a short commute into San Francisco, the mecca for nonprofit agencies where everyone is notoriously and grossly underpaid. Then there's the large number of single people from twenty-seven to forty-three. I'm no sociologist, but it seems like people here marry late and divorce a lot, and all that recycling and starting over creates a demand for cheaper living arrangements.

So in conclusion, it is completely acceptable in the Bay Area to have a roommate at almost thirty, and beyond. The caveat is that when two people in their almost-thirties and beyond start dating, and both of them have roommates, they will either break up sooner because it's just not worth it (especially for the woman— all those humiliating, postsex sneaks to the bathroom) or they will cohabitate sooner. That was what happened with Fara and her boyfriend. They'd been together four months, and now I was moving out.

It was a little humiliating, being dumped by Fara, like getting left by an alcoholic with perpetual body odor. The main problem with Fara as a roommate was that she was obsessed with the apartment and got subtly (and not so subtly) territorial about it. She'd lived there for four years, and I'd heard her say more than once, only half-jokingly, that she planned to be buried under the floorboards of the living room. If we had lived in a rent-controlled palace in New York, that joke wouldn't be as weird. In New York, it might not even be a joke. But it was an apartment on the lake in Oakland. I have my civic pride, but I do get those sorts of distinctions.

The other major problem was Fara's personality, which I definitely wasn't in the mood for that night. Even after quitting, I'd worked late, and by the time I got home, it was 7:30 PM and she had, as usual, commandeered the living room, this time for a reality TV party, or as she described it, "one of my famous reality TV parties." She's the kind of person who sends out e-mail invitations with phrases like "back by popular demand."

I hated that I had come to hate her. She was essentially harmless, and at least two-thirds clueless, and she'd done some nice things for me in our year together. Besides, I had too little energy left after my long workdays to waste any of it hating her. And yet, when I came in and saw her there, in $200 jeans and the feather boa that she was not entirely sure was ironic, and her dumbest friends Christina and Tracy were braying with delight at something she had just said, I was too weak to fight it.

"Hi, Nora," they chorused. Fara added a peppy "How was your day?"

I gave a halfhearted wave and exaggerated my exhausted gait as I headed for the kitchen. "I'm tired and starving," I said, hoping that would be the extent of my interaction.

Never one to read a mood and let it stop her, Fara said, "Nora, you have to see this. You, of all people, will love it."

"What is it?" I asked wearily.

"Just come and see." Now that I was moving out, Fara kept trying to cement our dubious bond. She tended to think people were closer friends than they were, and she was making it clear that she wanted to keep me in her menagerie.

I resigned myself to humoring her, at least until I was done eating. "Let me start microwaving, and then I'll be in," I said. I opened the refrigerator and peered in, looking for last night's takeout. I had a sinking feeling. There had been empty plates on the coffee table in the living room. I confirmed my hunch in the kitchen trash, then poked my head back into the living room. "You ate my takeout," I said.

"You know you're always free to eat mine," Fara answered sweetly. But she meant that in a metaphorical sense, a small consolation when I was bone tired from work and she, of course, had no leftovers because if she had had her own leftovers to serve, she wouldn't have eaten mine. Fara had a sort of perverted hippie mentality, which meant that she would give you anything she had, but also thought she was owed anything of yours. Our living together had been a clash of civilizations.

As you'd imagine, we'd had this particular takeout/leftover exchange before. I reminded myself, as I had so many times this past month, that soon I'd be out and this was a battle that I, blissfully, would never have to fight again. So I gritted my teeth, pulled open the freezer, and appraised its contents. Finally, out of spite, I selected Fara's frozen vegetarian dinner and started the microwave.

"Hurry, Nora!" she called.

To avoid another battle, I joined them in the living room. On the TV screen were two teams of grown adults grunting while playing tug-of-war. The tussle between the Red Shirts and the Green Shirts appeared to be at a stalemate. "Why would I love this?"

"They're all reality TV stars." Fara looked at me expectantly.

"But I hate reality TV."

"You like to think you hate reality TV. That's who reality TV is for."

Christina piped up. "I like the nice reality TV. Like those makeover shows. I tell you, I could just watch them flash 'before' and 'after' photos on the screen for hours."

"Exactly," Tracy said.

I wondered how late they'd be staying. I noticed that Tracy was wearing her pajamas, and resented her for being more comfortable in my apartment than I was. Fara's constant entertaining made me feel like a guest in my own apartment. I would have thought this was only in my head, but one day I actually received an e-mail inviting me to a party at my own apartment. Fara and I had words about that one, and while she initially seemed genuinely perplexed, she eventually offered what looked like a sincere apology. She's not all bad, I guess.

Fara eyed me. "You look fucked twice over."

"Thanks." I shot her an irritated look.

She corrected her tone to one of concern. "I mean, are you okay?"

"I'm more or less fine." I figured I should mention losing my job, mostly so that in case Dan or someone else let it slip, I wouldn't have to deal with her wounded outrage at not having been told. Not that I'd lost my job. I could go back in there tomorrow and tell Maggie I wanted to stay, that I would spend more quality time with the animals like she'd suggested, and it'd be like time travel. "I quit my job."

"Why? Did something happen?" Fara was sitting on the floor, her back against the couch, and she patted one of the cushions encouragingly. It was the seat next to Goliath, the cat she'd gotten from the animal rescue.

Goliath never ceased to horrify me. When Fara chose Goliath, he weighed thirty-four pounds. He was the fattest cat the shelter had ever seen. Now, it's one thing to love a cat that has gained some weight, but it's quite another to pick out a morbidly obese cat and declare him yours. Fara seemed to think Goliath was some sort of miracle showpiece cat. To paint a picture, Goliath was so fat that he couldn't sit down normally. He had worked out a system of sitting that was either excruciating or hilarious to watch, depending on your perspective. You could see the wheels turning for Goliath once he fixed his eyes on the cushion because being that fat, he needed to think a couple of moves ahead. For Goliath, sitting involved careful positioning, followed by a backward free fall. It made me think of a corporate retreat I'd attended a couple of jobs back, where we were mandated to fall backward into the waiting arms of our coworkers to prove we were one big, trustworthy family. Thankfully, Goliath was not my coworker.

"Nothing happened. I just quit," I said.

Before Fara had a chance to respond, I left to retrieve my food. Steeling myself, I returned to the living room and sat on the floor. Four humans sitting on the floor, one fat cat on a couch. *Eat. Eat like it's an Olympic sport.*

"You know what that was, don't you?" Fara said.

"Yes," I said, to shut her up. I hadn't even understood the question.

"You had an epiphany," she said knowingly. "Everyone seems to be having them lately. Lots of breakups, lots of job changes—"

"And one sex change," Christina cut in. "Hand to God. I can't tell you who it is. Though I guess you'll know someday."

"It's a really long process," Fara added. "You have to see a therapist first to prove that you're sane before they'll even start you on the hormones."

I wanted to finish my food so I could get out of that room, but my throat wouldn't cooperate. It seemed to have closed up on me. The enormity of what I had done had been held at bay by the day's busyness, and now the ramifications were washing over me. I'd been living hand to mouth. If I spent nothing between now and the first of next month, I could pay rent to Dan, but then what? How would I pay my credit card bill? Make my car payment?

"Fara, when I moved in here, did I pay a security deposit? Or the last month's rent?" I asked hopefully.

Fara thought for a moment, then shook her head. "You were a little strapped so we decided you'd just pay the first month's rent."

"Oh."

Definitely not the answer I wanted, though it was a key reason I'd ended up living with Fara. She could be magnanimous when she saw someone in need. Once when I was quivering with a 1:00 AM fever, she went out to the twenty-four-hour convenience store to get me juice. My gratitude for her willingness to dodge crack whores while wearing her pajamas was slightly tempered when she said, "I know I can be a pain sometimes, but the good thing about me is that I'll always be the first to get you juice."

"Nora, do you think you could put in a good word for me at your work?" Tracy inquired, eyes bright. "I love animals."

Fara's eyes lit up, too. "Oh, Tracy would be great at your job!"

This was how it was done in the nonprofit world. You're underpaid and you're overworked and you have to know someone to get the privilege. Tracy probably would be great at my job. I'd always considered myself underemployed—I had to, just to preserve a little dignity—but I decided that Tracy's fitness was the true mark of just how underemployed I was. There would be no reversal. I was moving forward without a net.

· · · ·

"You've got to be kidding me." Dan stared at me incredulously. "Tell me you're kidding me."

Needless to say, it wasn't the reaction I'd hoped for. During the drive to Dan's apartment (soon to be our apartment), I had reassured myself of the rightness, the inevitability even, of that day's decision. By the time I arrived, I was certain that Dan and I would spend the night toasting my—our—new life.

"I'm not kidding." I returned the stare, somewhat sulkily.

"It's not like I don't get it. There are days I don't like my job, either. But you've got to have a backup plan, right?"

"You don't *have* to."

He had assumed the physical posture of exasperation: legs stretched way out in front of the couch, head tilted far back and upward, hand raking through his hair.

"I thought you'd support me in this," I said.

He jerked his head upright. "Support you?"

The way he said the word "support"—I suddenly got it. He was afraid I was moving in with him to be a kept woman. In our time together, we'd developed certain unexamined routines, and one of them (probably derived from him making more than double my salary) was that I picked up the check for weekend brunches and he picked up the check for everything else. Maybe he thought that was my idea of a split, and that I planned to move in, cover a utility bill, and let him handle the rest. And I realized anew that six months is not a lot of time.

"*Emotional* support." I inwardly groaned at the clarification.

A flash of relief crossed his face. "But you don't seem to need emotional support. You bounced in here and announced you're jobless like it's a good thing."

"Because it is a good thing."

"Sweetie," he said softly, looking into my eyes with great affection, "it's not a good thing."

At that, I found myself stomping around the living room like the child he seemed to think I was. "You don't get to decide that! You"—I pointed at him—"are fine with being on the ten-year plan for your dream. And that's fine *for you*. I'm ready to go to the next level now. *I* am ready to kick my dream into overdrive."

"Your dream of being a writer," he said, without inflection.

"Yes."

"And you don't want to be a writer with a day job."

"Well," I faltered slightly. "I don't want to be a writer with *that* day job. I could be a writer like Kathy."

"A ghostwriter."

"Yes."

"If it's so easy to break in, why hasn't she helped you do it already?" he asked. It occurred to me that it was not an insensible question.

"I never asked her." Which was true enough.

"What makes you want to be a ghostwriter?"

"I don't know! I just want to be a writer." I sank down on the couch. "Stop it, this thing you're doing. This deconstruction of my dream."

"I'm not taking it apart. I'm trying to help you put it together. A dream needs to be broken down into goals, right? And objectives."

"What's the difference between a goal and an objective?" I asked. It was my turn to stump him.

"That's what I mean about the breakdown. You start with the dream: 'I want to be a writer.' Then you say, 'My goal is to write for travel magazines,' and then you look at the steps it takes to reach that goal and those would be your objectives." He stood up. "You want a drink? I'm doing a shot."

I shook my head and watched him walk to the beautiful mahogany bar he'd built into the living-room wall. He'd combed estate sales until he'd found one he both loved and could afford. He loved bars—not the actual watering holes, which he liked pretty well, but the bars themselves. He'd never been to bartending school, but he could mix anything and he came up with new concoctions all the time. Naively, that night I'd thought maybe he'd invent the Animal Liberation in my honor. Instead, I was watching with mounting anxiety as he downed top-shelf tequila.

Numerically, there are many software engineers in the Bay Area. Categorically, there are only two: those who want to stay in computers, and those who want to do something else. I only date the latter, and I've dated four of them. One wanted to be a musician, one wanted to be a cartoonist, one wanted to be a barfly, near as I could tell (which made for the temporarily arresting combination of the sexy bad boy in a programmer's body), and Dan wanted to own a bookstore with a liquor license. He figured it would officially combine the bookstore and the pickup joint. He had this vision of writers doing readings there and then hanging out at the burnished, turn-of-the-century bar drinking a

Scotch with him. It was an appealing vision for me, too. I liked the thought of being the proprietress of such an establishment, mingling with literati, maybe even being literati someday.

Dan's not one of those people who tells you all his dreams the first time you meet him. He's not the kind to doodle the floor plans for his bookbar on a napkin. I wouldn't want that kind anyway. Dream whores get boring after a while. When you're underemployed and you meet another person who's underemployed, telling your dreams right off the bat is the quickest way to establish your identity. But Dan didn't consider himself underemployed. He generally felt lucky to make a good living at something he just happened upon out of college, and he'd been living below his means for years to save up for the bookbar. He wasn't cheap; he just figured out what mattered to him and put his money there. If something didn't matter, he didn't spend on it. He could probably have started the business already, but he'd done a lot of research and was trying to do it at the optimal time with the optimal amount of capital, so he figured it'd be in five years or so. He got antsy sometimes, but mostly he was okay with the wait.

And I loved him for this. I loved him for his methodical mind and his patience. I admired him tremendously. From the first time I met him, I adored the way he tilted his head to really consider what I was saying, and the confidently long pauses he allowed to elapse between my question and his answer. I adored it, but it made me self-conscious about my own answers. I wondered if what I'd said stood up to that kind of scrutiny. Scrutiny's the wrong word, though; it implies appraisal and there was something wonderfully accepting about those pauses. It was more like I wondered if what I'd said deserved such consideration.

"I wish I was like you," I said sadly.

He sat down close to me, and his voice was low. "What you

did scares the shit out of me. You're someone who can just say, 'Fuck it, I'm gone.'"

I took his hand. "I'm just getting here."

"I know I didn't ask you to live here the right way. It should have been more of a thing, an event." He looked at me intently. "It was like we just brokered a deal. I should have told you that I wanted you to live here so you could be the central part of my life. I should have told you it was because you matter the most."

I teared up. "I feel that way, too."

"I just wouldn't have done what you did. But maybe it was right for you."

"It felt right. Just gut-level right."

"I hear that. But I'm big on backup plans. And sweetie, I love you, but you ain't got any."

"I know."

"I can try to help you come up with some."

"I'd like that." I kissed him. "Thank you."

• • • •

We didn't sleep together that night.

Rationally, I knew that wasn't a big deal. Couples of six months don't necessarily have sex every time they see each other. People have differing sex drives, and there are couples who have sex once a year, and if both people are satisfied with that, it's a perfectly fine arrangement.

See, I knew all that. And this was not the first time we'd slept in the same bed and not had sex. But it was the first time we'd had a meaningful conversation that ended with us validating the great love that we shared, and *then* climbed into bed and went immediately to sleep. Rather, Dan went right to sleep. I lay there wondering why he hadn't reached for me. Was he disgusted by my impulsiveness? Despite his declarations that he wanted me to be more a part of his life, did he doubt that I was a worthy partner? Was he regretting the decision for me to move in?

Or was he just tired? Could it possibly be that simple?

I reminded myself that for Dan, it absolutely could be that simple. He wasn't the one lying awake contemplating the state of our relationship. There was no evidence that he had stopped loving me during the course of the evening. There was no evidence that I had become repugnant or that he had lost his potency. We just weren't having sex that night, simple as that.

But why? *Why weren't we having sex?*

Sex was one of my habitual areas of overthinking. It was probably because the act of sex meant so much to me; it was when my brain shut off temporarily and sensation took over. Sex with someone I love is the best respite from meta-life.

I also subscribe to the "sex as the barometer of the relationship" theory. That means I look at the duration, connection, calculation, level of inventiveness, and overall quality of the sex; I try to read these like tea leaves. I've gotten better at recognizing the normal pattern of six-week fall-off and then the three-month fall-off, and I've stopped worrying about them as much as I used to. The later spikes and lulls, though, still tend to get way too much attention.

I was well aware that all that thinking was anathema to the delightful thoughtlessness of good sex itself, but I had cause to be wary. I'd had four relationships that ended at almost exactly one year. Each time, we started with strong chemistry that progressed to love and ended with me having almost no sex drive at all. And when my sex drive was low, so was my tolerance for my boyfriends' peccadilloes. I'd get critical of them, then I'd get critical of myself for being critical of them, and the whole relationship inevitably soured like milk. But I was determined to do it differently with Dan. This time I would crack the code of my meta-sex life, and everything would fall into place.

Dan let out a snort and rolled onto his back. I thought about waking him up by going down on him. Then we could have sex and I could, literally, put all these thoughts to bed. But did I actually want to have sex, or did I just want to prove something? Would I be using sex to quiet my head?

Oh, who cared? I sunk down under the covers, and reached for him.

Chapter 3

NORA

Age:	29
Height:	5'6"
Weight:	130 lbs
Occupation:	Back under construction
About me:	Under construction
About you:	Under construction
Last book I read:	*What Should I Do With My Life?*
Biggest turn-on:	Under construction
Biggest turnoff:	Under construction
Five things I can't live without:	Under construction
Most embarrassing moment:	The window incident

Dan was right: I had no plan. And every time he tried to initiate one of his patented dream/goal/objectives conversations with me, I wriggled away. I hadn't slept in four nights, and the glow of self-determination had burned out, replaced by the terrible realization that I had not a prospect in sight. I'd just been drifting along, waiting for something to lift me out of my life, as if a publisher from Condé Nast would go looking for a puppy on the animal rescue Web site and be so struck by one of my bios that she'd recruit me right then and there. I'd tripped into that job and even though I never meant to stay, I'd done nothing to leave: I'd long ago stopped looking at job listings or trying to network, and I couldn't remember the last time I'd considered the next step in my career. When was the last time I'd even used the word "career" in a sentence? Maybe meta-life was an elaborate scheme cooked up by my brain to avoid realistically thinking about the future.

On Sunday morning, Dan and I went to brunch, the meal that was always my treat. I'd been keeping my rising anxiety to myself because I didn't want him to think he was moving in with a basket case. (He'd signed on for the manicured neuroticism of, say, Bridget Jones; I couldn't suddenly give him Zelda Fitzgerald.) But that day, when he ordered a mimosa, it took a concentrated act of will to avoid screaming, "Are you trying to break me here?!!" My stomach was knotted with tension as I tried to distract us from the pink elephant, and brunch came to $38 plus tip. I said I had to go home and do some organizing for the move, which was true: I'd been spectacularly unproductive all week. But what I really needed was to talk to Kathy.

Kathy had been my friend for almost ten years. We'd met in a creative writing workshop in college at a time when we shared an unfortunate habit of writing in the second person (a side effect of reading too much Lorrie Moore). We were convinced we were naturals: we'd both won a slew of essay contests growing up, were extravagantly praised by teachers and family, and were generally acknowledged to be the best writers in our workshop. She loved my stories and I loved hers, with their gutsy protagonists and their even gutsier settings. She was addicted to travel magazines and confessed she'd never been anywhere she'd written about. I always suspected she was a bigger talent than I was, and I knew she was more driven, so it wasn't surprising that she ended up being the one with the successful writing career. It was surprising that it was ghostwriting, since Kathy seemed like a novelist waiting to happen. She'd take a mean author photo: her explosion of black curly hair around her striking, pale face. She wasn't pretty; she was formidable.

After graduating college, Kathy took a proofreading job at a literary magazine while I took an office job, figuring I'd send out some stories to magazines and be promptly scooped up by the literary world. In the beginning, I did things like mail a story to the *New Yorker* with a scribbled cover letter: "Just thought you might like this." By the end of the year, I was poring over every story published in *Seventeen* magazine and then creating a pastiche of their themes and styles, only to be rejected some more. Depressed and demoralized, I decided to travel for a while to clear my head. After that, I lived in a few different cities, tried out some jobs (none of them lasting more than a year), met some interesting people, drank too much, had relationships, and avoided thinking about how wildly unsuccessful I was.

Until now.

"You've reached the voice mailbox of Kathy Pecoe. I'm not able to take your call right now. Please leave your name and phone number with area code, even if you think I have it . . ."

Shit. I debated whether to call her cell phone. She was probably working; she worked a lot of the weekend. I shouldn't interrupt her. I could handle this on my own, at least for a while longer.

Plan, plan, just come up with a plan. How hard could it be? Break it down, like Dan said. What's my objective? To be a writer. No, that's the goal. Or is it the dream? Shit.

Go to the drawer.

It was like a command issued from my very soul. I stared over at the drawer in fright. The dresser drawer, which held my never-

finished everythings, dating back to college: short stories, novel-
las, novels, poems, plays, screenplays. I'd even managed to walk
away from a short short story—conceived as a two-pager, I went
to make grilled cheese at the end of the first page and lost my will.
I'd saved them all because I was a chronic recycler. One particular
character named Lucius popped up no fewer than six times in
completely unrelated works.

I hadn't written anything in at least a year, though I nursed the
assumption that deep down, no matter what, I was still a writer.
But if I opened that drawer, and read what was inside, I might
learn that I didn't have talent. I might learn that even my dream
was wrong. I'd have nothing.

No, I'd have clarity. I needed to know: did I have talent or
didn't I? If I didn't, I was going to walk away, once and for all. If I
did, well, that was another problem entirely. Taking a deep
breath, I opened the drawer.

Three hours later, I collapsed in despair on top of a libretto I'd
attempted my sophomore year. The best I could say was that I
was not untalented, but I surely didn't have enough talent to wait
around to be discovered. I'd actively have to do something, probably a lot of something. I'd have to practice my craft. I'd have to
figure out my market. I'd have to work hard, and suffer, and but-
tress myself against rejection, and take risks.

I was no good at those things.

Which was why, at that point, I started e-mailing everyone I
knew to ask for a job, any job. Some were people I'd met only
once, some were friends of a friend, some were men who'd tried
to date me. Finally a real-life application of my coordinator skills.
I sorted according to categories. Men who'd tried to date me got
e-mails that made no mention of my relationship status. "Friend
of a friend" e-mails featured a prominent mention of that friend

in the introductory paragraph. People who knew how the game was played—i.e., that everyone has to use any connection in a market like this—got to-the-point e-mails with a résumé attached. People who were more sensitive to exploitation got chatty e-mails that sandwiched my job situation in the middle of the update and had no résumé attached.

Taking action was calming. I'd never had a problem getting a job before, especially since I'd cultivated such low standards; something would come through. And just when I'd sent the last e-mail, the phone rang. I leaped for it. Kathy, with her impeccable timing. But something told me to check the caller ID first.

It was my mother, the very reason I had caller ID. My mother has always seen disaster lurking around every corner, particularly when it comes to me. She called every other week, and a maximum of five days could elapse between her screened call and my return call. If it took me longer than five days to respond, she called again and insinuated that I hadn't called her back because I had something to hide. But by varying the number of days between her call and when we actually spoke, I could manipulate the system so that we'd talk about every three weeks. During our phone calls, she asked the same series of questions, all designed to make sure I wasn't screwing up my life too badly. These calls did not in any way resemble normal conversation. When I made any overtures to find out about her life, she deflected them and acted like I was just trying to throw her off the scent of my own troubles. She'd tell me about my sister Casey's academic successes, but just about nothing else.

Please let someone e-mail me back in the next five days. Otherwise, I would have to call my mother back and confess what I'd done. I didn't even want to think how that call would go, but I knew what would come next. Panicked, my mother would increase the frequency of her calls. She might, at some point, start sending cash, which I would accept because I had no pride, but that would be far, far down the road.

Of course my mother would want me just to take another job, any job. Those e-mails were exactly what she would have told me to do. For the past two hours, I'd been channeling my mother. Less than a week and I was already selling out my dream. This was my chance to change my life, and I was giving up without a fight.

I paced, stared at the drawer, paced again, stared again.

You have no talent.

I have some talent.

It's not enough.

Well, not if I never take a chance. Not if I sit around waiting for something to happen.

All right, then. What is it you'll do?

I'll be a writer.

Specifically, what will you do?

Oh, shut up.

You're almost thirty. You own nothing. You have no savings. The Social Security system is collapsing.

I'm only twenty-nine. There's time. There's plenty of time.

Everyone else got on the publishing track years ago. They all got started when they were twenty-two, but they didn't just quit when things got hard.

I didn't just quit. I went to India. It was very spiritual.

It was cheap. You went because it was cheap.

I can do this. I can be a writer.

That means doing *something. What will you do?*

I'll take whatever job I get offered through those e-mails, that's what I'll do.

You mean you'll give up again.

I'm being realistic. I can't just drift along indefinitely. I'm not twenty-two.

Then give up.

But I didn't want to give up. Not yet. Not until I talked to Kathy. If anyone could help me, it was her. I called her cell phone.

"Hello?" she said, her voice rising above a din.

"Kathy, is this a bad time?" I asked. "Can you talk?"

"Nora?" she queried. She knew my voice, of course; it was just loud enough to need confirmation.

"Yes."

"Is something wrong?"

"Oh, yeah."

"Let me pack up my things. I brought my laptop down to a café because I couldn't stand being cooped up in my apartment for another minute. I've been working on this book nonstop." We chatted to fill time until she could get out on the street and give me her undivided attention. After another minute, the line was clear. "Okay. Much better. So, are you okay? I mean, fundamentally intact."

"No shattered limbs."

"Glad to hear that."

"But I'm going crazy. I don't know if what I did was crazy but necessary, or just crazy, but I quit my job and I have nothing lined up." Saying it out loud made it even worse. What had I been thinking? Oh, right. I hadn't been thinking. For once in my life, I decided not to think, and look what happened.

"Huh. Really?" Her response was inscrutable. She was waiting for more information.

"This was not the time to act hastily, right? I have no savings,

I'm about to move in with Dan, he probably thinks I'm a gold digger—"

"Has Dan said anything about you being a gold digger?" she asked calmly.

"No, but he wants to make sure I can pay my half of the rent. Which is pretty reasonable, actually, and soon I won't be able to. And then what'll happen to us?" I realized that my mother's brain would have followed that precise sequence, and ended on just that question.

"Let's go back a few steps. How did you decide to quit your job?"

"That's the thing. I just went with my gut. I went to work and I saw this dog and I knew. But my gut is not honed for moments like this, Kathy. There is nothing to suggest that my gut should be trusted."

"That's just not true. You've made plenty of gut decisions in your life, and lots of them have been right."

"No, they haven't. Because if they had, they wouldn't have led me here. I'm twenty-nine, and I'm pretty much a failure. Somehow I've managed to avoid that realization throughout my twenties, but there's no avoiding it now. I am going to be thirty years old, and I will have nothing. I will be nothing." I started crying at the incontrovertible truth of it.

"Are you having a blood sugar crisis?" Kathy suddenly demanded.

"What?" I asked, disoriented by the question.

"When did you last eat?"

I glanced at the clock and dabbed at my eyes. "Seven hours ago."

"Nora, you know you can't go that long without eating. Are you on a cell phone?"

"No."

"A cordless phone?"

"Yes," I sniffled.

"Bring me with you, and walk into the kitchen, and drink some juice, if you have it," she instructed.

"My problem is not my blood sugar, Kathy. It's my life." I couldn't believe that Kathy, of all people, was reducing this to a biological event. My life was a disaster. I was a disaster.

"Nora, come on. You know how this goes. When your blood sugar drops, you get irrational, but you don't see it."

"Maybe sometimes," I allowed, "but that's not what's going on now." But she had planted a small seed of doubt, so I figured I might as well follow her directions. Juice never hurt anyone. And I did remember making the discovery that a decent percentage of my relationship problems could be solved by carrying a Fruit Roll-Up in my purse. "I'm drinking the juice, but it's going to take a few minutes," I warned. "That's *if* you're right."

"Well, in the meantime, let's talk about me."

"I don't want to hear anything good. I love you, but if you tell me your book's been optioned for a telemovie, it's war."

"No, let's talk about my love life. Let's talk about my"—she said the next two words with absolute revulsion—"Internet dating. You met Dan in real time, so you don't know about this awful process. I'll fill you in."

"I had a profile up on a dating Web site. I just happened to meet Dan a few weeks later."

"So you never had to do the deed. Let me just ask you. I'm not Quasimodo, am I?"

I laughed. "You're great-looking. You know that."

"I've always thought of myself as reasonably attractive. And I'm generally okay with that. I've always thought, if I was given a choice to be reasonably attractive or drop-dead gorgeous, I'd go with reasonably attractive. But this Web site is messing with my head. I've been on it for a month now, and five guys have written me. Two were clearly troglodytes just writing to anyone. E-mails like, 'U R from Boston? Me too.' They actually used the letters: *U R.* And two were really, really old. Like fifteen, twenty years older than I said I wanted in my profile. Disrespecting my wishes from the get-go is always a turn-on. The last one was this really sweet, really homely guy and I wrote back to him to say I'd just started dating someone and that maybe I'd get back to him in the future if it didn't work out."

"Which was a lie."

"Of course. But I didn't want him thinking people don't write back to him because he's homely. I felt for him."

"Maybe he's just not photogenic," I suggested. I sat down on the couch and put my feet up on the coffee table. I realized how lucky I was to have my breakdown on a day when Fara was out of the apartment.

"He had ten pictures up there. And he was a different brand of homely in every one. One was 'grizzly man homely,' another was 'ski bum homely.' There was no denying it."

"Have you been on the Web site long?"

"A month. Which isn't that long, I know, but you get the most hits when you're new."

I remembered that from my brief stint. When you're new, you're at the top of the queue, and you have that first-day-in-a-new-school-midway-through-the-year allure.

"The worst part is that the Web site just added this new feature where you can see what other women are like you. I have no idea why someone dreamed this up. But basically, at the bottom of the screen when I log in, it actually says, 'Other seekers like you.' And you can click on their profiles and read about your competition."

"How'd you fare?"

"What's funny is that when I read that line about the other seekers, I was nervous to look down because I thought, well, it's New York. These women are going to be goddess neuroscientists. They'll be supermodels who've climbed Everest. I thought I could very well be crushed by feelings of massive inferiority, but I look down because I'm a masochist, and it's a million times worse. It's like Frumpfest '88. These women are not only unattractive, but when I click on their profiles, they're self-hating. Not self-deprecating, but actually self-hating. And the kicker is, they're not even smart! I don't even want to tell you the last book they read."

I made clucks of sympathy. "And everyone knows even though the question is the last book you read, you don't actually list the last book you read. You write down the book that conveys what you want the world to know you've read."

"Exactly! I'm lumped in with a bunch of women who disdain themselves, and appear to have every reason to. It's plain humiliating." She was no longer comically distressed; she was genuinely distressed.

"But you're the only one who sees it, right? The men who click on your profile don't see those other women."

"I'm convinced they've left their scent. I need to get in with a better class of women or I'm doomed."

"Maybe your profile could use a makeover. How are your pictures?"

"Okay, I guess."

"My theory is that you need to approach this like market research. Change a picture here, tweak a line there. Then you can gauge how different the response is."

"I can try it," Kathy said, sounding dubious. "I just know I don't want to be that woman who's 'looking for her partner in crime,' or who's 'equally at home at the ball game or the ballet.' That stuff makes me want to retch."

I laughed. "Did you write that in your profile?"

"I didn't use the word 'retch.'"

"That could be part of the problem."

"You mean I should have used the word 'retch'?" she teased.

"I just think you need to be careful when you're being acerbic, because it can sound bitter. It seems like men want to make sure you're fun and nonscary, which you are. I think that's why so many people write that ball game/ballet stuff. In San Francisco, all the women are equally at home in hiking boots or stilettos. You know, for the outdoorsy/sexy vibe." My friend Larissa was an Internet dating veteran and she and I had had discussions on the topic before, but I hadn't realized I could sound this authoritative. Weirdly, I was starting to have fun.

"It's hopeless! I hate self-promotion. Think about it, Nora. I'm a ghostwriter."

"But you're also funny and clever and all the things anyone could want in a partner in crime." I waited for her to laugh, but she didn't. "It's just that these things need to be carefully crafted. You want the pictures to show diversity, and you want them to be great but to actually look like you so that when you meet the guy, he's not disappointed. You want the profile to read like you on your best day, but you have to find a way to showcase your cleverness without too much sarcasm or irony because those can read badly. What you are, above all else, is a writer. This assignment is made for you." I had warmed to my pep talk so much that I had entirely forgotten my earlier misery.

There was a pregnant pause; then Kathy said, "Maybe the assignment is made for you."

"What do you mean?"

"Maybe you could edit my profile?" she asked hopefully.

I had to admit, I liked that my successful writer friend was soliciting my help. It was an ego boost I really needed just then. "That could be interesting."

"I'd pay you," she offered.

"No. Absolutely not."

"I insist. Think of it as your first paying gig as a writer." There was silence on the line for a few seconds, and I could tell she was thinking about something. Kathy was one of the only people in my life with whom silence really could feel companionable. "If this goes well, maybe you could market yourself. You know, be some sort of profile consultant. Think about all the people languishing on those Web sites, wondering why no one's writing to them. What they need is a smart, fresh eye to read and give them feedback. You could be—the Profile Eye! What do you think?"

I laughed. "That's the worst name imaginable."

"That's where you're wrong. The worst name is 'Yen for Books.' I couldn't think of anything when I was supposed to name my profile and after sitting there for way too long, I just typed it in."

"Kathy!"

"I know, I know. The more we talk, though, the better I feel. I mean, it's so obvious why no one is writing to me."

"You know, what's interesting about your idea," I said slowly, "is that there are all these people sitting around feeling bad about themselves when the fault lies with their profile. It could be a real self-esteem builder to have someone point that out, and then help with it. I mean, kind of a public service."

"A public service that pays."

"And I'd be a writer," I said, my excitement starting to rise.

"You would."

"Is there any way this could actually work?" I asked, desperately wanting her to say yes.

"Yes."

Chapter 4

YEN FOR BOOKS

Age:	30
Height:	5'9"
Weight:	130 lbs
Occupation:	Writer/Editor
Hometown:	Boston, MA; live in NYC now
About me:	If you're looking for a slip of a girl whose primary trait is acquiescence (and many of you are, even if you don't know it), keep scrolling. Words are my business and my passion. Heaven is a Sunday spent reading the month's accumulated *New Yorker* magazines.
About you:	Don't tell me about how brilliant and well-traveled you are; show me. Be sexy—the world doesn't have to think so, but I do. You should love what you do for a living, or you should be trying hard to get out of it. You live by your wits and could survive if you were transplanted to a distant country knowing only the words "mama" and "pancake." If you really want to annoy me, tell me you're not religious but you're spiritual.

Five things I can't live without:	Intense conversation, a great zinfandel, passion, compassion, the Strand bookstore
Last book I read:	Proust. I'm always reading Proust.
Biggest turn-on:	Proust
Biggest turnoff:	Men who don't read Proust
Most embarrassing moment:	Placing this ad
Smoke:	Sometimes
Alcohol:	Sometimes
Drugs:	Never
Wants kids:	Sometimes
Religion:	Agnostic

Kathy! What were you thinking?" I squealed.

"I don't know! Maybe I wanted someone who doesn't scare easy."

"Well, the good news is, I've diagnosed your problem. I mean, after reading this, even I was considering never e-mailing you again."

"Hey, I know it's bad. You don't have to rub it in."

"And you filled in every single category! I mean, putting in that you're an agnostic on top of all those Proust references—that's the death knell right there."

"Ha-ha." She paused. "You don't have to fill in all the categories?"

"No. You can skip around."

"Okay. I authorize you to remove the agnostic part and my weight."

"Oh, no. Your weight stays. That's the only reason you got any responses at all."

"Don't you have some work to do?" she asked mock-pointedly.

"I'm going."

We hung up and I reread the profile, more intently this time. The problem was, it didn't sound like Kathy at all. It didn't capture her kindness or her generosity or her playfulness. She did like Proust, but mostly she was using Proust as a punch line, and what kind of guy can you net with Proust as a punch line? And saying it was embarrassing to place an ad alienated any reader who'd been hardy enough to make it that far. Not to mention that opening shot about wanting an acquiescent woman, even if they didn't know it . . .

So there were two questions to be answered. The first was, Who was Kathy? The second was, Who was the target audience? I needed to blend those into one entirely authentic sales pitch, which wasn't the oxymoron Kathy seemed to think it was.

ANAGRAM

Age:	30
Height:	5'9"
Weight:	130
Occupation:	Writer/Editor
About me:	I was "One to Watch" in *Highlights* magazine when I was 11. (Look out, world!) Words are still my passion, and now my profession, and that's just pure good fortune. I'm a generous noticer. I'll bake a pie for anyone who needs it, because no one can be sad when there's pie around. I

	don't equivocate: when I'm in, I'm in all the way.
About you:	You're a poet, a scientist, a philosopher, a farmer, a scholar, a rugby player, a teacher, a carnival barker, a raconteur — be any or all of these, but be it fully. You're interested in travel and the arts and other people. You know when to shut up and just feel. You're sexy for all these reasons and some that only I'll get to know about.
Five things I can't live without:	Intimate conversation, a great zinfandel, passion, compassion, the Strand bookstore
Last book I read:	*New Yorker* magazines, March–May, on a leisurely Sunday
Biggest turn-on:	A well-chosen detail
Biggest turnoff:	Being uncomfortable with yourself
Most embarrassing moment:	Having my best friend rewrite my ad

"Nora!"

"Okay. I guess you can take out the last line." I paused a beat. "So, what do you think?"

"I love it," Kathy said, without hesitation.

"Now it sounds like you." My face flushed with pride and relief. I'd been so nervous reading it to her, waiting for the verdict.

"Really?" she asked, sounding touched.

"Definitely."

"You can do this. I mean, for a career. You could really do this."

My heartbeat accelerated again, with hope and terror.

• • • •

Kathy and I decided the best place to start my freelance career was Craigslist. That's because in the Bay Area, it's fairly common to manage your whole life through Craigslist, a Web site of classified listings that range from the mundane to the mind-blowing. Over the years, I've generally used it for the mundane: jobs, apartments, a bedroom set, and a car. People I know have found their massage therapists, child care workers, bandmates, pets, lost keys, and, in one instance, a reliable sex worker. When I first moved to town five years ago and knew no one, Craigslist introduced me to a hiking group, an adventure group, a meditation class, a wine-tasting club, and a loosely organized cadre of extremely hip knitters. Every time I forced myself to make an appearance, I managed to tap at least one person who was as misplaced as I was. I met one of my best friends, Larissa, at a gathering of Jewish singles, and I'm not Jewish. (It was a low moment, trying to pass. But I'm a mutt, and mutts don't get their own singles gatherings.) Anyway, Craigslist was free, and largely unpoliced, and yet somehow legitimate, which made it the perfect place to launch my new business venture.

I was so electrified with excitement that it was hard to make it through the next day of work, though I was grateful for another week of guaranteed income. I spent a lot of my time browsing dating Web sites, gleefully noting any clunker ads and thinking how soon I might be coming to their rescue. I felt like the right person with the right skills and the right idea at the right time, which was dizzyingly foreign to me.

I left work right at five. I'd decided that I wanted to surprise Dan with a special dinner that night, my way of saying, "Aren't you glad I'm moving in with you?" I was also going to surprise him with my new career plan. For the provisions, I went to the gourmet market, where I never shopped. I frequented the supermarket with its bright lights and Krispy Kreme display, where the perpetually harried filled their carts with salami and canned peaches. The gourmet market, on the other hand, is a place where people actually sign up for wine and cheese classes. The fish department only buys from sustainable fisheries to protect the local ecosystem, and at the meat and poultry counters, staff wear white chef jackets and recommend the best cooking preparation and a wine pairing. The produce is all organic and each fruit or vegetable has a sign in front of it explaining that it's from whatever region in the world currently has the best crop of that particular kumquat or gingerroot or what-have-you. It's where locals who could afford to care about their bodies and the world in equal measure shopped, and where I envied them in their serene, yoga-pantsed glory. They lived here; I was only a tourist.

I headed for the fresh pasta department and bought a pound of the butternut squash ravioli. The woman who sold it to me explained how to prepare it lovingly with a sage butter sauce, asparagus, and cherry tomatoes. When I added on some bread, the red wine she suggested, and flowers, I felt a twinge that I refused to interpret as guilt. I didn't have time for guilt anyway. I needed to get to Dan's home before he did or all was lost.

Once inside the apartment, I threw everything on the kitchen counter and hurriedly arranged the flowers in a vase on the table. As I debated whether to start slicing the bread or boiling the water for pasta, I looked around and realized just how little time I'd spent in this apartment without Dan. It seemed completely unreal to me that in a week, this would be my home.

I'd never moved into someone else's space before. I'd lived with boyfriends before (two, to be precise), and in one case, he moved into my apartment, and in the other, we'd picked out an apartment together. I would have preferred the latter route this time around, but Dan's rent was so low that neither of us wanted to give it up. My rent would be half what it had been at Fara's, and that reduction in expenses couldn't have come at a better time.

But it wasn't the apartment I would have chosen. First of all, it was carpeted and I'm a hardwood lover. I tried to get my fill of wood from the bar that runs the *entire* length of the living room. Yes, the bar was gorgeous, but it was from 1920 and didn't exactly blend with an apartment built in the 1960s. It did, however, match the mammoth entertainment center on the perpendicular wall. I was daunted by that living room.

The bedroom was more hospitable. It's small and it was going to be a challenge to fit everything in, but I felt sure I could make it work. I had a spot picked out for the drafting table I use for a desk, right under the window. A window that opens. *We'll be happy here*, I thought as I started chopping the asparagus.

When Dan opened the front door, the table had been set and dinner was just a few minutes from being ready. *I'm finally getting my timing down.*

"Oh, baby!" Dan said, smiling broadly and embracing me. "You are a find, you know that?"

"I know that." We kissed, and while I felt a stirring of passion, I felt a greater desire to eat. I realized I was ravenous. When his hands started to move down the front of my shirt, I gently shrugged him off. "Dinner's going to be ready in five minutes."

"It'll keep, won't it?" he said playfully, reaching for me again.

"I'm really hungry. You just walked in on this smell; I've been smelling it for a while now. I'm practically salivating." There was a defensive note to my voice that bothered me. I wanted to sound as light as he did.

"It's cool. We can eat." And it did seem to be cool with him.

He tossed a cherry tomato in his mouth and smiled at me as he leaned against the counter. "This was a nice surprise."

I handed him a glass of wine and pecked his cheek. I still felt the tension of having moved away from him, though he didn't seem aware of it.

"So you made it through another day," he said.

I raised an eyebrow at him quizzically.

"At your job. At your brutish job." He waggled an eyebrow back at me.

"I was no Cinderella there today. They barely got a half day's work out of me." I drained the ravioli and started arranging our plates. "Sorry I didn't get any salad."

"Don't apologize. This is great." He touched the back of my hand lightly. I felt myself glowing slightly at his appreciation as I brought our loaded plates to the table.

"I didn't even notice the flowers before. Man, you are a find," he said again, shaking his head. It was something he'd told me on our third date, and until the past five minutes, only once or twice since. I smiled at the memory. "Thank you." He held my gaze for an extra few seconds before picking up his fork.

I watched him eat, feeling my nervousness surge. I really wanted him to approve of my—well, Kathy's—freelance idea. I thought if he approved, it would mean I was doing the right thing. I hadn't told anyone else about the idea yet, and it felt like expensive wedding china, like something precious and easily broken.

"I ended up having kind of an exciting night last night." I was shooting for casual, but landed on labored instead.

"Yeah?" He glanced up, but continued eating.

"I was losing it, actually, totally panicking about leaving my job, and I called Kathy and we just stumbled onto this great opportunity."

He nodded in that "go on" way, his face betraying nothing.

"Maybe opportunity is the wrong word. Or at least, it's not a ready-made kind of opportunity."

He nodded again, making a face of approval. My heart leaped, then I realized it was because he was gesturing at the ravioli with his fork. "These are delicious. You didn't stuff them yourself?"

"No. They came from that market on Seventh."

"Wow. We've gone upscale." He squeezed my hand. "Baby, this was so good of you."

"I try." It was good to be appreciated, but he was ruining my flow. I plunged in again. "The opportunity is for me to write profiles on dating Web sites. Have you ever been on those?"

He shook his head. "I've heard of them. Never been on one. It's, like, advertising for dates."

"Right. That's the point."

He did a little shudder.

"I had a profile on one for a while. But then I met you," I said.

"And you could get hired by the Web sites to write profiles for people? *Dating Profiles in Courage. Let Us Now Praise Famous Daters.*" He smiled wryly, still focused on his plate. When he joked, he never looked for my reaction.

"No, I'd be a freelancer. I'm going to put an ad on Craigslist and offer my services to the people who have profiles and aren't getting a good response, or to people who've been too shy to put profiles up, or, you know, to anyone else who answers the ad." *Say it's a great idea. Say I'd be a natural.*

He cocked his head to the side. "Sounds interesting. Do you think it'll work?"

"I think I'd be good at it."

"I'm sure you would. But"—he furrowed his brow almost imperceptibly—"do you think it'll work, you know, getting people to hire you?"

My heart sank slightly, but I tried not to let it show. "It's a big market. Lots of people do Internet dating now."

"A lot of people looking to get laid. I was listening to some radio station and this guy called in and said he'd slept with three different women that weekend. The DJ says, 'How'd you do that?' and the guy says, 'Two words for you: Mymate-dot-com.' Complete idiot. Those aren't two words."

I tried to conceal my irritation. Didn't he get what big news this was? Why was he telling me anecdotes about radio call-in shows? "But what do you think of the idea?" I prodded.

"It seems clever." He didn't shrug, but it seemed like he should have.

He probably didn't mean it to be dismissive, but it stung. "And clever ideas fizzle out, right?" I said it more sharply than I'd intended.

"I wasn't criticizing. I know you'd be good at it. I just don't know if you'll get enough people from Craigslist to make a run of it." He pointed at my plate. "Aren't you going to eat? It's good stuff."

I popped a ravioli in my mouth to placate him. He was right. They were good. He was always aggravatingly right. I chewed another ravioli to work out my rising annoyance before speaking again. "I don't know if I'll get enough people, either, but I think this is my time to try, with my rent being so much less. I think it's worth trying."

"Sure."

"And hopefully, if I do the profiles well, I'll get word of mouth." I started in on the wine, hoping it would relax me. I told myself Dan wasn't doubting me, he was wondering about the market, but it still felt discouraging. I knew it wasn't fair to ply him with food so that he'd be enthusiastic about my idea; I just hadn't realized that was what I was doing until right then. "And I can send out e-mails to everyone I know asking them to tell their friends." I figured I could use the same lists I'd made the day before to beg for nonprofit jobs. "Oh, this might be jumping ahead, but I want to ask your permission for something."

"What's that?" I wished he'd stop being so fixated on dinner.

"People might want to know my credentials for doing this. And I thought I could tell them that you and I met over the Internet. More specifically, I want to tell them that you liked my profile and contacted me." I looked at him intently.

"I wouldn't have to meet them, would I?" He seemed perturbed at the thought.

"I don't see why you would."

"But if you're sending the e-mail out to people you know and asking them to send it on to their friends, there's the possibility I could meet those people someday."

Damn his scruples. First he couldn't even feign excitement, now he was throwing up roadblocks. "What are the odds that even if you did happen upon such a person, say, at a dinner party, they'd actually try to confirm that we'd met online? It doesn't make sense."

"I just don't want to have to lie."

"It's a white lie."

"Well, it's a full lie," he said.

"A white lie doesn't mean half a lie; it means it's the kind of lie that doesn't matter."

"Let me think it over."

"Are you serious?" I burst out, exasperated.

"You want to rewrite our history. Don't I get to think about it?"

"Here's the thing," I explained, summoning my patience. "It's like white lying at a job interview. You might say you have skills that you don't actually have because you can learn them, and if you admitted you didn't have them up front, you'd never get hired. In this case, the reason it's a harmless lie is because I am qualified to do this, I just need to get in the door." I looked at him beseechingly. "I won't even tell people unless they ask."

"Why don't you say you met your last boyfriend on the Internet?"

"I thought of that, but then they'll know that it wasn't a lasting connection."

"Are you really going to start using phrases like 'lasting connection'? I don't know if I like this."

"I can't even tell if you're joking."

"That's because I don't know if I'm joking."

"Please. It's not a big deal." I let out a sigh. "I can't believe we're having this conversation. I was only asking you as a formality."

"Nice."

"You know what I mean. I just didn't think it would matter to you."

"It's one thing to lie to some phony in human resources, but it's another thing to instill false hope in the kind of desperate people who need to hire a matchmaker."

"Now you're saying I'm predatory?"

"That has never crossed my mind." He brushed my cheek with his forefinger. "You tell them whatever you decide is right, okay?"

"Okay." I decided to take that as an expression of confidence. I would have done what I wanted anyway.

Chapter 5

LARISSA

Age:	32
Height:	5'4"
Weight:	That's why there are pictures, silly!
Occupation:	Environmental lawyer for the little guy
About me:	Idealistic. Whimsical. Hardworking, but somehow I always find the time and the energy ☺. I believe chemistry can be found in unlikely places. And I believe that it's not whether you fall; it's how you get back up that counts.
About you:	My kids will be Jewish no matter what you are, so just be well-adjusted, honest, quick to laughter, and basically nonpolluting (you don't have to bring your own bags to the grocery store with you, but it's nice). If you're easy to be around and love a classic movie, this could be the start of a beautiful friendship.
Five things I can't live without:	The ocean, caffeine, good company, brown paper bags, and, well, love (there, I said it)

I can't believe you're going to be doing the Internet dating thing. That's my turf," Larissa said. She lifted books from my shelf and placed them in the box at her feet. It was moving day, and she'd generously offered to help me with last-minute packing.

"Spine-side down," I directed.

"Really? I've always done it the other way."

"It's completely counterintuitive, I know, but when I worked in a bookstore, that's how they did it." I crossed back to my closet, where I was transferring the hanging clothes to suitcases. "Sorry. Didn't mean to cut you off."

"It's okay. I was just thinking that now you're going to really see what it's like out there."

"Oh, I know what it's like. I was out there six months ago."

"But now look at you."

I surveyed the mostly empty room. "Yeah. Look at me."

"Did I tell you I'm on a new dating site now? You know, the one I laughed at a few months ago. Well, desperate times, right? It's the one where they match you based on these exhaustive questionnaires. I filled mine out last night; it was like taking the LSATs again."

I laughed. "How'd you score?"

"I guess I'll know soon enough. The site's going to do the matching for me. Everything's a science now."

"How many sites are you on now?"

"This new one brings it to four."

"That sounds tiring."

"Not really. I'm old news on three of them, so no one writes to me anyway. The depressing part is that I keep seeing a lot of the same guys, with slight modifications depending on the site. Like, on the sexier site, they add virile flourishes. Of course I tart it up sometimes, too. But it bugs me anyway. I mean, the whole point of being on multiple sites is to get access to new people. If I keep seeing the same ones, it defeats the purpose."

"But you're defeating their purpose, too."

"I know." She paused. "I have this new bad habit of tracking my ex-boyfriends by their profiles. Remember Jason? He's on the market again."

"Tell me you don't want Jason back."

"No. I want the schadenfreude. I hate when their profiles disappear because it means they've met someone, and I love when they reappear because now they're in the same boat as me. I can even tell how their last relationship went by the changes they make in their profile. Jason's last girlfriend must have been clingy because now he's all about finding an independent woman."

"You're right; this is your turf."

"I'm just going through the motions, really. I still miss Dustin. Six months, and according to Debbie, I'm still in denial."

Debbie was Larissa's therapist. "Meaning you don't believe he's gone?"

"Most of the time, I know he's never coming back and that there are a million reasons why I don't want him back anyway, but I've still got moments where I'm sure he was the one for me and that one of these days he'll realize it."

"What does Debbie make of that?"

"She says it's part of the grieving process." Larissa counted off on her fingers: "Denial, anger, bargaining, depression, acceptance. She even gave me an acronym to remember them. DABDA."

"Catchy." I held up a belt I hadn't worn in three years and squinted at it critically before throwing it into the suitcase. "I'm so jealous that you can afford therapy."

"I'm so jealous that you never started it. I mean, every week I go in and I discover some new subpar aspect of myself. I some-times think I should stop while I'm ahead, before I find out any-thing else."

"But you've already opened Pandora's box. There's no going back." I zipped up the suitcase. "Every time I move, I swear this will be the time that I do it right. I'm going to get organized, I'm going to go through everything and throw out the crap I've been hauling with me from apartment to apartment, and every time I leave it all to the last minute and just throw it into boxes. And some of it's never actually come out of boxes since the last move."

"You could go through everything when you're moved in and make a donation."

I shook my head. "No one does that. You either donate before you move, or it stays yours until the next time."

"So lately," Larissa said, "what Debbie and I have been work-ing on is goal setting."

I groaned. "What is it with that horrible word right now? That's what Dan wants me to do, too."

"Therapy goals are different. They're like, How will you know when you're done with therapy? How will you know when you've fully evolved?" She placed a self-deprecating emphasis on the "fully evolved."

"And?"

"Goal setting has taken up three sessions!" She actually threw her hands up to indicate her frustration with herself. I couldn't remember ever seeing anyone do that outside of a bad sitcom. "That's three hundred dollars. And Debbie's like, 'Well, there's your problem. You don't know what you want.'"

"Maybe Debbie's your problem. If you don't develop any goals, you're never getting out. It's sort of a fantastic scam, isn't it?" Seeing the anxiety on Larissa's face, I added hastily, "I don't really mean that. You've gotten a lot of good things out of therapy."

"I thought I had, because I was so much happier for a while there. But then I realized: I was happier when I was with Dustin. I was just all-around happier. So I went to therapy every week and we talked about my father and I felt proud of myself for staying committed to the process. That's another thing Debbie talks about: my commitment to the process, so that if I leave, I'm someone who can't commit. Now, I know I have a lot of shortcomings, but that is not one of them. I've broken up with two men in my life. Two! And I've been in, like, five hundred relationships. I am not afraid of commitment."

"So if you quit therapy, it would actually be progress. You'd break up with her instead of waiting for her to do it first." I was only half-joking.

"Sonya thinks I should quit, too."

We exchanged a look that said, "Well, obviously." Sonya was our self-possessed friend. That's actually how we thought of her. She was also our successful corporate friend, our new mother friend, and our able-to-do-math-and-her-own-taxes friend. Even if we occasionally got frustrated with her pragmatism, we could never end our friendship with her because she occupied so many important niches.

"Have you seen her recently?" I asked.

"Last week. She's doing great."

"Of course she is," I said. Sonya was always doing great. She needed Larissa and me to balance out her charmed life. I didn't want Sonya's life; I just wanted her certainty about it. Larissa, on the other hand, pretty much wanted Sonya's actual life.

"So that's it." Larissa taped up the top of her box and stood up. "You're pretty much packed."

"I know." I gave a nervous smile. "This could be bad, you know? This could be a hideous mistake."

"Dan's great."

"I know *he's* great. You do realize that if something goes wrong with this, it's going to be my fault."

"That's just garden-variety self-doubt."

"It's happening so fast. I mean, don't you think it's entirely too soon for us to live together?"

She walked over, put her arm around me, and gave me a squeeze. "When's Dan getting here?"

"I'm going to call him when I'm ready."

"Are you ready?"

Just once, I wanted to answer yes and mean it. But this wouldn't be that time.

. . . .

Later that day, I was unpacking, alone, in Dan's bedroom—our bedroom, now—but I didn't feel like I was really alone. The wraiths of my past relationships were right there with me: the six-weekers that had never grown into anything; the three-monthers that seemed to hold so much promise; the four that had each lasted a year, two where we lived together; relationships that had exploded; relationships that had imploded. This time around, I didn't want to stay too long, or leave too early.

That's when it hit me. This whole move was motivated by fear. I'd thought it was money, which wasn't good, either, but the truth was worse. I'd rushed into this because I wanted to know whether Dan and I were going to last, and the quickest way to find out was to live together. That's the perverse logic of fear: if it's going to blow up, might as well blow it up fast.

"You're so quiet," Dan said from the doorway.

I looked up, startled. I should have been finished with this room an hour ago. It was like unpacking while suspended in maple syrup.

"There's a lot to get done," I said.

"There's time."

I sat down on the bed, facing away from him. "I'm thinking that maybe this was a mistake."

Long pause, then Dan came and sat beside me. "Why do you think that?" he asked evenly.

"Just knowing me." I was suddenly on the verge of tears.

"I know you," he said, "and I'm glad you're here."

"I'm crying. It's the first day we're living together and I'm crying. Doesn't that freak you out?"

He shook his head.

"Is this going to work?" I asked urgently.

His eyes were trained on mine. "If we want it to."

"You're right," I said finally. I stood up. "We should get some dinner."

"My treat," he said, smiling.

· · · ·

Two days later, at 4:57 PM, I sat staring at my computer screen in the animal rescue, terribly conscious that in three minutes, it would no longer be my computer screen. There it was, the draft of my ad. Once I clicked on the "post" icon, it would be out there. *I* would be out there, an Internet profile consultant, open for business. All I had to do was click on the "post" icon.

My finger trembled on the mouse. *Just click. All you have to do is click.*

But I couldn't. I was leaving the only job I'd ever really done well. I was leaving the best coworkers I'd ever had, and the kindest boss. I was leaving the only job I'd ever held down for more than a year. Though ironically, I couldn't even say I'd stayed so long because of my boss, or my coworkers, or the good work I'd done. I'd stayed because the older I got, the more times I performed this dance, the less sure I was that something great was waiting for me on the other side. I definitely wasn't sure now. Just click this button—and then what?

Full minutes passed. It was now after five o'clock. I'd cleared out my desk the day before, had my good-bye lunch with everyone, and now all I needed was to post my ad, get my purse, and walk out the front door.

You can't sit here all night.

It was starting to look like maybe I could, when I heard footsteps. I hurriedly clicked, turned off the computer, and looked to see who it was. Oh. The one coworker it wasn't hard to leave behind.

"Hey, Nora," Estella said. "I guess this is it, huh?"

"I guess it is."

"Denise told me you're going to do something on the Internet . . . ?" she asked, pushing back her hair and resettling her bag on her shoulder.

Just to clarify: I didn't hate Estella for being gorgeous. I didn't hate her at all, in fact. I simply didn't care for her, because her every gesture seemed calculated to underscore just how good-looking she is, and that's just annoying.

"I am," I said. I didn't want to say more, especially since I was still feeling raw about the ad I'd just sent into cyberspace, but she kept looking at me expectantly. I gave in, and went on. See, she always got what she wanted. "I'm going to help people work on their Internet dating profiles."

"Huh." She nodded, considering.

"Yep." I wondered if I had to wait for her to walk away, or if I could just announce that I was leaving.

"So you're going to help people write their profiles?"

"I can help with writing, editing, whatever they need." I sped up as I spoke, hoping to give the impression that I needed to get going.

"What if they need a makeover? Then what will you do?"

"Nothing. That's not my job."

"Because some people, it doesn't matter what they write, they're going to have problems." She bobbed her head solemnly, as if in sympathy for those less fortunate.

I shrugged. I hadn't had many nonwork conversations with Estella, and hadn't seen her elitism on display before. It wasn't pretty.

"I mean, men only care about the pictures." She leaned in like she was going to reveal a secret. "A ton of guys write to me, and it's so obvious they didn't even read what I wrote. I'd say men are dogs, but that's just an insult to dogs, you know?"

I was assimilating the fact that Estella needed an ad, just like the rest of the proletariat, when Maggie came down the hall. My anxiety about the ad momentarily abated, replaced by sadness that I wouldn't be seeing Maggie five days a week anymore.

She was holding a small pastry box, which she set on my desk. "Open it," she said, smiling.

"Oh, Maggie!" I lifted the lid, prepared to coo. Inside was a cupcake, with its icing shaped into the figure of—a Dalmatian. Maggie had brought me a dog cupcake. Well, no one at any other job had ever brought me baked goods on my last day. I stanched my disappointment. "That's so sweet, Maggie. Thank you."

I stood up and hugged her.

"You've meant a lot to us," Maggie said. "I wanted to do something—"

Estella cut in, "You got that at Gorman's, right?" She glanced at me. "That's where she gets all of them."

I wasn't really surprised by that. Everyone sensed that Estella was Maggie's least favorite staff person; she had to feel at least a little slighted. Maggie would never be rude or mean; she just wasn't as warm toward Estella as she was toward the rest of us. Which was strange, since Estella was phenomenally gifted with animals and I was someone who ran away at the first sight of drool.

"I did get it at Gorman's," Maggie said, not looking at Estella. "So what will you be doing now, Nora?"

"She's going to write Internet porn," Estella said. She waited for Maggie's reaction, which was minimal, then laughed loudly. If Estella couldn't be the favored child, she'd be the rebel.

"What are you actually doing, Nora?" Maggie asked, giving Estella no reinforcement.

"I'm going to be freelancing," I said. My nervousness returned just saying it, though luckily, with much less intensity than earlier.

"That sounds exciting." Maggie flashed a maternal smile at me, and it seemed like we were going to leave it at that, which was how I wanted it.

Maybe sensing that, and still in bratty-sister mode, Estella said, "She's going to help people find dates. You should tell her about it, Nora."

Maggie waited politely. I was annoyed that Estella had forced us into this and I fought the urge to glare at her. "Well," I said, "people are going to hire me to help fix up their Internet dating profiles."

"You've just got to wonder why people can't do it for themselves. I mean, what's going on there?" Estella said.

"That's not a very charitable thought, Estella," Maggie chided. She turned back to me, her face serious. "That's going to be very delicate work. These are people who are probably already feeling insecure about themselves. You'll have to tread lightly."

"I know," I said. But honestly, I hadn't thought much about that part of it. I'd thought more about the writing, the part I knew I could do well.

"Nora, I think your job is to meet people and instill confidence. It's about meeting these wounded souls and mending their bruised egos. You need to help them access the best in themselves, and that's what you write about."

I wilted before her. I wanted to protest, *I'm not a healer, I'm just an amateur writer who doesn't need any more pressure.*

She must have seen it in my face, because she said quickly, "I'm sure this is going to be just the thing for you, Nora."

I looked up at her, eyes shining, not above digging for reassurance. "You really think so?"

"Absolutely."

"You'll be good, Nora," Estella said. Was she just trying to get on Maggie's good side? Looking at her, it was impossible to tell. I decided to take it as genuine.

After a final round of hugs and one last look around, I stepped outside. *You'll be good, Nora. This will be just the thing.*

I reached into the pastry box, bit off the head of the Dalmatian, and headed for the train.

• • • •

By the following morning, I'd gotten four e-mail responses to my ad. When I'd posted my 1992 Honda Civic for below blue book value, I'd gotten 150 in three hours, but who's comparing?

I thought how excitement and anxiety felt the same in my stomach, and I couldn't even tell which one I was experiencing more acutely as I sat staring at my in-box. *This is a good start. This is a good start. This is a good start . . .*

Chapter 6

CANDACE

Age:	32
Height:	5'2"
Weight:	120–140 lbs (Is it around the holidays?)
Occupation:	I'm in banking.
About me:	I was raised in a close-knit family in Southern California. I still go home for most holidays because my mother is the best cook. Now I live in San Francisco with my cat, Rudy. I named him after the movie *Rudy*, which is about this short football player . . .

I recognized Candace immediately. She wasn't the only brunette with shoulder-length hair, but she was the only one who kept looking up from her book expectantly. There weren't many people in the café, which was how she'd wanted it.

"Candace?" I asked.

"Nora?" she responded, smiling. "What a stupid thing to say. Obviously you're Nora. Do you want to sit down?"

"Sure," I said, taking the seat across from her. "It's nice to meet you in person."

"It's good to meet you, too." She leaned in, lowering her voice. "I'm kind of nervous. Is that normal?"

I nodded. She was my first client, but it seemed normal enough. I certainly felt nervous, though I hoped I wasn't project-ing it quite as openly as she was. I reached into my bag and pulled out the profile she had e-mailed me the night before. I decided the best way to combat my own anxiety was to minimize the small talk and leap right in. "So I read this, and it's—you know, it's not too bad. I just think it could use some pruning."

"Pruning? So you mean taking things out?"

"It's a little wordy."

"Oh." She seemed disappointed, like she'd gotten a bad grade on a test.

"Did you spend a lot of time on it?" I asked, with what I hoped sounded like sympathy.

"I did, actually." She already looked crestfallen. *Tread lightly, wounded souls:* Maggie's words echoed in my head.

"There's a lot of good stuff in here. It's just my experience that often, in this business, less is more. Sometimes men are reading a lot of profiles, and so you want to grab them and then leave some mystery. You know what I mean?"

"I think so." She tried to smile.

"Like, when you describe yourself, that paragraph is fourteen sentences long. So that could be a little intimidating."

"But what do you think of the sentences themselves?" She looked at me keenly. I noted that her eyes were her best feature, hazel and long-lashed. She looked older than thirty-two. Maybe that was because she was wearing her work clothes, and she worked as a loan officer.

I hesitated. "It reads kind of like an essay. And that's not a bad thing," I added quickly. "But you have to remember this is a marketing pitch. You want everything to be targeted. Nothing extraneous."

"What parts are extraneous?" Her eyes narrowed just slightly. She'd gone from doubting herself to doubting me. Maybe Maggie was wrong. Maybe I shouldn't baby them. Maybe I needed to make it glaringly apparent to Candace just what a disaster her profile was. Maybe I needed to break her down and build her back up, like in boot camp.

"The really long sentence about your love for Rudy, for example. The cat, not the movie, though we might want to rethink the other one, too." I was no therapist, and I was no drill sergeant. I hoped I was landing somewhere in between.

"She's really important to me."

She? "I know, and that's great. But this first section—that's where you want to hook them. And you have to think about the most desirable aspects of yourself and lead with those."

"Some men like cats."

"They do. But some men don't like women to like their cats too much."

"Then those men are bad matches for me."

That was not a good exchange. It was time to pull out the big guns. I took a deep breath. "When I first had my profile up, almost no one wrote to me, and the ones who did all seemed like freaks or perverts. Later on, I had the exact same pictures up, but a lot more men were writing to me, and they were quality. One of them is now my boyfriend. It took some time for me to learn how to write a profile, and then I helped my friends do it, and now I do it for a living. I know this must be weird, meeting with someone who's telling you that your paragraphs are too long and that you shouldn't talk about your cat. You must be feeling kind of defensive. I'd feel defensive, too. But I'm not criticizing you at all, the flesh-and-blood you who's sitting here with me. I'm making suggestions about how to best represent yourself so that you can get what—and who—you want."

Thankfully, the speech worked. Candace visibly relaxed. "I just can't believe I'm paying someone to help me market myself on the Internet. Next thing you know, I'll be auctioning myself off on eBay."

We both laughed. "Trust me, I sometimes find myself doing surprising things, too."

Candace surreptitiously glanced around the room, then said, "I'm not really thirty-two. I'm thirty-five."

"Oh."

"I know, it's stupid to lie about that. All my friends say, 'Well, what'll happen when he finds out?' and I say, 'Who's this he you're talking about?' If I could pass for twenty-nine, I'd write that. Your stock falls at thirty, everyone knows that. And it falls again at thirty-five, so I figured at least I'd try to get in before that second drop. The irony is, writing thirty-two hasn't gotten me shit, either."

"So maybe you should stick with thirty-five." But I knew what she meant. My own stock was falling as we spoke. If Dan didn't work out, I was well aware that there might not be that many men left on the floor of the exchange. I could see them, walking out one by one, and then two by two, as the ticker tape showed me dropping by quarter points, then half points—

"If I write thirty-five, then all I'll get are men over fifty writing to me."

I blinked. Oh, right. Candace. *Stay focused.* I picked up my pen. "Would you consider dating men over fifty?"

She snorted. "No. That's like admitting it's over for me."

"What if he was really handsome and owned his own plane?"

She laughed, then leaned in again conspiratorially. "You want to hear something funny? My mother's paying for this."

"For me?" I was oddly flattered.

She nodded. "She'll do anything for grandkids."

"Do you want kids?" I thought I remembered her profile saying that she didn't want kids.

She shrugged. "Probably. I doubt it'll happen, but if I had the choice, then probably."

I glanced at the profile on the table in front of me to confirm. "You put 'no' on this."

"I didn't want to scare all those guys off. I figure the last thing men want is someone with aging eggs who's going to push for kids right away."

"But you're not sure if you want kids. So you're not going to be pushing."

"But they don't know that. They'll just see my age and assume."

"The problem is that by saying no, you get the men who either don't want kids or who are frightened of women who do want kids. And you lose the men who might like to have a family someday, which might be what you want, too."

"So what do you think I should do?"

"I'd put 'not sure.' My theory is that ambiguity is best, as long as you don't seem like you're actually hiding something. For example, if you seem to be avoiding a direct question or talking around it, that's not good. But if you just leave room for interpretation, that's good." It had taken a little while, but I was feeling it now. I was in my element.

"My profile doesn't leave much to the imagination, does it?" she asked.

"Not as it stands right now. But we've got a lot to work with, right?" I smiled at her, and she smiled back.

"That we do."

This one was in the bag.

• • • •

I arrived at the apartment still exhilarated from my triumph with Candace. Dan was lying on the couch reading a magazine, and I leaped on him.

"Hey, you," he said as I buried my face in his chest and he wrapped his arms around me. "I'm guessing it went well?"

I lifted my head. "It went *amazingly* well. We had a lot of laughs, we made some big improvements in her profile, I drank two cappuccinos. It was a good night."

"You seem like someone who drank two cappuccinos."

I pretended to sock him, then straddled him instead. I bounced up and down. "Hey, you wanna?"

He laughed. "So that's what's passing for foreplay these days?"

"No, this is." I stripped my shirt off, then began to kiss his neck and downward. When I reached his belt buckle, Dan grabbed me by the shoulders and pulled me back up. His hand was on the back of my neck, forceful and insistent, as he kissed me. There was never anything tentative about Dan sexually, and I loved that. He went for what he wanted, and if he was rebuffed, he backed away without shame.

I remembered the first night we slept together. It was our second date and I hadn't seen his apartment yet. I found the bar strange and fascinating, and I just assumed Dan would offer an explanation of where it had come from and why. He didn't. He began to mix a drink so confidently that I thought he must have done it a million times before, but he said he was making it up as he went along and he christened it the Nora. He didn't say this the way most men would have, looking at me and waiting for my reaction. He just said it casually as he poured the drink into a cock-tail glass. It was strong, the Nora, and I said so. *Is she?* he asked.

I thought Dan was at once the best and worst flirt I'd ever met. All those long pauses and intermittent eye contact. But I was buzzing from his nearness before I had even taken a sip. Finally he kissed me. I was perched on the bar stool, Dan was standing on the other side. As I shifted my weight on the stool, my skirt splayed out so that I could feel my panties against the leather and my stomach was flat against the side of the bar and Dan's hand was roaming my face, my neck, my hair . . .

He made me wait. I was debating whether to jump over the bar, or yank his arm, or tell him he'd better get over here already. I wondered whether he was a sadist. Then I wondered if he was a masochist. I was starting to worry that he didn't feel what I did, that he wasn't even attracted to me if he could hold out so long, when he grabbed my face in both his hands and said, "Wait." He came around behind me and lifted me off the stool so that we were both standing. His chest was against my back, and we were both breathing hard. He slid my underwear off, and I could hear him unzipping his pants. He put his arms under mine, and then stretched us both out against the bar. As he entered me, I tensed my muscles around him, and when I finally released, we both went limp.

"Good trick," I said over my shoulder, so spent that I started laughing.

"Yours too."

We fell to the floor. I realized I was dampening my skirt and possibly his carpet, but I didn't want to move yet. I was waiting again, waiting for him to take hold of me. I'd grab him if I had to, but I wanted him to do it. It would mean more that way.

He began stroking my hair. I turned my head and looked at

him. His face looked more vulnerable to me now. It was a good face: not handsome exactly, but solidly crafted. He had gray blue eyes and those are rare. He had a small scar above his eyebrow, just a slight indentation of uncertain origin. I wanted to hear the story behind it someday.

"Thanks for coming," he said.

It was my first indication of just how strangely corny Dan could be. We both laughed, and he moved closer to me.

"I got it from an estate sale."

"What?" I asked, confused.

"The bar. I know you were wondering. I looked a long time for it."

"It's beautiful."

"I know it doesn't exactly go with this room, but I plan to have it forever. When it fits somewhere, that's where I'll stay."

Now, a little more than six months later, we were lying on the couch, my head pressed to his chest. We had just finished making love, and I couldn't tell if my forehead was damp with my sweat or his. I tilted my head to look at the bar, and thought about what an unusual first time that had been. Dan's sexual confidence was not something I'd found in many other men. It was quiet, but undeniable. He was purposeful, and his ego never seemed to bruise. It was just one way in which Dan seemed strangely impenetrable to me.

He nudged me out of my reverie. "We got sidetracked for a while there. Tell me more about your night."

I was suddenly gripped by a sense of foreboding, as if this moment were a mirage, and there was something darker behind it, or beyond it. It was the sensation of being buried up to my neck in sludge. I feared that everything would bog down sooner or later: my relationship with Dan, my freelancing. Either I hadn't really been good with Candace, or if I had, it would turn out to be just shy of what was really needed. I would never get enough clients, I would never make enough money, I would never move forward. That was what it always came back to, the idea that I would never move forward. It was my version of a panic attack, only I could breathe just fine and my heart didn't speed up much—and it could last all night. I would have preferred the kind that Larissa had, the kind that peaked in ten minutes and then you got on with things.

"I'm suddenly really scared," I said. "Could you talk me down?"

He clutched me more tightly and spoke softly into my ear. "You're going to be okay. Better than okay."

"Do you think so?" I asked. It was already working; the darkness was subsiding.

"You were glowing when you came home. You nailed it."

"I did, actually." I smiled slightly, remembering. "I think I did a good job with the writing, but the other thing was, she just looked so hopeful. She started out tense, and at the end, she looked hopeful. I don't know that I've ever had that kind of direct effect on someone before."

"Well, not through your work." Dan kissed the top of my head.

"You know what's weird? That's the effect you just had on me. In a matter of seconds. It's crazy, the way you can do that." I settled more deeply into his arms. "I can do it to myself sometimes, but you're so much better at it."

"It's easier for you to trust someone else. I tell you it'll be okay, and you take my word for it."

"That might be true. I wish it wasn't true, but it probably is," I said sleepily. The day had finally caught up with me.

"Let's go to bed," Dan said, reading me perfectly. He shifted me around so he could stand up, then offered me his hand.

· · · ·

I still hadn't told my mother about quitting my job. I'd had one conversation with her since giving notice, where I managed to answer all her questions without lying, but avoided telling her what I'd done. It was my most sophisticated verbal circumlocution yet, which is saying something because when it came to my mother, I'd become pretty crafty over the years. Now that I could claim one freelance success, I was ready to bite the bullet and return her phone call.

As I dialed, I felt nervous, and then frustrated with myself for being nervous. After all, the worst that could happen was that she'd be disappointed in me and I could handle that. I was used to her low-level disappointment. Now it might be a higher wattage, but that was entirely survivable.

"Hi, Mom," I said. I looked down and realized I was clenching and unclenching my fists, the hallmark of a healthy mother-daughter bond.

"Nora! Finally." It seemed like her happiness at hearing from me was always tinged with reproach.

"Sorry it took me a few days to get back with you."

"I'm used to it," she said. "But how are you? You sound pinched."

"I'm fine."

"So you and Dan are getting along?" She was on script. She turned on the faucet, and I could hear the water running. She was doing the dishes while we talked. I had "finally" called and she needed something else to occupy her.

"We're doing well." I'd be on script, too. For a little while, at least.

"You've been getting out?"

"Yes, I have."

"Going to the movies? Have you seen anything good at the movies?" That was a new one, actually.

"I haven't been to the movies in a while. I can't remember the last thing I saw. What have you seen?"

"Oh, just some garbage." Vintage Mom. For once, she had made what looked like a foray into normal conversation by asking me about movies; then when I followed up, she negated the whole thing. "And you're eating well?"

"Pretty well."

"I sent you that article on the low-carb diet, didn't I?"

"Yes. But I don't need a diet." I was trying not to sound pinched, whatever that meant.

"The article was about why people shouldn't do those low-carb diets." I generally threw out the articles she sent me unread, and she always caught me like this. But she kept sending them. Why was my mother booby-trapping my mail?

"I don't diet anyway." We had at least another two segments to go before this show would be over. I couldn't wait until we got to the Casey part of the call. That was the only time my mother actually answered questions at any length. When we got to Casey, I could always breathe again. Sometimes I tried to go there prematurely, and my mother would steer me back to the remaining topics in my own life that she felt still needed excavating.

Casey is my thirteen-year-old sister. She was adopted when she was three, so she and I have never lived in the same house together. Because of the infrequency of my visits, Casey and I don't know each other very well. We talk on the phone sometimes, but she doesn't open up easily. She's smart and sweet and painfully neurotic. She has all sorts of nervous tics and perfectionist tendencies and she's proof that my mother is to blame for my meta-life. I mean, Casey's not even from our gene pool and look at her. When I entered adolescence, my mother's snooping skyrocketed and I suspected the same thing was happening now. I also suspected that I was being routinely used as a cautionary tale to keep Casey on the straight and narrow. And leaving my job on a whim would surely, in my mother's mind, be one for the annals.

"And you're still not working out?" she asked. That particular question was designed to rhetorically showcase her disapproval of my lifestyle choice.

"No."

"It's going to catch up with you, Nora. I know you think it never will, but you're almost thirty. That's when the metabolism slows down. Believe me, I know. I was built like you, remember."

"Um-hmm." I wanted her just to hurry up and get to the work questions, because once we arrived there, we'd stay awhile. I glanced at the clock. I'd requested that Dan shout to me in ten minutes that we were late. He'd asked me what we were supposedly late for, and I said he didn't need to worry his pretty little head about that, he just needed to play his part and then keep his yap shut. That made him laugh. He liked the word "yap."

"And how's work going?"

Finally. "I have a new job, actually."

"Really? You didn't even mention that you were looking."

"I'm not looking. I'm building my own business."

"Well, that's enterprising of you. What kind of business?"

"I'm a freelance writer and editor." I was trying to say it with the inflection I thought a real freelance writer and editor would use. I felt somewhat fraudulent, as in, *I'm not a freelance writer and editor; I just play one during conversations with my mother*.

"And freelance means that it's not steady work. Isn't that what freelance means?" The worry had already set in. If I acted fast, maybe I could stave off panic.

"It means you contract with different people to perform a service, instead of all your work coming from one source or employer." I'd practiced that answer, and was pleased with my timing and pacing.

"What service are you performing? And is this really a growth industry that you're getting into?" Despite my efforts, she was going to panic. She wasn't there yet, but I could feel it.

"It is a growth industry. I'm helping people with their Internet dating profiles."

"*Pornography*? Is that what you're doing?"

Why did people keep saying that? "Of course not. Internet dating is a completely acceptable way to meet people. It's getting more popular all the time. I'll send you an article about it." I didn't really have an article, but the offer allowed me to both stress my legitimacy and take a jab at my mother.

All I could hear was her loud breathing. But at least she'd stopped doing the dishes.

"It's going really well so far," I said. "Kathy's helping me do it." My mother loved Kathy. She thought Kathy was "a real go-getter."

"She is?" At the mention of Kathy, my mother's breathing normalized instantly. It occurred to me that I should start having Kathy do these calls for me. Both my mother and I would probably be happier that way.

"She is. I actually worked on her profile. She was my first paying client."

"You let Kathy pay you?"

"She insisted. And she said she would have paid me double, it was so good." A white lie. Kathy would have said that, I'm sure, but she didn't conceive of quality in monetary terms. My mother, on the other hand, did.

"And people other than your friends have started paying you for this service?"

"Yes. They're paying me well for it."

"Where do you get these clients?"

I hesitated, but I couldn't think of any answer but the truth. "I placed an ad. There's a Web site—"

"So these are complete strangers? Anyone with a computer can arrange a meeting with you? That's how thousands of young women get killed every year." Her voice was getting louder with each sentence.

"Mom, calm down."

I could hear my mother trying to heed my suggestion, which was progress for us. "This seems dangerous." She tried to keep her voice level. "Does Dan approve of this?"

"He supports me, yes."

"And he goes with you to meet these people the first time?"

"He has a job and a life."

"So he lets you go off to meet strangers."

"Mom, stop this right now. Dan is not my father. He doesn't 'let me' do things. We talk and he gives me his opinion and he respects my ability to make my own choices." I was getting as huffy as she was, which was exactly why I hated these conversations. They reminded me of our similarities, while I generally tried to think only of our differences.

"How very enlightened of him. He supports you in endangering yourself. I don't know what kind of—"

"Stop right there, Mom. Say one more word against him, and I am hanging up this phone." Now I'd had it. This battle over my inadequacy had been going on for fifteen years, and I wouldn't let an innocent bystander take shrapnel.

She was quiet, perhaps trying to gauge how serious I was. Most likely, she was finding another tactic. "I'm just saying that he should—"

I wished I hadn't been on a cordless phone so that I could have slammed the receiver into a cradle. That would have been much more satisfying than clicking the "End" button, even if I did punch it three times.

Almost immediately I regretted hanging up on her. I regretted it for the following reasons, in ascending order: 1) It was juvenile; 2) Worse, it made me look juvenile; 3) I'd seemed defensive, and my mother would construe that I must have something to hide, which would increase her worry; and 4) Most important of all, now that she was worried, she would call more, creating more opportunities for me to horrify myself with my own behavior.

But right then, I needed to focus. I had to decide if I was going to call her back, wait an hour by the phone to see if she called me back, or hate the sound of my phone ringing until she did. Calling her back immediately was the move most likely to alter her perception that I was destroying my life. I could apologize for my behavior, say that I was a bit stressed with all the change, but that I was confident about my abilities and there was nothing, absolutely nothing, for her to worry about.

I do realize that I'm far too reactive to my mother. In between phone calls, I nurse the fantasy that someday I'll outgrow it or, better yet, become so incontrovertibly successful that even a champion neurotic like her couldn't poke holes in my life. Larissa once suggested I find a therapist who would do conference calls with my mother and me so we could heal our relationship. I said I'd prefer to give my money to someone who could impersonate me during phone conversations.

Dan called from the other room, "Honey, we're going to be late!"

"Shut your yap," I muttered as I redialed my mother's number.

Chapter 7

NORA

Age:	29
Height:	5'6"
Weight:	130 lbs
Occupation:	Internet dating consultant
About me:	Under construction
About you:	Under construction
The last book I read:	*The 7 Habits of Highly Effective People*
Biggest turn-on:	Under construction
Biggest turnoff:	Under construction
Five things I can't live without:	An income of at least $1,500 a month, plus four others
Most embarrassing moment:	The window incident

So I finally have my therapy goal. It's been months in the making, many tears have been shed, but here it is." Larissa made a trumpeting sound. "I am going to live more in the moment!"

It was, frankly, underwhelming. I couldn't help thinking that the goal—not its achievement, merely its articulation—had probably cost her a thousand bucks. "That's great, Larissa," I said, trying not to let my true feelings show. She had seemed so delicate lately, ever since the matching site had paired her with men who were professionally successful and interpersonally crippled, with seemingly identical upbringings to her own. I speared a cucumber and thrust it in my mouth to avoid a follow-up remark.

Larissa read me instantly, though. "After all that time, anything was going to seem anticlimactic."

"You're probably right." And she was. But still, all that she could have bought with a thousand dollars . . .

"It's a good goal, right?"

"It's a great goal."

"So why do you have that look on your face?"

I put down my fork. "Every time you and I get together, we review your therapy sessions. Essentially, we analyze your analysis. And now your goal is to live more in the moment, and I applaud that. I really do. I'm just wondering about the method for reaching that goal."

"Therapy," she said, like the star pupil she'd always been.

"Right. What I'm saying is, living more in the moment is about thinking less. It's about less analysis. Isn't it kind of paradoxical to live more in the moment by analyzing more in therapy? I mean, can something be both the disease and the cure?"

"Debbie and I have already gone over this," Larissa said. "Through more concentrated analysis, I free myself of the need to analyze in the moment."

"So what you're saying is that you confine your analysis to the therapy session. Once you leave Debbie's office, you're in the moment."

"Exactly. See, it's not about disease and cure; it's about disease and vaccination. I swallow an attenuated form, and then I'm protected."

Vaccination against meta-life. It was a compelling idea that I didn't buy at all, but debating the point with Larissa could only end with hurt feelings. She was invested in this, financially and emotionally. "I guess I can see that," I said, hoping she was ready to let this go.

Thankfully, she was. "So I need to tell you about Liza's wedding."

"Oh, right. I'd forgotten about that."

"I don't think I told you this, but Liza set me up to share a room with this guy, Martin. His story is much worse than my Dustin story. He got married less than a year ago, and his wife decided after a month of marriage that it wasn't for her, he wasn't the one, and they got it annulled. Can you imagine? I guess they'd been together for like seven years." Her eyes were wide. She took a sip of diet soda. "I have no tolerance for these women who don't know themselves at all. She couldn't dump him on the eve of the wedding like a decent person?"

I shrugged. "Buyer's remorse?"

"It's gross, in my opinion."

I didn't want to point out that her vociferousness might be more about being unceremoniously dumped by Dustin than about Martin's plight. "So how did you wind up sharing a room with Martin?"

"It was a Sunday-afternoon wedding, but I had to be there the day before for this spa-day bachelorette party and the pre-wedding dinner on Saturday night. And between the spa day and springing for a wedding gift, the whole affair was costing me a fortune, so when Liza called a few weeks back and said she had this harmless guy for me to share a room with, I agreed. I wasn't thinking that anything was going to happen. He's still heartbroken, I'm still heartbroken—"

"Precisely why something was going to happen."

"How do you know anything happened?" she asked coyly.

"If it hadn't, you wouldn't be dragging out this story."

"So Martin is a textbook harmless guy, like Liza said. He's the groom's cousin from the Midwest, stocky and corn-fed and soft-spoken. He flirted with me sort of ineptly during the prewedding dinner, and of course, we both had a few drinks, and then we went upstairs to the room together." She paused dramatically. "The shocking thing was not that he moved in. It's the way he moved in. The door shut behind us and he pounced. He grabbed me and pushed me up against the door and jammed his tongue down my throat."

"Classy."

"I know, right?"

"So you told him to stay on his side of the room?"

"No. I made out with him for a couple of hours."

"Why? Did his technique improve?"

"It did, actually. I was into it for stretches of time."

"The endorsement every man wants to hear."

She shrugged. "He's the first guy since Dustin. What could I expect? It's good to get it out of the way with someone who doesn't matter and who I'll never see again."

"I just hate when these guys skip the preamble. It's one thing if you've had some seething sexual tension all night long, but it doesn't sound like that. What made him think he could just jump you?"

"Circumstance," she said with certainty. "Weddings. All the movies about weddings. I was going to be a bridesmaid."

"He didn't even wait until you actually were a bridesmaid."

"He couldn't. This was his moment of opportunity. I was driving home the next day right after the wedding."

"So you made out with him for a couple of hours, and then what?"

"That's it."

"You didn't sleep with him?" I asked, a little surprised. I'd just figured that if she wanted to get her first rebound out of the way, she would have gone all the way.

"No. I made it clear that wasn't happening. Like, he kept trying to go down and I kept saying, 'No, I don't want you to do that,' and then, 'No, I *still* don't want you to do that.'"

"Have you noticed how the tides have turned on oral sex in the last couple of years? They're all leaping face-first down your pants now."

Larissa considered. "You know, that's really true."

"Remember dating five years ago? Men didn't try to go down before you'd had sex. Now it's just a regular part of foreplay."

"I'm not into that," she said emphatically.

"Into oral sex?"

"Not before we have sex the regular way. It's too intimate."

"I agree. All of a sudden men act like that's between third base and home plate and I think it's more of a grand slam." I paused. "So why didn't you sleep with him?"

"Because of Dustin." She lowered her eyes. "I know, I know. It's just, the kissing was fine and I was getting turned on, but I also felt like Dustin's image was barely at bay. It was like, I wasn't actually thinking about Dustin, but I could, at any second, and then it would be unbelievably painful and I'd start crying and I'd be there with this stranger to comfort me, not Dustin. I thought if I had sex with Martin, Dustin would definitely break out of his pen."

"Maybe it would have been cathartic. You'd be there with someone who gets what it's like to be left by someone they love. You could have both started crying and comforted each other."

"That's a completely heinous thought."

I thought for a second. "You're right. It is." I took a sip of wine. It was so nice to be able to drink in the middle of the day. "So you didn't sleep with him. Was that awkward? I mean, did you stay in the same bed?"

"Definitely awkward. For the last half hour, I was preoccupied with how to end things gracefully. I was trying to decide what my obligation was in terms of getting him off. I mean, I'd made it clear that there wouldn't be sex. He took his own pants off, but I never reached down there. But then, it *had* been a couple of hours and his erection was pressing into me the whole time."

"But he'd been such a Neanderthal when you first got into the room."

"Exactly! And the irony is that if he hadn't jumped on me, if we'd hung out in the room and talked for a while, I probably would have had sex with him."

I nodded in complete understanding. "I wonder how many men get that."

"The good ones get it intuitively; the rest never do."

"Don't keep me in suspense here. Did you or didn't you?"

"I gave him a hand job."

"Larissa!" I didn't like Martin. I was hoping he'd walk away with nothing. Actually, blue balls would be preferable.

"But listen to this. When I reached for it, that's when I discovered that he'd brought his own lube. He grabs my hand, tells me to 'hold my horses,' and goes into the bathroom to get it. 'Hold my horses!' Can you imagine? Maybe it's a Midwestern expression, I don't know. When he came out of the bathroom, I almost changed my mind. I mean, that's pretty forward, bringing your own lube into a hotel room with a woman you don't even know."

"Maybe he was planning on using it on himself."

"In a hotel room with a woman he didn't know?"

"Good point."

"But I gritted my teeth and did it, like the good girl I am."

"Ah, the good girl's dilemma: to jack them off or not to jack them off."

"And after all that, the next day at the wedding, he basically ignored me. He didn't do it pointedly or anything. He smiled at me from across the room a couple of times. He just never came to talk to me. I went up to him once while he was in conversation and he introduced me, then went back to his conversation about astrophysics or something. He didn't even shift the topic to be a bit more inclusive. And he underscored this decision by saying, 'This must be a real laugh-a-minute for you,' or something like that. At that point, I just walked away."

"And he never asked you to dance, even?" I wasn't surprised by his breach of etiquette by this point in the story, but I was still disgusted on Larissa's behalf. I mean, one hand job equals at least one dance.

"Not one dance. It's not like I was expecting him to be my date just because we fooled around in the hotel room, but it would have been gentlemanly for him to at least check in with me occasionally. You know, the occasional conversation, maybe a dance or two. But pretty much nothing. That's while we're inside. When I went up to him to say good-bye, he offered to walk me to my car and once we got there, he actually tried to kiss me again."

"And did you kiss him?" I asked, smiling at what I suspected the answer would be.

"Yeah. I didn't want to be rude."

At that, we both cracked up.

"Okay. Enough about Martin," she said. "Tell me about how things are going with you and Dan."

"Things are good." I stuffed some bread in my mouth and looked away.

Larissa gave me a knowing look.

"They are! There's nothing wrong at all. It's been two weeks of us living together and no problems, really."

"So you're happy?"

I reflected for a few seconds. "It's complicated, you know? I'm stressed out. Rent is due in two weeks, and I've only had the one client. That went great, and I figured there were more where she came from, but no one else has panned out. A few people e-mailed me to ask more questions and I wrote them back and then never heard from them again. I never responded to one guy because he seemed to think I was an undercover hooker. When I go home today, I'm going to work on my ad and post it again. Though it's kind of disheartening. I mean, I'm advertising to help people write their profiles and I can't net anyone with my own ad."

"It'll just take a little time, that's all. I mean, you're good at this. You said your profile for Kathy worked wonders."

"She did say that." I sat up and squared my shoulders. "Right? She actually used the term 'miracle.' That's got to mean something, right?"

"Of course it means something."

"'Of course' is what people say when things are most definitely in question."

"I don't. I'm a lawyer. One wrong word can get you sued." I laughed, and she continued. "You're just panicking. You made a big change, and now you're panicking. You just need to stay the course."

"I want to, but I'm getting really anxious. I have all this free time now, and I spend most of it wondering why I ever thought this would work out for me. It's kind of crazy, actually. I turned down my leads for nonprofit jobs, and I can't go back to them and say I made a mistake. So now I have no leads for real jobs once this fails."

"That's why you've got to go all in. Like, in poker. You've got to bet everything you've got and hope for the best. Often it scares off your opponent and they fold."

"First of all, I don't have an opponent. Secondly, since when do you play poker?"

"I've been watching poker tournaments on TV. They're oddly fascinating."

"I would never have pictured you using your limited free time to watch televised poker."

"All single people watch way more TV. You want to hear people talking." She shrugged and ate the last bite of her sandwich. "But you didn't exactly answer my question about Dan. You started talking about your career instead."

"It wasn't instead. That's my answer. I'm stressed and I'm panicking, so it's hard to be fully happy about anything. And you know how much I love Dan. But I've been so on edge, and I'm just so nitpicky. It's not that stereotypical stuff, where he leaves the toilet seat up or dishes in the sink. It's meaner than that. It's like, he says something and I dissect it in my head. I think, 'How can I spend my life with a man who says that?' And there was nothing wrong with what he just said! I know that, but I can't stop thinking that way. So then I get frustrated with myself, and I think how Dan's the only thing I've got going for me right now and I'm going to screw it up. And this just goes around and around. It's a brutal cycle."

Larissa nodded sympathetically. "I've got my own set of head games. They sound similar to yours, just in the past tense. Like, if I hadn't done x, y, and z, Dustin wouldn't have left me."

"Do you think Dan's going to leave me?" I studied her face attentively.

"I want to say no, because I'm your friend and because I think Dan really loves you, but my radar is pretty bad when it comes to male behavior. Honestly, reassurance from me is worse than none at all."

• • • •

Dan and I went to one of our favorite restaurants that night, a small Ethiopian place dimly lit throughout by lamps. I'd spent much longer on my hair and makeup than usual, and as we sat on the floor on silken cushions drinking honey wine, Dan ran his finger along my cheekbone in a way that told me my efforts were appreciated.

Dan never talked much about his work, and I didn't have any to speak of, so at times, conversation was slow going. I kept smiling at him, determined to keep everything wonderful. I knew that I was attaching far too much significance to every moment of our dinner, and instructed myself to stop, but I wouldn't listen.

"So Larissa went to a wedding last weekend, and ended up with this stranger."

"Happens a lot."

"I know. But this was kind of weird, in my opinion. They'd never met before, and the bride basically set them up to share a room so that they could both save money."

"Right." He gave me a knowing look that I didn't like very much.

I pushed on. "So, Larissa wasn't planning on being with anyone because she's still torn up over Dustin. But she and this guy, Martin, are at a dinner the night before the wedding and she said he flirted a little with her, no big deal. They go back to the room together, and he basically mauls her against the doorjamb."

"He got violent?" Dan looked more interested at this point. Was he someone who needed violence to get into a story? Should I throw in a car chase, too?

"He didn't literally maul her. But he was really aggressive with the kissing. Oh, I didn't tell you the most important thing, which is that Martin is supposedly still heartbroken because he recently got left by his wife after a month of marriage."

"Did he tell Larissa he was heartbroken?" Dan poured wine from the decanter into my glass, then into his.

"No, because they barely talked. He just jumped her, tried to get sex, and then ignored her the next day at the wedding. Kind of tacky, don't you think?"

Dan tilted his head. "Which part?"

"Trying so hard to get sex and then ignoring her the next day."

"Trying hard to get sex seems pretty normal. It's a wedding."

"It's the night before a wedding."

"As I see it, there should be a clear boundary. Either nothing is going on, or there should be sex. Either it's changing into your pajamas in the bathroom and separate beds, or there should be sex."

"Are you serious?" Who was this man?

"Sure. It's a wedding." Dan took a swig of his honey wine as I continued to stare at him.

The server arrived with our food: a large round tray of *injera* bread, dotted with various stews and meats. Dan immediately yanked off a piece of *injera,* scooped up some red lentils, and popped it in his mouth, oblivious to my reaction to his theory.

"You think a woman shouldn't be able to say no to sex?" I questioned.

"You're missing my point here. If a woman says no, a man should stop what he's doing. But what I'm saying is that it's normal that he'd expect sex when he's fooling around with a woman in her thirties the night before a wedding."

"She's heartbroken!" I exclaimed.

"How does he know that? She was kissing him, right? He's touching her?"

"Well, not totally." I lowered my voice. "He kept trying to go down on her. He barely knew her, and she repeatedly told him to stop."

"Sweetie, I'm just saying, the guy's not a rapist."

"I'm not saying he's a rapist!" I said it louder than I'd intended, and the people behind us glanced over, then put their heads together in consultation. "I'm just saying the whole thing was a little—uncouth."

"I'm sorry." He put his palms up in a gesture of faux surrender. "I guess I just don't share your outrage. She's a grown woman getting into it with a man in a hotel room. I'm not saying he's a prince. I mean, if it were me, I would have assumed that it was the 'change into your pajamas in the bathroom' kind of arrangement."

"Right. You'd play the nice guy because that's what would get you sex." I narrowed my eyes at him.

"I wouldn't be playing anything. And this guy probably wasn't playing anything, either. He just went for it. And when you're thirty, you're in a hotel room together one night only, it's not making out; it's foreplay. It's her right not to have sex with him, but then she can't get angry when he's not acting like her wedding date."

"She didn't expect him to be her date. She just expected him to be civil."

"Was he rude at the wedding?"

I fought my rising frustration. This wasn't how I wanted things to go. I'd just been making conversation, and now here I was, annoyed at him once again. And why was I always the one to work so hard at conversation anyway? Why was Dan so content to eat in silence while it made me want to crawl out of my skin?

Stop this. "No, he wasn't rude exactly," I said through tight lips.

"Why is this getting you so upset?" Dan asked.

"I don't know. I just—I thought this conversation would go differently."

"You thought I'd agree with you." I thought I detected the faintest trace of a smirk, but I ignored it.

"No. I just thought it was sort of evident what it all meant."

"Oh, right. You didn't think I'd agree with you. You just thought I'd agree with you," he teased, taking my hand.

I decided to try one last time to get him to see my point, though I had the discomforting image of me as a pit bull with her jaws locked. "Here's what I'm saying. He pressured her to get sex, and then he wasn't nice the next day. And that's kind of jerky."

"And what I'm saying is that it seems like it should be all or nothing: rebuff the guy right from the start, or finish him off. Don't just leave him hanging." Apparently, Dan could be a pit bull, too.

"She didn't leave him hanging. She got him off, even though she didn't want to."

"Well, then." He shrugged his shoulders, as if the discussion were now over. He seemed to think Larissa's hand job was a personal victory.

I let out an exasperated sigh. Maybe just *one* more try . . . "But she gave him clear signals the whole way, that's all. Like the way she kept stopping him from going down. She was letting him know from early on that there were boundaries."

"Okay." He was eating some lamb with evident pleasure and didn't seem terribly interested anymore.

I took a drink of my honey wine and a deep breath. *I can let this go. I can.* "Have you noticed," I asked conversationally, "that men are going down far earlier than they used to?"

"What do you mean?" he said through a mouthful of peas.

"They go down now before you've even had sex with them. It's invasive."

"They're letting you know they're sensitive. And that they want you to go down on them. Plus, some men really like it. I really like it."

"Do you do that? Go down on women before you've had sex?" I realized how curious I was, since he was generally so discreet about his previous sexual relationships. If we ever broke up, I'd probably appreciate that. But not until then.

"I have."

"Well, why didn't you do that for me?"

"Because you think it's invasive."

"You didn't know that then!" I protested.

"If we could go back in time, I would go down on you on our first date so that we would never have to have this conversation." He looked at me, waiting for a smile in return. The longer he held the look, with his lips pursed in amusement, the more I wanted to laugh. And the longer I held back, the more ridiculous it seemed. But I still couldn't let go. What was that?

"Nora," he said, and everything about him at that moment said that he loved me. So I cracked.

Chapter 8

VINCENT

Age:	36
Height:	6'7"
Weight:	Don't own a scale
Occupation:	Plant pathologist
About me:	I got my PhD in agronomy and horticulture in 1997, and spent a few years dabbling in plant genetics and soil science. At the age of 33, I was a foremost expert in Sudden Oak Death. Currently, I'm fascinated by parasitic nematodes. Just devastated by them. Sometimes I dream about them . . .

Vincent was my second client, and we were meeting at the botanical gardens, where he worked. Even though I knew he was 6'7", it was still jarring to arrive at the Japanese plant display to find this hulking man, with his shock of whitish blond hair, waiting for me. He extended an enormous hand in greeting.

"Nora," he said. When he smiled, his eyes nearly disappeared. His features were surprisingly soft and gentle in a slightly ruddy face.

"It's nice to meet you, Vincent," I said, squinting up at him, my hand enveloped in his.

"Let's sit down." He led me to a bench near the Japanese pool, where we sat side by side, gazing out.

"I've never been here before," I said. "This is really beautiful. What are those trees called? You always see them in Japanese wall scrolls."

"Japanese maples," Vincent supplied.

The pond was ringed by boulders and shaded—as I'd just learned—by Japanese maples with leaves of varying shades of red, orange, and green, as well as bamboo. In the center of the pond was a small island, also surrounded by boulders, with an iconic tree growing out of it. Its leaves were a golden orange burnished by the late-afternoon light. It was so lovely that I fought my nervous inclination to get right down to business, and tried to just take it in.

"There are some dogwoods, too. Bamboo, of course." He pointed. "Redwoods. Got to have a nod to California, right?" He glanced at me out of the corner of his eye, and I smiled. I liked Vincent. "The thing I like best about Japanese gardens is that they're not overly concerned with flowers. They're heartier than that. They're all-weather. It's not just about the spring, you know?"

I nodded. We fell silent for a few minutes. There were no other people, so there was only the sound of birds twittering.

"Did you think it was strange that I suggested we meet here?" he asked, turning to face me fully.

I was about to give him a quick no, but there was something urgent in his face that told me I should consider my answer more carefully. "I was going to suggest a café, which would have been my natural habitat. This seems to be yours."

He faced the pond again. "That's what I was thinking, too," he said, with some measure of approval.

Was he testing me? I wasn't sure. I wondered if there was something challenging about him picking his own turf for our meeting. Maybe he could smell how much I needed this gig. My face was getting hot, and my stomach was tightening. Maybe my mother was right, and I shouldn't be meeting strangers. Maybe I had no business doing this job at all. *Stay calm and don't talk first*, I counseled myself. *You don't know enough. Just let it play out.*

The next five minutes of silence were agonizing. When I finally cast a surreptitious glance at his face to gauge our progress, I saw that he looked completely serene. He wasn't trying to make progress at all. I envied him.

I took a deep breath and then exhaled. It was louder than I'd intended. He looked over at me and smiled slightly, then lowered his eyes shyly. We both looked back at the water. Yes, I needed this gig. But it had been a long time since I'd sat by a pond and watched the light change. I was going to analyze this meeting to pieces later; it seemed like I might as well try to enjoy it now.

Another five minutes, then ten, passed without either of us speaking. Peculiarly enough (or naturally enough), there didn't seem to be any tension in it. I remembered a meditation class I'd attended once to learn how to manage my stress better. My thoughts refused to be harnessed, and it felt more like an exercise in frustration tolerance than stress management. The more I sat there trying to make my mind go blank, the more flares it set off in rebellion. I talked to someone after the class who seemed so much more successful than I had been. All she said was, "You know, it's hard." I waited for her to say more, but she just smiled. *Zen bitch*, I had thought, figuring she was hoarding the secret of the universe. But that was probably it. It was hard, and it was frustrating, and you had to push through, and when presented with a situation like that, I did what I'd always done: I never went back.

Now here I sat, looking at the beauty, and thinking of my failings. Why did I always have to do this to myself?

And why was I always so self-obsessed?

I wanted to talk. I needed to talk. I wanted to ask Vincent how he sustained that look on his face for so long. I wanted to find out how he was able to revel in silence. I wanted to know how he quieted his mind. I imagined him spending his days meandering through the gardens, breathing in and out slowly, savoring the moments. I could see him inside a greenhouse, tending to the sick plants, talking to them, stroking their leaves with his big hands.

The sun was dipping faster now, and it was getting colder. I put on my sweater and hugged myself. It was a pleasant tactile sensation, a diversion from my sudden vague longing toward Vincent.

"Do you know anything about mindfulness meditation?" he asked.

I was startled to hear his voice in the stillness. Could he have known I was thinking about meditation? Well, among about twenty other things, but still. It was a little jarring. "No," I said.

"The idea is to embrace reality with all your senses. It's like being the most awake you've ever been, all the time."

"Being in the moment?" I thought of Larissa.

"That's one way of putting it." He turned toward me. "It's about insight and concentration and focus. But it's not about clearing your mind. You focus on a physical object, or your breath, and then you just let your thoughts pass by."

"What do you mean?"

"Like I said, you're not clearing your mind. You're just noticing. And noticing is a big part of being, as you said, in the moment." He was becoming more animated as he spoke. "So you notice all your thoughts, but you don't judge any of them and you don't judge yourself for getting distracted. You just let it all go by, and you refocus on your breath or on the object you picked."

"Is that what you were doing while we sat here?"

"I was trying. I just started taking a class, and this is my favorite place to practice."

"I can see why." I paused; then I had to ask. "What made you start talking about it? Did you read my mind?"

He laughed.

"No, I'm serious," I said. "I was sitting here thinking about meditation and about how bad I am at it and about how you seemed to be in this profound Zen state and then you tell me about mindfulness meditation."

"I don't read minds, that I know of. I didn't know what you were thinking about, but suddenly that topic came to me. It's happened before. People have told me that they've been thinking about something, and then I brought it up out of nowhere."

"That's wild," I said, with some delight.

He nodded, but didn't answer.

"We could use that in your profile," I said, thinking aloud. "We wouldn't write it like you're clairvoyant or something. We'd write it like you're highly attuned. Mind reading is creepy; attunement is sexy. Women love attunement."

"Huh." Vincent turned his focus back to the pond.

"Do you want to sit here longer and meditate?" I realized that might have sounded harsh and tried to soften it. "I mean, I'm fine with that. It's just getting darker, and I won't be able to write in the dark."

"I didn't think we'd write out here. I have an office over there." He gestured toward a building in the distance. "We could head inside, if you'd like." He shambled to his feet. Good Lord, he was big. Even though it wasn't my job to give fashion tips, I wanted to tell him to stop being so—well, shaggy. He was wearing faded brown corduroys, with ink stains on them, and an ill-fitting plaid shirt. He didn't seem overweight, just bulky.

We walked toward Vincent's building. "I haven't seen any other people," I said. "Does anyone come here at night?"

"Not really. There aren't any lights. The people who come here most often are art students, and they come during the day. They paint the pond and the footbridge." He pointed. I hadn't even noticed the ten or so suspended planks of wood with their delicate arch, decorative rather than functional. The bridge seemed like an afterthought. It was interesting that students considered it the most worthy subject. I found the trees much more striking.

Vincent unlocked the door to his office and ushered me in. It was disappointingly ordinary. I had pictured him surrounded by fanciful plants, maybe as big as he was, but there was just a desk with a chair behind it and a chair opposite, one bookshelf, and what looked like a standard-issue herb garden and some plants sitting on the windowsill. "I don't spend much time here," he said, with a note of apology in his voice. He gestured to the guest chair.

The setup made me feel like I was interviewing for a job, and I said so.

He smiled. "Sorry. Maybe we should go to a café."

"No, that's okay. I think we should switch sides, though. Just so I can write."

He vacated his chair immediately. I thought that spoke highly of him (that he was accommodating, didn't have control issues, etc.), and with the right wording, we could work that into the profile.

Even with our seating reversed, it wasn't ideal. Our time outside had had a pleasant looseness to it, and now we both seemed more stiff and formal.

"You must really love it here," I said, trying to recover the earlier atmosphere.

"This office?"

"No, the gardens."

"I do." He said it wistfully. "I've never wanted to leave."

There was something in the tense he used and in his tone that made me ask, "Are you thinking about leaving?"

He nodded, with evident sadness.

"Why?"

"I want a wife," he said.

I know it might sound strange, retrograde even, but when I looked at Vincent's face, my heart jumped. Not because I had any romantic interest in Vincent (my momentary attraction had vanished), but because it was the purest statement of desire and longing I'd ever heard a man utter.

It took me a few seconds to gather myself enough to respond. "And you think you need to leave to find her?"

He nodded again. "They're not my people out here. I like them fine, and I like a lot of things about San Francisco. Part of why I decided to take that mindfulness-meditation class was because I thought I'd never get the chance to do that in Nebraska."

I noticed that his manner of speaking had changed. I could hear the Midwest in him; when outside, as he spoke about meditation, he'd sounded more like California. "If you leave, you're going to Nebraska?"

"I'm from Nebraska."

"I've never been there."

"It's a passing-through place for most people. I know it more intimately. I've studied it from the soil up." He still had that wistful look on his face. "But I love the plants here in California. You know those five things I can't live without? Well, three of those plants are native to California."

I glanced at my printout of his profile.

"Betulaceae, also known as the resin birch," he said. "*Cypripedium californicum,* or the California lady's slipper. And *Eriastrum luteum.* Those are just three. If I'd had room, I'd have listed a whole lot more. Those are native to California, and you can find them somewhere else, but I get the highest concentration of the most plants that I truly love here."

I could see that it pained him to think of leaving. "It seems like you could find a wife here. I know lots of women in the Bay Area who want to get married."

"Women don't write me back," he said.

"We'll fix that." I tried to inject the three syllables with all the certainty I could muster.

"I hope so. This is it for me. You're my last-ditch attempt to stay here. If we rewrite and nothing happens, I'm packing up."

I was Vincent's last chance. It hit me hard to hear that, because I felt like in a way, Vincent was my last chance. He and all the other clients. If I couldn't get things right this time . . . Then there was my relationship with Dan. I was almost thirty. Sometimes everything in my life felt like last chance.

"Well, we'll do what we can." I wasn't sure if I was up to this mission, but I was prepared to give it all I had. "The first thing I noticed was that in the section where you describe yourself, it reads like a CV. You just sort of present your credentials and your areas of study. I think you included the subject of your thesis."

"I did."

"I know you love what you do," I said gingerly, "and you love the world of plants, but your profile seems—academic. The passion isn't coming through, you know?"

"I'm not a writer." He got up and started watering the plants on his windowsill with what seemed like great tenderness.

"We can work on the style later." His watering was a little distracting, but I kept going. "Right now I'm concerned about content. Nearly everything is about plants. In the section where you described what you want in a woman, you mainly wanted her to be tolerant of you searching for different plant species on your days off from work."

"Yes." He sat back down heavily and started cracking his knuckles. It was the loudest knuckle-cracking I'd ever heard, possibly because they were the biggest knuckles I'd ever seen. It was apparent that he didn't want to do this. I understood that. No one likes to take the steps that could be their last.

"I'm just trying to figure out the best approach for your profile. I know it's not all that fascinating," I said apologetically. My inexperience was showing. So much hinged on getting this right—for both of us—and I was already letting us down.

"I'm sorry. I don't mean to make your job harder." He averted his eyes. "You've got your work cut out for you, that's for sure."

"I just need to get to know a little bit more about you, and what you're looking for, that's all."

"I understand." He forced a smile.

"We were talking about what you were looking for in a woman."

He nodded and thought about it. "I want a woman who can enjoy the things I love. I want her to share those things with me. That's why I wrote the profile the way I did. I'm putting what matters way up front."

"You mean what matters to you," I clarified gently.

"Right. If our relationship is going to work, that should be what matters to her, too. I don't want to find a woman and change her. I want her just the way she is."

"Which is interested in plants."

"Which is in love with plants," he corrected, his gaze intense.

"That could maybe be a little"—I tried to choose the word carefully—"limiting." He didn't seem entirely sure what I meant. "Internet dating—all dating—is a numbers game, don't you think? You want to get the most responses you can because that's the most opportunities to find what you're looking for. Do you know what I mean?"

"I haven't had a date in three years," he said. "I'm not about posting big numbers. Love isn't basketball for me. Love is more like"—he paused to think—"soccer."

"Sometimes those games end scoreless."

He frowned. "I guess they do."

"You haven't had a date in three years. Let's just try to get you back in the game. Call it basketball, soccer, backgammon, it doesn't matter. We need to get you out there."

He nodded and gave me a smile. "What do we need to do, coach?"

For the next three hours, we hunkered down and worked, question by question. Finally I declared the profile complete. We'd included his enjoyment of soccer, documentaries, and Cuban food. We mentioned his desire to learn Japanese someday and his very passing desire to brew his own beer. We waxed rhapsodic about the way Nebraska looks at night, and compared it to the beauty of the California coast. Vincent was now looking for a woman with a deep appreciation of nature, someone who would love foliage drives and long walks with a caring botanist to guide her. After a hairy negotiation, of the five things he couldn't live without, only two were plants. One was a native Californian, the other native to Nebraska.

I read the profile aloud, with satisfaction. Then I said, "You sound sweet, loving, hardworking, and just a little quirky. I think it's perfect."

Vincent nodded, but he was frowning again. I'd gotten used to that expression during our hours together, so I wasn't unduly concerned.

"Is there anything you think we've left out?" I asked as a formality. I was ready to wrap up here. A second job well done.

"Yeah. Me."

"I haven't known you for long, obviously, but I think it sounds like you. I mean, everything in there is true. It's you, just reassembled."

"I sound so . . ." He struggled to find the word. "Well-rounded."

"Right. That's what we were aiming for."

"But I'm not well-rounded. I'm obsessed. I've been obsessed with this world since I was a kid, and it's who I am. And any woman who went out with me would know that after an hour, because I'm not going to act like someone I'm not." He was obviously agitated, but fighting to contain it.

"I'm sorry," I said. "I messed this up, and I'll redo it for free."

"No, no," he said, immediately contrite. "It's my fault. You did exactly what you were supposed to. You're performing the service I paid for. I'm just realizing it's the wrong service."

"But we can fix it! Really, we can." I wasn't thinking about the job or the money, but about last chances.

"No," he said firmly. "My first profile wasn't broken. It was accurate. You see those men in movies who love plants and they can tell women all about them in some grand romantic way. I've never been able to do that. I've never been able to woo a woman like that. I've never even had the guts to try. I need a woman who just plain finds this stuff fascinating. I can't make her find it fascinating, because I'm not that kind of a talker. I can tell her a whole lot of information, and if she likes that, if she likes having a man explain a plant, it'll work out. You said the old profile was too dry, but I think that's the way I am."

"But you're not dry," I said desperately. "When we sat on the bench and you told me about mindfulness meditation, you weren't dry at all. You could tell what I was thinking about before I even said anything. And if you weren't interested in things other than plants, you wouldn't be taking those classes. You just have a limited view of yourself."

He still looked pained, but he was thinking about it. "I don't know," he said finally.

"Maybe this new profile really is you. We didn't lie about anything. We just turned down the volume on the plants, and turned up the volume on the other things."

His shoulders were slumped. Then he drew himself up, and said resolutely, "I really thank you for how hard you've worked and for your time. Of course I'll be paying you for it."

He wasn't going to use the profile, no matter what I said. Why should he trust my assessment of him? I'd known him four hours; he'd known himself thirty-six years. But I knew that this was a bad decision. I felt sure that it was his own limited view of himself that was causing him to limit the number of people who'd have access to him. I also felt sure there was some woman in the Bay Area who liked plants just fine, but would love Vincent.

"So you're going to move back to Nebraska?" I said, trying to keep my voice neutral.

"I'm going to think that over a while longer." He looked around his office. "I really do love it here."

"It's beautiful," I agreed.

He smiled. "It was so much clearer when I was just giving it one last try. Now I've got to face this thing head-on."

"I know what you mean. The moment of truth, right?"

He nodded, still smiling sadly. Then he walked to the door and showed me out.

• • • •

There was no exultant ride home this time, and certainly no romp with Dan. I wanted to be alone to brood.

I kept running over the night in my head, trying to figure out where I'd made the wrong turn. Had it been before we'd even met? Had I been promising too much? Vincent had put so much faith in me, and I just hadn't been able to deliver. I had a cookie-cutter formula that was failing me on my second client. But it had seemed like such a no-brainer: make people seem interesting, earnest, funny, sweet. Round them out.

Maybe this job was too much responsibility for me. I didn't know what kind of qualifications a person should have to tinker in other people's love lives, but I didn't have them.

I could always go back to coordinating, back to answering phones and making flyers. If I got lucky, I could even author the flyers. Or maybe I could go back to school. Graduate school would be a nice reprieve from the world for a while, if I could just figure out what to study.

I wished I could stop picturing Vincent's pensive face, that look he had as I was leaving his office. But finally it came to me that his face hadn't only been sad. I mean, there was sadness, but there was something else in it. Resolve, maybe. He'd had the look of a man who was at least choosing his poison. He'd spent hours letting himself be repackaged, and at the end of it, he turned it down.

I'd told Estella I wasn't doing makeovers, and then I'd written a profile where the client was unrecognizable to himself. But it wasn't my job to change people, or to round them out. It was, as Maggie had said, my job to see the best in people and then to convey that to the world. It was like that hair color campaign from years back: "You, only better."

I could do this. Me, only better.

But first, I tried one last thing to help Vincent.

I knew there were dating Web sites for people with very specific interests, like for pet lovers or atheists. I decided to search for one for plant lovers. I combined and recombined words like "botany," "flowers," "plants," and "horticulture" with "love," "lover," "dating," and "mating." An hour later, I sent Vincent an e-mail saying I hadn't found anything yet, but I would keep looking, and I hoped he'd hang in there.

On a whim, I looked up mindfulness meditation. Persuasive as it was, I decided that I was temperamentally unsuited for it. Which probably meant it was just what I should be doing. But at the animal shelter, I'd learned that it was generally true that you couldn't teach an old dog new tricks.

I never did hear back from Vincent.

Chapter 9

LARISSA

1. My dating life has been:
    a. Entirely unsatisfying.
    b. Unsatisfying with small pockets of satisfaction.
    c. Satisfying half the time.
    d. Satisfying most of the time.
    e. Just how I like it.
2. In a mate, what's most important is:
    a. Style.
    b. Substance.
    c. Sass.
    d. Panache.
3. As a child, I was:
    a. Stubborn.
    b. Obedient.
    c. Mischievous.
    d. Confused.
    e. Maudlin.
    f. Happy.
4. When something goes wrong, I think:
    a. Better make a quick getaway.
    b. That was your fault!
    c. I'm not sure whose fault that was; let's talk about it.
    d. You know, that was probably me. It's always me.

5. My personal philosophy is:
   a. The more the merrier.
   b. Never too old to try something new.
   c. I'll sleep when I'm dead.
   d. Don't worry about me; I've been through worse.
   e. Don't leave me here all alone!
6. At a party, I'm most likely to:
   a. Talk to everyone—new people are possibilities!
   b. Talk only to the people I know.
   c. Stand against the wall and wait for someone to talk to me.
   d. Get embarrassingly drunk.
   e. a & d
   f. b & d
   g. c & d

*S*omething I didn't mention earlier—probably because I try to forget it myself—is that I met Dan at a party. The reason I dislike this particular fact is that the party was at my apartment, and Dan was there because he was a friend of Fara's. Not a close one, and definitely not as close as she liked to think.

So far, you've only seen the variety of Fara friends who hang out at other people's apartments in their pajamas. There's this whole other echelon—who really only show up for gatherings of eight or more, which makes them more quasi-Fara friends—who are monumentally, intimidatingly fantastic. Some of them are just achingly hip but not accomplished, and some are less hip but more accomplished. Some are what I would actually call brilliant. Fara's circle of (quasi)friends is proof that what you get in life is not what you deserve, but what you're willing to reach for. It's how schlubs land supermodels.

Anyway, when Fara's überfriends used to descend on our apartment in their perfect clothes with their funky glasses and their expertly dyed hair (the kind you're supposed to know is dyed), I would wonder why they couldn't be there just to see me. My most intense (yet entirely platonic) girl crush is on Fara's friend Sabayu. That's right, she's a white girl named Sabayu. A little affected, yes. But you should see her. Huge blue eyes magnified by her leopard print glasses, a thrift store T-shirt with just the right scarf, and always the best shoes. Dan had once said in admiration about her, "She's so *now*," and the staggering unhipness of his remark let me know why he was with me. He'd since decided that Sabayu was all flash and he had little use for that wing of Fara's friends. I thought he was probably right, but somehow my own feelings for Sabayu remained essentially undimmed.

Fara was having a party to celebrate her thirtieth b-day. Yes, she actually hyphenated it on the invitation. Was it meant ironically, or did she not want to blind us with the full word, like the way Jews write "G-d"? When I read her e-mail, I thought that the most pronounced difference between hipsters and the rest of us was their confusing deployment of irony. Or at least, it was confusing to me. They seemed to understand each other pretty well. It was better than a secret handshake. Well, whatever Fara had meant, her b-day celebration would be my first time seeing the apartment she now shared with Bart.

"Do I look okay?" I asked Dan. I was in front of the full-length mirror that I had installed on the back of the closet door, and he was lying on the bed reading.

He looked up. "You look good," he said, though his tone seemed noncommittal.

"Come on, what do you really think?" I urged.

"Do you really want to know?"

"Yes."

"I think you're trying to borrow a few elements from Sabayu, and you should just stick with what you know."

He was right. I wasn't passing. I was like a minstrel show. I ripped the scarf from my neck. "I hate being around those people!"

"Only some of the people look like Sabayu. A lot more look like us."

That was exactly the point. Anyone could look like me; I wanted to look like someone who was hard to imitate. I wanted, perversely, to imitate people whose personal style made them impossible to imitate. I dropped onto the bed in frustration. "I've been spending all that time in San Francisco and I just can't get it down."

"The people you're talking about spend all their time 'getting it down.' They go to thrift stores three times a week and spend the rest of their time in bars so they can scope each other out and see what the newest thing is. I saw this guy the other day wearing leg warmers. Leg warmers!" He wrapped his arm around my waist. "You don't want to be someone who decides you should, oh, I don't know, wear a petticoat on your head just because nobody in twenty-first-century San Francisco has gotten around to that yet, do you?"

I laughed. "No."

"Well, all right then." He said it in his Rodney voice, inflected with a cockney accent. He often turned into Rodney when he thought I was being high-strung.

Taking his cue, I stood up and marched around the room. I was now Mrs. Pimmbottom, the ultimate high-strung grande dame. Rodney was my houseboy. "Most certainly not!" I declared, my British accent crisp and upper-crust. "It simply won't do!"

"Would the lady like a bath?"

"The lady is getting ready for a ball! Rodney, honestly," I said, with great exasperation.

That's when Dan/Rodney jumped around the room like the orangutan he was. No one ever said a houseboy had to be human. He started hooting.

"We are displeased." I sighed, turning back to the mirror.

Dan leaped at me, arms akimbo, and began grooming me. His monkey hands were in my hair, searching for lice, fleas, and other detritus. Every time he found something, he ate it, at which point his monkey noises became gentler, the monkey noises of escalating satisfaction. It was really very soothing, being groomed.

I don't remember quite how Mrs. Pimmbottom and Rodney came about. I think maybe Dan started acting like a monkey one day and I decided the appropriate response was to act like a disapproving English madam. There was something uniquely delightful about it, and more and more, we found ourselves spontaneously in character. Our scenes were all variations on a theme: Rodney wasn't a very competent houseboy and Mrs. Pimmbottom pretended to chastise him, but she secretly got a kick out of his antics. Let me make the disclaimer that these characters did not extend into our sex life. I'm no prude, but my fantasies have never included bestiality.

For me, Mrs. Pimmbottom and Rodney were the first fully realized characters to appear in the context of an intimate relationship, but they were on a continuum with the kind of play I'd experienced in every long-term relationship I'd ever had. I've never talked to my friends about this, but I've seen them do it, too. I once saw Dustin and Larissa talking to each other at a dinner party when they didn't think anyone else was listening and she was using this Kewpie doll voice I'd never heard. It wasn't sexy at all; it was this very specific, grating, childlike voice. But Dustin didn't seem to find it grating at all. He was totally into it.

My theory is that all adults still want to be kids, at least a little bit, and we get to indulge that part of ourselves the most once we actually have kids and can take them to please-touch museums. In the meantime, we use the safety of intimate relationships. We roll around in bed and we squeal and we pout and we talk in voices we'd never use with anyone else. The closer we get to another person in an intimate relationship, the freer we are to enact scenes that gratify our kid parts.

I considered Mrs. Pimmbottom and Rodney a testament to the solidity of my relationship with Dan. Our first month of living together had had its ups and downs, but the second month had been good to us. Now going into our third month, I was feeling cautiously optimistic. I know cautious optimism doesn't sound like high praise, but for a meta-lifer, it is. Lately I'd even been catching myself not thinking. I'd be lying in bed with Dan in the morning, just feeling completely content, and I'd suddenly realize, "Hey, I'm lying in bed with Dan, feeling completely content," and then "Hey, I'm thinking about my contentment. Stop that," and from then on, it'd be ruined. I couldn't regain that initial feeling of blissful unawareness. Once I was hyperaware of the good feeling, all I wanted to do was make it last, but by wanting that so much, I killed it. I was killing what I loved.

But back to my original point. Dan and I were happy.

• • • •

As we stepped inside my old apartment, I was struck by how radically it had been altered. I felt a twinge of resentment, since I hadn't been able to make a single change to the apartment in the nearly one year that I'd lived there. Not that Fara outright forbade me. It was just that the first time I brought something new into the living room (a small decorative lacquer box, to be precise), her response had been a most effective deterrent. Clearly aggrieved, she stared at it for an uncomfortably long time, then said, false brightly, "Next time, we can go shopping together!" She kept trying out different spots for it on the coffee table and then the end table, back and forth and back and forth. It was like watching Baby Jane. Fara was so pained by the box (and the thought of us shopping together was so odious) that I ceded the common areas entirely.

But Fara had allowed Bart to bring in his enormous black leather couch and easy chair, which even I could see had destroyed the feng shui of the living room. And I knew Fara cared about feng shui because she had books like *Feng Shui for Your Cat and You.* (Or maybe *Feng Shui for the Cat in You?*) The tapestry on the wall had been replaced by a framed poster of Van Morrison. Even the rug had been changed from the imitation Persian to one that was, get this, *fuzzy* and *green*. The Asian-inspired armoire was still there, with its doors open to reveal the TV inside; Fara had always been adamant about keeping it closed when the TV was turned off. Did that mean that Bart actually planned to watch television during the party? Or did he want to prove to his friends that he still had a television? My annoyance at Fara turned into pity. Was this debased decoration what she thought it took to hold on to a man?

"You came! You came!" Fara called. She launched herself at Dan and me, hugging him first, then me. She smelled like cheap booze. I wouldn't have known the difference before Dan, but now it was overpowering. She smiled back and forth between us. "How are you?"

"We're good," Dan said. He casually put his arm around my

waist, and I leaned into him. It was fun being so obviously, easily coupled.

"You look good together," she said. "You look happy."

"We are happy," I said.

"Well, I'm happy for you." Fara surveyed us as if we were her personal handiwork. "I don't mean to brag, but I did bring you two together."

"That's true," I said. Pity was already morphing back into annoyance.

"How's the Internet dating thing going?" she asked. Before I could answer, she went on. "What's funny is that Bart and I met over the Internet. I wonder who I would have met if you'd fixed my profile."

Huh. "It sounds like your profile didn't need to be fixed," I said in an attempt at diplomacy.

"Yeah, well." Fara looked down and away, and when she lifted her head, she'd plastered a smile back on.

"Are things okay?" Dan asked. He moved toward her with concern. Bless his heart, he cared. I was just curious to hear about her car crash of a relationship. Then I reminded myself that karma might exist, and I decided to care, too.

"It's a process, you know?" Fara's gaze was unexpectedly probing. She was looking for chinks in our armor. "I mean, you two must know, right?"

"It's definitely an adjustment," Dan said, his tone reassuring.

"Exactly!" Fara said as if he, alone, got it. It occurred to me that it was not impossible that if Fara had just a little more to drink that night, she'd try to seduce Dan and chalk it up to her emotional distress. I had no real evidence for this suspicion, but that didn't stop me.

I draped my arm across Dan's back. It wasn't actually the most comfortable position, but it wasn't about comfort. It was about establishing dominance.

At that moment, Goliath waddled over and rubbed himself against Dan's right leg. Dan extricated himself and squatted down to pet Goliath.

"How great is he?" Fara asked, gesturing toward Dan.

"Pretty great." My smile was tight. I wanted Dan to stop touching that beast, wash his hands, then thrust his tongue down my throat.

I was surprised by the sudden force of my jealousy, but I liked it. As Fara excused herself to greet other guests, and Goliath moved on to the futile task of stuffing himself under the coffee table, I looked at Dan and found his sex appeal had skyrocketed. I grabbed him and kissed him.

"Mmm," he said when our lips parted.

"You want to do it in my old room?" I said, in what I hoped was a sultry voice.

Dan shifted away from me slightly. "That would be a little rude, wouldn't it?"

"To Fara?"

"To the party."

"You really think they'd miss us that much?"

"Maybe later," he said. He pecked my nose in a way that told me we would not be retiring to my old room that night.

I felt a little rejected, but mostly relieved. I sometimes made bold suggestions, and then when I was taken up on them, I spent the whole time worrying that we needed to hurry up, that someone was going to walk in, that I'd mess up my dress, that we'd miss the opening credits. The theory was always better than the practice.

"Nora." It was Sabayu. She was working a geisha look that

night, and on anyone else, it might have been stupid or even kind of tasteless. But not on Sabayu. Not my Sabayu.

"Sabayu!" I hugged her. I knew I was being too enthusiastic. It was part of why I could never join their ranks.

"Hi, Sabayu," Dan said, clearly underwhelmed by her arrival.

"Hey, Dan." She turned to me. "I am so jealous."

"Are you serious?" I could not have given a lamer answer if I had all night to come up with one.

"Of course I'm serious. You did what I wish I had the guts to do. Just march in there and quit."

"I always thought you had a great job." Sabayu is a curator's assistant at the Museum of Modern Art.

"I'm speaking metaphorically," she said.

"Oh."

"So you don't want to quit your job, you just think that if you did, it would be something you wouldn't necessarily have the guts to do?" Dan interpreted, with just the slightest hint of derision in his voice.

"Precisely." Sabayu smiled at me. "What's it like? Escaping the grind?" She somehow made ordinary phrases sound exotic, like she'd coined them.

"I love it," I said.

I wasn't just trying to keep pace with Sabayu. It was true. The first month had been lean and I'd panicked, but once I'd picked up enough clients to pay my bills, I relaxed and settled into my new lifestyle. In the morning, I answered the e-mails and calls of prospective clients, caught up on some reading, or ran errands that I used to hate because the stores were jammed with other people doing their shopping after work. I'd discovered a wonderful produce market, and I began to grocery shop like a European: every two or three days, everything fresh. I made regular lunch plans with friends; I even revived some old friendships to keep my dance card full. In the afternoon, I might meet a client, but it was more common to meet them in the evening. Most of my clients were in San Francisco, so if I was going to see a client at night, I would often go early and roam the city like a tourist. I'd visited Grace Cathedral, eaten dim sum in Chinatown, toured Alcatraz, walked the Golden Gate Bridge, and watched the sea lions sun themselves on Pier 39. I planned to walk the Crookedest Street in the World, Lombard Street, sometime soon.

"So you write dating ads for people, right?" she asked. I nodded. She had the silkiest voice. "What sort of people do you meet doing that?"

I cast her an appraising glance. There had been a note of condescension in her question, as if she were inviting me to mock my clients for her pleasure. "I've been lucky. I've met some great people," I answered honestly.

She nodded, seeming ever so slightly disappointed. So I hadn't misread her intentions. Now it was my turn to be disappointed.

We kept talking long enough for the end not to seem too abrupt. I asked questions, she gave me elliptical answers, and then she disappeared into the crowd. I was okay with seeing her go.

I spied Larissa across the room, deep in conversation with one of Fara's ex-boyfriends. I felt a moral responsibility to rescue her. Any man who had seriously dated Fara was not part of the dating pool.

I interrupted with a smile, saying that Larissa and I needed to go outside for a smoke. Neither of us smoked, but she followed me. She wasn't protesting, so maybe she'd decided on her own that he wasn't a viable prospect.

"Want to walk?" she asked. "I could use the air. I think I've been drinking a little too fast."

"Sure."

We instinctively headed toward the lake. There weren't too many walkers on the path and there were none who were dressed like us. Larissa was wearing sort of a bustier contraption and had about a yard of cleavage. She grabbed hold of my arm as we walked. She wasn't kidding about drinking too fast.

"Are you okay?" she asked with concern.

"What do you mean?" I responded, confused.

"I mean, are you still happy?"

Her question hit me hard. Yes, her timing was peculiar from the drink, but she knew me inside out. My rent was cheap; my man was wonderful; my business was picking up speed. I could pay my bills twice over, and I made my own schedule. This was a good life. This was *the* good life. But for how long could I sustain happiness?

I hadn't even formulated an answer, when Larissa blurted, "Well, *I'm* miserable! I hate single life. I can't be alone. Debbie thinks I've taken a huge leap backward in the past week, but she's wrong. I had never taken any steps forward. I'm working constantly because I can't stand to be idle. I can't stand to be with myself." She bumped against me as we walked.

"Why don't you want to be with yourself? You're one of my favorite people to be with."

"That's just it. If I met me, I think I'd like me a lot. If I met me back at that party"—she motioned in the direction of Fara's apartment—"I'd think, 'She's funny, she's smart, she's a fucking lawyer!'" Larissa seemed like she was about to cry. "But that's around people. By myself, I crumble. All alone, there's nothing funny about me, and my intelligence is all in service of making myself feel like utter shit." She looked at me. "What am I going to do?"

"Oh, Larissa," I said. "I wish I knew."

We walked along, not speaking. "I want to turn around," she said. "I want to go back. If Collin's still there, I'm getting his number."

"I told you, he dated *Fara*. It could never work."

She jutted her chin out. "Well, I don't need something that'll work forever. Dustin was supposed to be forever. I need someone to take up my time. I need someone to take up my mental space. I need someone to find me charming. I need someone I can be good company for." She spun around on her heel, and I followed her as she headed back to the house.

"I just think you should be with a man who's worthy of you," I said. But even as I said it, I realized I was just spouting what I was supposed to say. Why should we wait around for people who are worthy of us? If we like ourselves most when we're with someone, anyone, should we be alone to prove a point? Alone didn't seem to be working for Larissa. My smart, attractive, capable friend was drunk and stumbling around a lake that smelled like sewage, and if what she wanted was a man, who was I to stand in her way?

I caught up with her. "That was a stupid thing to say. You don't need to be with someone who's worthy of you."

"Really?" she asked, eyes shimmering with gratitude.

"Yes. If you want to be with someone who's plainly beneath you, you won't hear a negative word from me."

She hugged me, then started chattering as we walked. She was the only person I knew whose mood swings rivaled mine. That's the kind of thing you can build a friendship on. "You want to hear a confession?" she asked.

"Of course."

"Remember that dating site that's supposed to do the matching for you, based on surveys?"

"The one that gave you all the total losers."

"Well, what I didn't tell you was I lied the first time around. I tried to answer things the way that would get me the best men."

I thought of Candace. How common was lying in a dating market this tight?

"And it just came to me last night: I got the men who were doing the same thing! I got the men who had also lied to look good. So at two AM last night, I filled the whole thing out again, completely honestly."

"I'm surprised the Web site lets you fill it out again. I mean, you were supposed to be telling the truth the first time, and they already gave you your matches."

"I made up a false identity."

"You used another name?"

"No, I'm still Larissa. But I set up a new e-mail address and I used a different credit card and little things like that. I had to, if I wanted to finally be honest."

"Could you get in trouble for that? I mean, is it fraud?"

She waved a hand. "I know fraud. This is just dating."

We started laughing, and soon we were back at the party. Fara's ex-boyfriend had clearly moved on to another girl, but Larissa handled it well. I set her up to talk with Dan while I approached Alex, a friend of Fara's whom I knew to be a decent photographer. At least, I knew he'd taken the only good pictures of me on record. I'd hoped he'd be there tonight because I had a proposition for him.

Alex leaned in to kiss my cheek. "It's been a while," he said. "I don't have anyone to flirt with when I come over here anymore. Bart's not my type."

Alex was corny, but harmless. What he neglected to mention was that I never responded to his flirting, except to roll my eyes, though I suspected that was the reaction he actually wanted. He was someone who'd be more comfortable pulling a girl's pigtails than giving bedroom eyes. "It has been a while. What have you been up to?"

"Different things." Alex never gave a straight answer. I knew he was some kind of artist with a day job, but I didn't know what kind of art or what kind of day job. "I hear you're an entrepreneur now."

I laughed. "A freelancer, actually."

"Hey, they're not that far apart. Get a little more ambitious, and you're an entrepreneur." He held up his glass as if to toast me.

"It's funny you mentioned that, because I've been thinking about expanding the business." I was glad I'd had a few vodka tonics. I was feeling pretty loose. "I know you take great pictures. You've taken some great ones of me, and I'm notoriously unphotogenic."

"Hard to believe."

"So you know I'm helping people with their profiles for dating Web sites, right?" He nodded. "Well, that's only part of the battle. The other thing is the pictures. If the pictures aren't working, no one will ever read the text. So I was thinking that maybe I could help people with their pictures, too."

"Which is where I come in," he said slowly.

"I was thinking that when I advertise my service, I could include that as a possible add-on."

"Like when people are buying a car, and they get options."

"Right."

"That sounds great to me. I'm in." He smiled.

"Really?" I beamed. It just seemed disconcertingly easy.

"Let me give you my number. We can work out the details later."

The birthday cake appeared at just the right time. Alex and I had exhausted our conversational reserves and it gave us a graceful exit. Everyone moved toward the kitchen, where Bart was carrying the cake, which blazed with thirty candles. I returned to Dan and Larissa. Dan smiled at me and laced his arm through mine, and I rested my head on his shoulder.

Bart started off the singing. "Happy b-day to me," I jokingly sang in Dan's ear. The rest of the room sang the real version, and Fara looked completely in her element. She preened and did those "Who, little old me?" gestures. Bart put the cake down on the table, and Fara held her long hair back, positioning herself to blow out the candles. She ballooned her cheeks comically, then blew. The candles flickered, then roared back to life. Trick candles, at the birthday party of a thirty-year-old woman. Bart laughed loudly and pointed at her. He actually shouted, "Gotcha!"

Fara tried again, with the same result. Obviously. She continued to play along, but I could see that she was embarrassed.

I would have expected to revel in this moment: in her humiliation, in her obviously failing relationship with an infantile sadist. But I actually felt bad for her. Was this what adulthood felt like? Well, I didn't care for it a bit.

"Let's go home," I said. I didn't want to watch anymore. With the candles to light our way, Dan, Larissa, and I filed silently toward the door.

Chapter 10

NORA

Age:	29
Height:	5'6"
Weight:	130 lbs
Occupation:	Internet dating consultant
About me:	Under construction
About you:	Under construction
Last book I read:	*The Rough Guide: San Francisco*
Biggest turn-on:	A man who knows how to play
Biggest turnoff:	Under construction
Five things I can't live without:	An income of at least $2,500 a month. The clarity that it takes to answer this question.
Most embarrassing moment:	The window incident

A few years back, Larissa, Sonya, and I were nearly inseparable. We all lived in Oakland and even when we had boyfriends, we made sure we saw each other at least once a week, though it was usually more often. It was a pact, actually. That might sound juvenile, but it seemed necessary. We had lost too many female friends to relationships, and we were determined not to go down that road.

But then Larissa fell in love with Dustin, and Sonya got a great job in San Francisco and decided to move there. San Francisco's just a few miles from Oakland, but the traffic's often grueling and the bridge became a psychological hurdle. I got tired just thinking about the trek, and Sonya apparently did, too. Soon Sonya and I were every-other-week friends, with long voice mails or e-mails in the interim. After a while, there were fewer visits and fewer messages, but no ill will. Sonya's social life had migrated to the city, and while I still loved her, there had been some pretty serious drift.

That day, when I got to Sonya's apartment, she opened the door with a crying baby balanced on her hip. She waved me inside, apologizing. "Palance won't go down for his nap, so he's a little cranky."

I'd heard his wails from outside, so I was prepared. "Don't worry about it at all," I said.

Palance was nine months old. And yes, I was shocked, too, when I heard that name. Sonya's husband, Chris, had this weird affection for Jack Palance, and Sonya defended the name on the grounds that her son was probably the first Palance on record. Someone probably held the record for longest time spent on a unicycle while eating saltines, but that didn't make it right.

"Can I get you anything? A drink?" Sonya offered. She was jiggling Palance on her hip. "You're okay, pumpkin. You're okay," she comforted him as he erupted into fresh sobs.

"Nope, I'm okay, too." I settled on Sonya's beige couch. Directly in front of me was a screened-in fireplace. "New screen?"

She nodded. "Babyproofing. He's crawling like mad now. This front room is pretty much done. Our bedroom is still a death trap." She paused. "Did I just say that? I'm becoming a lunatic."

"You're just being careful."

"No, I'm a lunatic," she said matter-of-factly. She settled herself on the floor and whipped out her breast. Palance finally stopped crying as he suctioned his lips to her. "This is what I do all day long. He cries, and I give him the boob. He's going to grow up to be a pervert. Tits will be the only things that soothe him."

I laughed. Palance stopped drinking and turned his head to gaze at me. He was a beautiful baby. I don't say that about all babies. Some of them are discolored, some are goggle-eyed. I can say that, because I'm not their mother. But Palance had enormous blue eyes and milky skin, which didn't even seem blotchy from all his crying. Sonya's breast was still exposed as she waited to see if he'd resume interest, so I kept my eyes locked on Palance. It was disconcerting, trying not to look at Sonya's engorged breast and erect nipple. I knew her when it was half that size. I was relieved when Palance started feeding again.

"So you're meeting a client later today?" Sonya asked when she finally snapped her nursing bra shut and pulled her shirt down over it.

"I was supposed to, but she canceled. I asked if she wanted to reschedule, but she said she'd changed her mind."

"Does that happen much?"

"It's happened a few times. And there was that guy I told you about, the one who paid me, but then didn't want to use the profile."

"He sounded sweet. I wanted to find him a wife myself."

"I know." I took a second to reflect on Vincent. "He never wrote me back. I wonder what he decided to do."

"It's easy enough to find out. You could just call the botanical gardens and ask for him. If he comes to the phone, hang up."

"I don't want to stalk him. I just wonder. I've heard back from a few people who said the profiles worked, but not from the others. I guess I should just be glad no one's asked for their money back." I'd been feeling more self-doubt the past few days, and that day's cancellation had me on edge.

"You're not a magician. You probably did the best you could with what you had." That comment was Sonya in a nutshell. It was why she never had insomnia.

"It's just been occurring to me that if my rent wasn't so low, I wouldn't even be able to do what I'm doing now. I mean, this isn't really a growth business."

"Didn't you say that you get a better response to each ad you run?"

I waved a hand dismissively. "That doesn't mean anything."

"It doesn't mean anything because you're getting scared. You're scared of success." Palance was crawling around the floor now, looking content. He stopped every so often to gaze back at me curiously. I smiled at him before he continued on his way.

"Well, the good thing is that a fear of success is one I'll never have to confront." I realized how self-pitying I sounded, and told myself to stop it. I could at least stop myself from saying it, even if I couldn't stop myself from feeling it. Maybe I truly was incapable of sustaining happiness.

"Hey, what are you doing to yourself here?" I thought for a second that Sonya was talking to Palance, but she wasn't.

"I know, I know. My business is coming along fine; everything's good; I get to sit here with you and your beautiful baby in the middle of the afternoon. There is no reason on earth for me to feel this pit in my stomach. But I do. That's what's so frustrating about it."

"Maybe you could use an antidepressant," she suggested.

I tried not to feel offended. She was just trying to help.

"I'd be on one, but I'm worried it would come through my breast milk," she said.

"Then you'd have one contented baby." Since when did Sonya need to consider antidepressants?

"Ha-ha. I'd really love to do it. I have a friend with obsessive-compulsive disorder and she went on an antidepressant—I think it was Paxil—and it did wonders for her. She needed to count all the time. Count her steps, count the tiles on the bathroom floor. As you'd imagine, it was totally interfering with her life. But she's basically cured."

"Won't it all start back up the minute she stops taking Paxil?"

"Probably. But she'd rather be on a drug the rest of her life than live like that."

"Do you think I'm obsessive-compulsive?"

"Of course not." She watched as Palance tried to stand up using the couch for support. He stayed up for a few seconds, then fell down. "Yay!" she cheered. Palance wavered between laughing and crying for a second, then chose laughing. She said to me, "I'm trying to train him not to cry at every bump. Cheering helps."

I wanted to talk about me some more, but then, I also didn't. "What's so loopy about you?"

"I don't know where to start."

I felt like something momentous was about to pass between us. I mean, Sonya was the kind of person who recommended antidepressants, not someone who wished she could take them. She was someone who made a choice and never looked back. Like having Palance. She and Chris had only been together three months when Sonya realized she was pregnant. She was thirty-five, and while she'd previously been fine with the fact that she might never have a baby, she gave it careful thought and reversed her position. With a minimum of fuss, she decided that she'd have her child with or without Chris. And since it was Sonya, it turned out that Chris (who, at forty-two, had never wanted kids before) wanted the whole package. She was also okay with not getting married, and when Chris proposed, in typical Sonya fashion, she took a week to think it over. On her wedding day, she was the calmest bride I'd ever seen, completely unfazed by walking down the aisle with her pregnancy bump. Then during the twelve weeks of maternity leave from her corporate VP job, she decided that she wanted to stay home with Palance and she'd been remarkably at peace with that decision, too. Or so it had seemed.

"Actually," she said, "I do know where to start. Let's start with the muffin."

"Okay," I said, laughing in advance.

"Palance is still a lousy sleeper, so I'm not sleeping. Let me just make that disclaimer first." She arranged herself into a more comfortable position on the floor and cooed again at Palance before diving in. "So last Friday, Palance and I go to the supermarket to pick up a few things. On the drive there, I realize I haven't eaten anything all day and I start fantasizing about a muffin. Like really fantasizing. I can practically taste the thing by the time we pull into the parking lot. We go inside and I pick up one of those muffins from the self-serve bakery case, the kind you put in a waxy bag, and I throw it in the cart. The cashier rings us up, we go out to the car, I settle Pal into his car seat, and I look through the bag. I want my muffin right that minute. I don't even want to drive home first. I want it now.

"It's not in the bag, and I figure I just need to run in and reclaim my muffin. So I look at Palance, and he's all comfortable, and I'm kind of peeved at this point, not at Palance, but at the cashier. I think it'll just take a second, so I pull into the handi-capped space right in front of the supermarket, lock up the car, and run in. And my blood pressure is elevated, my heart is racing, and I don't know why, but I'm thinking the muffin is the only thing that can help." She stops. "That's actually what I'm think-ing. Can you imagine?"

I nodded. I most definitely could.

"I go up to the cashier, and I say, 'Sorry. I must have left my muffin.' He says he threw it out. He pulls it out of the trash un-derneath the register, and it's still in its bag so I think, 'Fine, I'll work with that.' But he won't give it to me. He says I need to pay for it. I'm suddenly livid. I say, 'I already paid for it!' And he's like, 'No, I didn't ring it up. It was left in the basket, so I thought you didn't want it.' I'm like, 'Oh, no. I wanted it. I still want it.' I reach for the muffin and this kid, this twenty-year-old kid, actu-ally pulls his hand away. He says, 'You need to pay for it.' I say, 'I don't have any money. My purse is in the car. My *son* is in the car. I just ran in for the muffin.' He says, 'Well, you still need to pay for it.' And here's the craziest part—well, the craziest part up until this point. I say, 'I'm starving!' How melodramatic is that? I'm still carrying a spare tire from the baby, and the thing is, I ac-tually believed it!"

At that, we both started laughing.

"So now I'm actually begging this kid to give me a muffin. I'm a grown woman, I've had a career, I've got a baby—who I've locked in a car—and I'm begging for a muffin. But I'm really thinking, 'There's no fucking way I'm leaving here without this muffin.' It's like, this is my line in the sand. I've given up everything to have this baby and I'm going to have my fucking muffin!"

We were laughing again, but I also felt a little sad. Because for practically the first time since I'd known her, I thought I heard regret.

"And the guy doesn't budge. I'm actually losing this battle. Later, I tell Chris and he says, 'Well, the kid didn't owe you a muffin.' And I was like, 'He was pulling my muffin *from the trash.* He made the error and now he wanted me to pay for it.' You know Chris. He's basically like, 'The kid had to do his job.' I could have killed Chris for that."

"Chris doesn't understand our logic," I said. "He's a letter-of-the-law man. But you and me, we want things to be right. We want them to be fair. And it seemed only fair that if you had to run back in, the kid gives you your muffin."

"Exactly." Palance had begun to cry again, and Sonya once again lifted him to her chest. "So I lose, and I go back to the car. Oh, but before I do that, my parting shot to the kid is, 'You're mean.' And I meant it so deeply. I thought he was doing the meanest thing imaginable, and I didn't care that I was playing the mom card and trying to shame him for not giving a starving mother a muffin. So *then* I go out to the car and I drive a few blocks, and I think, 'Fuck that little punk.' I pull a U-turn and go back. I leave Palance in the car again in front of the store, and I storm back in. I go right up to the guy, who is in the process of ringing up this woman's groceries, and I throw my grocery bags on the counter and say that I want to return them. I announce that I will never be shopping there again, and that he can have my Preferred Customer card, too. The kid's a little flustered at this point, and he says he needs to finish with this woman, and I stand there waiting and glowering. And the funny thing is that it's all women in this line, and apparently they'd been talking about me, and one of them pats my hand and says, 'We were going to buy you the muffin, dear.'"

"Like they were moms who'd had those days, too?"

She nodded. "It was kind of a nice solidarity, or at least, nice to know they thought I was out of my mind for a reason. So I stood there, and the kid tries to do the return, and he can't get it to go through, and he calls the manager, who never comes. The minutes are ticking and I'm thinking of Palance outside, and my righteous indignation or my hormones or whatever are wearing off, and I'm just starting to feel really, really ashamed. I'm starting to see myself clearly, so I ask the kid for his name and for the manager's phone number and I say that I'm going to file a complaint and I storm out."

"Did you do it?" I asked.

"No. They'd probably give the little Nazi a raise."

"When you said you saw yourself clearly, what did you see?"

Sonya got quiet. She patted Palance's back, as if to reassure him in advance. "That I'm seething a lot of the time. They wouldn't let me come back to my job part-time, and I don't blame them really. I was hoping they'd value me so much that they'd make an exception, but they obviously didn't. With jobs like mine, they don't want part-time people. I didn't want to be with Palance full-time, and I didn't want to leave him full-time. My choices stank. But I chose Palance, and of course that's the right one. I didn't want him to be in day care all day. I didn't want to miss big swaths of his life. But sometimes I feel like I'm just losing it. I'm losing me. I mean, who was that muffin-starved freak?"

I nodded sympathetically. "But he'll get bigger, and he'll go to school. You can go back then."

"I know. I tell myself that all the time. It helps me get through the day. And that frightens me. I stayed home with him because I wanted to be with him. But all that keeps me going is knowing that someday I won't have to." Sonya wiped at her eyes. "I'm sorry. This isn't much fun for you."

"You don't need to be sorry. I'm glad you trusted me with all that."

"But didn't you know? It was just a funny story." She let out a hiccupy laugh. "People say that motherhood's hard, but they don't say in what ways. They don't say how many ways."

I hesitated for a second before asking, "But are you glad you did it?"

"Oh, my God, yes. That's what's so confusing. It really is like people say. It really is the greatest, hardest thing you'll ever do."

"I think that's what they say about the army."

"You know what never occurred to me before? That every choice you make negates other possibilities. If you have this, you can't have that. Maybe I've been blessed not to have realized that before, but it's so glaringly apparent to me every day now."

I knew what she meant. I felt it every day, too. I liked my profile job, but it didn't seem like forever. And if I kept choosing to do this thing that wouldn't last forever, wouldn't I be taking myself further from my true calling, whatever that was? "Do you think your calling was to be a mother?" I asked.

Sonya made a face. "Not at all."

"Was your calling to be a corporate vice president?"

She thought about that longer. "Not exactly."

"But the corporate job would be more of a calling than being a mother?"

"I guess for me, it's just a weird question. Callings are for creative people like you. You're waiting for the muse to strike. I just decided what would fit me, and what would let me live the way I wanted to live, and it turned out pretty well for a while. I'm not searching for inspiration."

Maybe that was my problem. I constantly expected to be moved or engaged in some way. It was what fed the meta-life. And the crazy thing was, even now, even after hearing the muffin story, I envied Sonya more than I ever had. There were hard choices, but she knew what she absolutely couldn't live without.

"Do you want to take a walk?" Sonya asked. "It's a gorgeous day out. I could put Pal in his stroller. That usually soothes him."

"Aha! So there is something besides the boob."

"I guess there is."

Chapter 11

ESTELLA

Age:	26
Height:	5'8"
Weight:	115 lbs
Occupation:	Animal rights worker
About me:	I'm from a family of fiery women, and I keep things spicy. I like the heat, in the kitchen and everywhere else.
About you:	You rise to a challenge.
Biggest turn-on:	Men who aren't afraid to go after what they want
Biggest turnoff:	Men who come on too strong
Last book I read:	*Maxim* magazine
Favorite movie:	*Y Tu Mamá También*
Five things I can't live without:	Satin sheets. Scented oils. My dog. Whipped cream. You.

*I*n theory, I still liked my lifestyle. I definitely still told people how much I liked it. But in practice, it was wearing seriously thin. I was tired of all my mini-trips to the grocery store; they no longer symbolized European sophistication and instead seemed like the mark of a shallow life. (American) people who are doing things in the world do not go to the market three times a week. And acting like a tourist in San Francisco had gotten old. I'd sat on the pier and contemplated the ocean no fewer than seven times. I'd ridden cable cars and carousels. I'd gone to museums venerating the history, culture, and art of five separate peoples. I'd never celebrated diversity so much in all my life, and it dawned on me that it was because I didn't have a life of my own. What I had was the kind of solo vacation that starts out exhilarating and just gets lonely and long.

Reality had set in. Unless I quadrupled my rates or worked four times as much, writing profiles would always provide me with only subsistence living. For it to be a viable career, I'd have to become a true entrepreneur, with an actual business plan, a marketing strategy, and the willingness to work myself into the ground. I'd never thought of myself as someone who'd ever run a business, unless it was through some elaborate sitcom setup, like I'm trying to bake a cake and I mess up the recipe and end up with the strongest adhesive known to man. I'd only ever imagined success coming through a sequence of lucky bumbles. Besides, writing profiles was a good enough way to pass the time and make a buck, but it didn't approach the level of a calling. I knew it was ridiculous to be almost thirty and still waiting for the muse to strike, but that's where I was.

I started romanticizing my days at the animal rescue. I missed being part of something with a clear purpose. I missed knowing what my paycheck would be every week, meager as it was. I actually missed having a structure imposed by someone other than me. I missed being part of a team of people carving out their small piece of goodness in the world. I missed the clarity, predictability, and simplicity. In short, I missed nearly everything that I had fled from in the first place.

So that's why I was having lunch with Estella. She wasn't the person I would have chosen, but she was the first person from the shelter to extend an invitation. Given the transparency of her e-mail, it made sense that it was Estella. I'd always suspected her of being an opportunist, and her e-mail didn't remotely camouflage the fact that what she really wanted was free advice for her dating profile. I was game because I remembered how she had insulted the people who needed my help, and I wanted to rub her nose in it at least a little. I also wanted to feel superior to one of the most breathtaking people I'd ever seen. And it was a reason to stop by the shelter, which I'd been meaning to do.

My nostalgia was tempered the moment I opened the door. There was my old desk, right at the head of a long corridor lined by cages. I was struck by the smell and the sounds of a hundred animals penned up, and I hadn't even re-experienced the sights yet. It was strange to think how inured to it I'd become. Now that I could take it all in fresh, I realized that I'd have to compare my current life unfavorably to something else.

Denise jumped up from my old desk to hug me. We exchanged excited greetings, then I took a good look at her. She had cut her hair into a sleek bob and finally looked twenty-three instead of seventeen. "You look fantastic," I told her.

She fluffed her hair. "I've gone urban."

"Eventually all you Midwestern girls fall." I glanced down the corridor. "Since when do you work the front desk?"

"I'm just covering it while Regina's at lunch. She's cool, but she's not you." It was apparent that Denise had really missed me, which was gratifying.

"Probably not. I bet she actually likes the animals."

Denise laughed. "Deep down, you liked them. I know you did."

"I didn't hate them," I conceded. "I'd forgotten what they smelled like, though. It's amazing what you can get used to."

She nodded. "I barely notice it." She unleashed a huge smile. "I'm so glad to see you!"

"It's really good to see you, too."

"I was thinking of you the other day, about how cool it would be if someday you turned your animal bios into a book. Like, a coffee-table book or something. You were so good at those."

"Thanks."

"Like, *really* good. I can really see the difference now. When you used to write them, people came in and they acted like the animals were rock stars. Like, 'Omigod, there's Rocco!' And sometimes they'd quote your bios. You had, like, a hundred different ways to say a dog was good with kids."

I was actually blushing. Man, I needed help.

Denise affected a more serious expression. "I don't think I ever told you how much I respected the way you left. I mean, I hated to see you go, but you did what you had to do. Most people don't go with their instincts like that. Now, dogs—they go with their instincts. Which is why I love them."

"That compliment shows that you're in the right line of work." I liked knowing that some people land where they're supposed to. Anyone could see looking at her that Denise had.

"I haven't even asked about your work yet. What's it like?"

"It's picking up." I tried to sound noncommittal, hoping she wouldn't ask more.

"I knew it would work out." She beamed at me. "So what brought you here? Do you want to volunteer?" she teased.

I laughed. "Actually, I'm going to lunch with Estella."

"Really?" She looked surprised.

"I know. It's kind of weird." I looked around, suddenly realizing how unusual it was that ours was the only human activity in evidence. "Is Maggie around?"

"No. They all did a run to the pound."

"Estella too?"

"Yeah. That's why I was surprised you were here to see her."

Sweet Denise. I thought she'd been surprised because she couldn't imagine Estella and me being friends. I sure couldn't. "What time do you think they'll be back?" I asked, fighting my feeling of annoyance. Here I was, doing Estella a favor, and she was standing me up.

"I'm not sure. They've been gone awhile now."

I thought about a course of action for a minute, then said, "I've been craving the *shawarma* from the Middle Eastern place up the street, so I'm going to grab a sandwich. If Estella gets back soon, could you tell her she can come join me?"

It was true that I was craving the *shawarma.* I had eaten at the storefront Lebanese restaurant with its peeling paint and scarred formica floor at least once a week when I worked at the shelter. It wasn't a particularly friendly establishment, which I appreciated that day as I fumed about Estella's rudeness. It was run by a family and the sulky nineteen-year-old who had waited on me about fifty times showed not a flicker of recognition as I ordered my sandwich. My irritation turned inward, as it was wont to do. I berated myself for not bringing a book. When I ate alone, I always hid behind a book, even when there were only eight other customers in the joint, like there were that day. I was thinking that there had to be a more dignified way to make a living than this, when I remembered that Estella wasn't paying me.

For the first five minutes of my wait, I was still hoping she would come so I wouldn't have to sit alone, but then my plate arrived. I decided that if I ate fast enough, I could escape with my moral superiority. But in the midst of my maniacal chewing, Estella appeared, striking as ever and slightly out of breath.

"I ran all the way here." I supposed that was in lieu of an apology. She settled herself across from me and pointed to my half-finished sandwich. "That looks good. I'm starved."

I swallowed an enormous bite and wiped my mouth with a napkin. I tried to modulate my annoyance because she wasn't really that late. Now I was stuck helping her. "It is good," I said. "Have you had the chicken *shawarma* here?"

"No. I think I'll try it, though." She called out, "Somar, can I have a chicken *shawarma*?"

And at that, the nineteen-year-old's face lit up. "Sure, Estella! I'll get you one."

Oh, for Christ's sake.

"So, Nora. How *are* you?" Estella now fixed her smile on me.

"I'm good. But you don't have much of your lunch break left, so maybe we should talk about you," I said, preferring to skip the niceties and get right to being used.

"You know, I'm not so good," she said. She pushed her long hair back behind her ears and thrust her face a little bit forward. It was what I thought of as her signature move, the one that highlighted just how perfect her tanned face was. The only flaw I could detect was a little bit of acne around her hairline, and I was glad to see it. Then her hair fell forward and it was concealed again. She even had a trick for that.

"What's wrong?"

"I need a man. A good man." She studied my face, waiting. I stared back. "And I know you're still helping people work on their profiles, so that must mean you're pretty good at it. Otherwise, you'd need to get a job like the rest of us, right?"

"I'm all right," I said. But in spite of myself, I felt a little flattered. I mean, in a way, I was different now. I might have been tired of whiling away the hours in art museums, but it was undoubtedly a luxury most people didn't have.

"I thought maybe you could help me work on my profile. It wouldn't take too long. Only as long as this lunch, I promise." She smiled brilliantly. "I've got it right here." She pulled a few pages out of her handbag and slid them across to me.

"You do know that I normally charge people for this." I continued to eat and didn't reach for the pages. I was going to help her, of course, but professional pride and my own ego dictated that I at least say that much.

"You know the kind of money I make. I can't afford your rates." She had the barest trace of a pout.

"Do you actually know my rates?"

"Well, no." Her eyes flitted away. "I just know that I can't afford anything."

"I guess it depends how bad you need a man." It occurred to me that I was being slightly sadistic. But why resent Estella? I wasn't beautiful like her, but I'd never had trouble finding men. And I had my own business while she was still essentially a glorified dog walker. Not even that glorified. I picked up her papers.

The tagline above her profile read, "I Look Good And I Taste Even Better." I almost choked on my sandwich with suppressed laughter. Her pictures were equally ridiculous in their over-the-top sexiness. In one, she was actually bent over lacing up her knee-length boot. Another was a full-length shot of her in tight jeans with her midriff exposed. Before moving on to the text, I said, "Just to clarify, you do get plenty of responses."

"Yes. But they're all jerks!"

I continued reading, trying to resist my impulses to wince, roll my eyes, or guffaw. I put down the paper. "This is all wrong," I said. I wasn't in the mood to sugarcoat. You get what you pay for. "I mean, every sentence drips with sex. All that stuff about being fiery. Even that line about your dog . . ."

"There's nothing in there about me having sex with my dog!" Estella's cheeks flushed with indignation.

"I'm just saying, on the list of things you can't live without, he's sandwiched in between scented oils and whipped cream."

"It's about getting noticed. It's innuendo." I could see her trying to keep the defensiveness out of her voice. She probably realized I hadn't done anything for her yet, and could easily walk away.

"The guys who contact you, how do they treat you?" I asked to underscore my point.

She dropped her eyes and when she raised them again, they were blazing. "It's not my fault that men are assholes!"

"I didn't say it was. But if every man that comes to you based on this profile is an asshole, then something's wrong with the profile, right? That's why you e-mailed me, isn't it?" It came out more condescending than I'd intended, so I softened it into something I'd said perhaps a dozen times already to other clients. "It's a weird thing, having to market yourself."

And like at least twelve before her, Estella quieted, then exhaled. "It is weird. I mean, how am I supposed to know what to write? I'm not intellectual."

"I just think we could cool this thing down, flesh it out with things you're interested in." I'd slipped into "we" mode unconsciously. Force of habit. "You want to include things that are unique and surprising, things people can't tell by looking at the pictures. Do you know what I mean?"

"I guess." She looked troubled. "I'm not sure I'm very unique."

It was a surprising admission. "Of course you are," I said immediately. "Everyone is, right?"

Estella shook her head no.

Apparently she was an absolutist. "You're uniquely firm in your opinions. You know your own mind, and you won't back down." I didn't necessarily mean those as compliments.

"Lots of people are like that."

"No one else at the shelter is."

She thought about it, then looked a little less dejected. "I guess that's true."

"Let's go at this another way. I'll just ask you something, and you'll give me a spontaneous answer, okay?"

She laughed uneasily. "Okay."

"What's the most charming, quirky thing a guy has done for you?"

Estella twirled her hair for a long minute, then finally said, "My laundry. I came home once and my boyfriend had gotten my roommate to let him in and he'd hauled like four loads of laundry down to the Laundromat. He didn't even have a car."

"That's good stuff. Write that down." I pushed the pages back toward her. "See, the fact that you can enjoy a gesture like that makes you more approachable. I think this profile is scaring off a lot of decent guys. Reading this profile, I'd have no idea that you could be happy with some loads of laundry. Maybe guys are even scared off thinking they couldn't satisfy you in bed." My new business card could read: NORA BISHOP, DIME-STORE PSYCHOLOGIST.

Estella laughed. "My last boyfriend was impotent half the time. If they beat that, I'd be happy."

There was no ready answer.

"That's so funny that you thought sex was the most important thing to me. Not at all." Another hair toss. "But it's the most important thing to men. Which is why I mostly hate them."

"Let's leave that out of the profile."

We both laughed. It should have been one of those break-through moments: The beautiful person reveals just how ordinary she is, the ordinary person realizes her own beauty, and the scene sings with life-affirming connectedness. But this was not one of those moments. This was me phoning it in. And what's so affirming about helping someone like Estella weed out the great unwashed masses?

"Could you give me some other pointers?" Estella asked, looking peppier by the second.

"Changing the pictures can do a lot. The pictures clue people in about how to read the profile." It was more of my usual patter. "Different pictures could really help. Maybe some that are less overtly sexual." That last part was new.

"I don't really have a lot of pictures of myself. I don't even own a camera. I just had my friends take these for the profile."

So she did mastermind the boot-lacing picture. I knew it! "There's a photographer who's taken pictures of some of my other clients and they turned out great. But I'm pretty sure he won't work for free."

"I could pay him."

Oh, now she could pay. "How much?"

"How about half of his going rate?" It seemed her bout of insecurity had passed.

"I'm not getting into that," I said firmly. "I'll call him and tell him you're interested in pictures. He'll contact you, and you can negotiate then."

"Thanks, Nora." She maintained eye contact. "Really, thanks."

"You're welcome. You're picking up lunch, right?"

"Of course," she said, wide-eyed, as if she couldn't believe I even had to ask.

• • • •

I wasn't surprised when I got Alex's voice mail a week later. "Thank you so much for introducing me to Estella. She's incredible. What a sweetheart. We walked all over her neighborhood taking pictures, then took some more back at her apartment. We got some great shots. I'm just hoping she never has to use them. It was the best date I've had in . . . I don't know how long, and it wasn't even a date. Do you know if she's got any other guys on the string right now? Could you maybe put in a good word for me? . . ."

Chapter 12

LARISSA

Age:	32
Height:	5'4"
Weight:	115 lbs
Occupation:	Professional do-gooder
About me:	Sensual, silly, and soulful. Open to new experiences.
About you:	Surprise me.

"Climb aboard," Dan boomed.

So this is what we've been reduced to.

Well, it was eleven o'clock, and I was tired anyway. Climbing over Dan rather than aboard, I went into the bathroom and started brushing my teeth. I slowed my motions when I realized my gums were starting to bleed from the force. I needed to release tension somehow, and it wasn't going to be through sex.

In case you're wondering, what you just heard was Dan telling me to mount him. Now, there are maybe, *maybe* three ways a man saying "Climb aboard" to indicate woman astride can be sexy. Dan projecting his voice like a jolly skipper is not one of them.

Still *in that voice*, Dan called after me, "Hey, where'd you go?"

I reached over and slammed the bathroom door, then spit into the sink. There was no denying it. My profile writing wasn't the only thing being phoned in. Dan and I were in a rut.

I put down the toilet seat and sat down, resting my chin on my hand. All the signs were there. We watched a lot more TV together. Dan was watching sports more often, and while he patted the seat cushion next to him, he didn't seem too bothered when I read in the bedroom instead. We didn't talk as much or as intently as we used to, and we fell into Mrs. Pimmbottom and Rodney a lot. One minute we'd be having a lackluster conversation and the next Dan would be making ape noises. But the most damning evidence of all was our sex life. We were only having sex at night, even when we had all weekend to spend together, and we were having it the same way. Our movements seemed choreographed. We were both able to come reliably, because we knew each other's buttons and we pushed them. I was on top about 80 percent of the time. At first, Dan's preference for that position seemed enlightened, and besides, it was my favorite. But recently he'd explained it as "a combination of my two favorite things: having sex and doing nothing." He meant it as a joke, but I was not amused. I thought there was more than a grain of truth in it. What bothered me most was that predictably enough, my sex drive had dropped. I was now content with once a week. If that.

I flushed the toilet and returned to bed.

"Are you okay?" Dan asked. "Is your stomach bothering you?" He must have inferred that from my flight.

"A little." It wasn't a complete lie.

"Come here." He enveloped me in his arms and stroked my hair. "I could go buy you some ginger ale."

"That's sweet. But I'll be okay." I laughed and pulled him tighter. "You're the only person I know who believes completely in the healing power of ginger ale."

"Well, you're the only person I know who completely underestimates the power of ginger ale. So there." He kissed my neck. "I was thinking that we should take a little drive this weekend, maybe go up to wine country. What do you think?"

"I'd like that. But who's driving home?" I added teasingly.

"Whoever does less drinking."

"That's probably a bad setup."

"We could stay overnight in a bed-and-breakfast," Dan suggested.

This was my first indication that maybe he thought we were in a rut, too. I seized on it and immediately began brainstorming. "Most of the good places in wine country are booked up way in advance, and have a two-night minimum on weekends. We could try to stay in one that's a little less chichi. I could look up some places on the Internet and—"

"That sounds like a pain in the ass. Let's just do something else then. Drive along the coast or something."

His immediate dismissal of the idea at the first impediment made me wonder if I'd read him wrong initially. Maybe he thought everything was fine, that this was the normal course of a relationship. Maybe it was.

"That sounds really nice," I said, squeezing his arm. "Let's do that."

"Yeah. Let's do that." His voice was drowsy. "Good night." With one final hug, he rolled away and went to sleep.

I noted that he hadn't tried again to have sex. But I told myself things were fine. It was all perfectly normal. We were just your average tired, normal couple. Except that Dan was, once again, the only one sleeping.

· · · ·

"Why didn't Dan want to come to this? It seemed like it'd be right up his alley," Larissa said loudly into my ear, trying to override the cacophony of the bar.

"The whole thing's just too close to his bookbar idea," I answered. "He prefers to pretend it's not happening."

"He'd better move on that idea soon. Anyone in here might get to it first." Larissa rotated her straw, then took a sip of her drink. Her third drink. It was our first bar, and she was already on her third drink.

"What time is the first reader anyway?" I asked. I was getting antsy. I generally didn't like bars this crowded. Someone kept elbowing me in the back, but by the time I turned around, I couldn't tell to whom the offending elbow belonged. I felt like a dog chasing her tail.

"Relax." Was she actually slurring? She looked at her watch. "It was supposed to start five minutes ago."

"I didn't expect there to be this many people. I thought they'd all be down the street at the bar with the travel writers."

Larissa nodded in agreement. "I thought the hipsters would all be at blog writing over at the Irish pub."

"I guess that's why we're not hipsters. We can't even guess what they're into."

"This topic must be so unhip that it's hip."

"Oh, right. It's always coming around again, isn't it?"

Every year, San Francisco hosted a literary festival that kicked off with a night of readings at staggered times at different bars, all within walking distance. There were at least four readings going on in each time slot, so you had to choose which was most interesting before going on to the next bar an hour later. There were about five slots before last call. Larissa and I had gone together for the past three years. To lessen the hipster intimidation factor and, in her case, increase the chances of picking up a smart guy, we tried to pick the most unpopular events in each slot. So this year, we'd selected "Postmenopausal Writers on the Meaning of Life" for our appetizer. And now here I was with a welt on my back. This city never failed to surprise me.

The crowd was actively quieting; people were shushing and pointing toward the makeshift stage. A woman of about sixty had clambered onto it. She had silver hair pinned up in a bun, and was wearing a long velvet skirt that nearly brushed the floor. "I'm Sonora Watson," she said, her voice scratchy but warm, like vinyl. There was polite applause, a few scattered whoops. She lowered her head slightly to indicate her humility. Since I didn't know who she was, the gesture left me with the reverse impression of arrogance. "I must confess, I was surprised to be invited to this gathering tonight. I'm embarrassed to say that I didn't even know young people were drunkenly stumbling through the streets once a year in the name of literature." Larissa and I laughed along with the crowd. There was something inviting about Sonora, a magnetism that we were all feeling. Well, we had all been drinking. It was the advantage of reading in a bar. You got a loose audience.

"I'd like to read a piece that I'm not entirely sure is finished," Sonora continued. "I'm hoping that I'll be able to tell by your reaction just how much work is left to do. I don't know how strictly it adheres to tonight's topic, but here is my inherently flawed, hopefully worthwhile attempt to approach 'The Meaning of Life.'"

Sonora went on to read a first-person account of a twenty-three-year marriage, with each year allotted one paragraph. Every word of every paragraph was perfectly tuned; there wasn't a wrong note. I found myself wanting to believe it had been her own marriage, though I reconsidered when the husband died midway through the final year. That last paragraph contained the narrator's remembrance of her husband's wedding vow, when he swore that he'd never be afraid to let her change him, especially if it was for the better.

The crowd froze for a few seconds after she had finished, as if she had asked for a moment of silence. Then we exploded into applause. She stood in the spotlight with what appeared to be tears in her eyes, repeating her earlier head bow. I tore through the literary festival program to see her bio. Each participant in the festival wrote their own. Hers said, "Sonora Watson is a retired psychotherapist living in Napa, California. Her first story, 'The Stanislavski Method,' was published in a literary journal she's sure you've never heard of."

"She's a therapist," I hissed.

"Go to her!" Larissa said passionately. She said it as if this were the penultimate scene of a romantic comedy, and I had to catch Sonora at the airport before she left me forever.

"She's retired," I said, realizing how disappointed I was.

"How beautiful was that?" Larissa sighed.

The next speaker was taking the stage, and she and Sonora briefly embraced. The woman said something into Sonora's ear that could only have been praise, and then Sonora stepped down from the dais. As she tried to move through the crowd, she was waylaid by audience member after audience member. I had never seen so many people simultaneously moved by a performance.

"I want to talk to her, but what would I say?" I asked Larissa. I monitored Sonora's progress with a sidelong glance. Within minutes, she might be right next to me and that would be my only chance. I needed to think quickly.

"I don't know. I guess tell her how much you liked her writing?"

"Everyone's already telling her that," I said, almost in despair.

"Well, what are you trying to get from her?" Larissa's question was surprisingly cogent for someone who'd just polished off her third drink in under an hour.

"I want her to come out of retirement and help me." I didn't really mean that, except that I did.

"Do you think that's realistic?" Now, that question was the caliber I'd been expecting.

"Of course I don't think it's realistic."

"You keep thinking. I need to find the restroom." She tottered away on her three-inch heels.

I wasn't even listening to the reader onstage. I was staring at Sonora. She was talking to three twenty-something women. Or were they in their early thirties? And actually, Sonora wasn't saying anything. She was just listening. They seemed to be bombarding her. *We're all looking for the secret.*

Suddenly Larissa was back and grabbing at my arm. "We need to leave," she said, panicked. "Right now."

"Why?"

"Dustin's here. And he's with someone." She was on the verge of tears. "And she's really, really cute."

"Did he see you?"

"No. That's why we need to get out now. I can't talk to him. I'm a mess. I don't want him to know I'm a mess." Tears were streaming down her face.

"Are you sure that he's *really* with her, that they're not just friends?"

"She's hanging all over him. And I didn't even get to pee!" she wailed. "I got out of line when I saw them."

"Let's go then," I said resignedly. "We'll catch the end of travel writing, or at least use the bathroom." I took her arm and we fought our way out the door. I cast a last, sad look back at Sonora, who was being accosted by yet another animated female. It was just as well. I still hadn't found anything to say. I'd once seen Bono in a restaurant and had the same problem. I knew I couldn't just go up and expect him to say something brilliant; I'd have to say something first that would inspire brilliance. I had to make them *want* to be brilliant for me. I didn't end up talking to Bono, either.

I tried to comfort Larissa as I led her to the next bar and it seemed to be working. But when we were almost at the door, she shrank back in terror. "I can't go in there," she said, shaking her head frantically.

"We don't have to stay. Let's just use the bathroom, and then we'll go home." I made my voice as dulcet as possible.

"What if Kevin's in there, with his wife? Or Sean, with his fiancée? Or Phillip, with his wife? What if I just keep seeing them?" She leaned against the front of the Laundromat next door. The elderly Asian woman inside looked out at us curiously, then resumed her folding.

"Your exes won't be there. Especially not Phillip. I bet he's illiterate."

Larissa started out laughing, but then she was crying. "I bet Dustin's engaged to that girl. I bet they were standing there listening to that story and thinking that would be them in twenty-three years." She wiped her eyes with the sleeve of her coat. "Except for the cancer part."

"I'm sure he's not engaged. He was just on a date. You've had dates since you two broke up."

"What does that matter? I'm never getting married, Nora. I'm never going to have the meaning of life." She sank down to the ground, her back pressed against the glass.

I sat down next to her. I could smell fabric softener. "First of all, that's not true. But second of all, who says that's the meaning of life? It was a beautiful story, but if you actually think about it, it's kind of hokey."

"There's nothing hokey about loving someone with all your heart and having them love you the same way." Larissa looked offended that I would ever suggest otherwise. But at least she stopped crying. "And that's the thing, Nora." She welled up again. "That's not how anyone has ever loved me. That's why they leave me. And then as soon as they do, they meet the love of their life. It's happened again and again and again. They break up with me, and a few months later, they're engaged. A few months after that, they're married. The year after he broke up with me, Kevin's wife was having a baby. I'm everyone's good-luck charm, but mine."

I didn't know what to say or do as she sobbed. I hurt for her, but her accounting of history was accurate. It wasn't impossible that Dustin really was engaged to the girl at the bar. When he left Larissa, he told her he'd been "mentally gone" for over a year; he just hadn't ended things because he thought it would destroy her. I was furious when I heard that, furious at his egotism and furious that he would actually tell her that. But Larissa said that she'd kept at him for hours, trying to remind him of all that they'd had so that he'd change his mind. She came to believe that in his own way, Dustin had been doing her a kindness by telling her that. He was helping her give up hope.

She was right, though. There was nothing hokey about a great love to span a lifetime. In Sonora's story, years three, seven, twelve, and (obviously) twenty-three had been painful. Some years had been boring. But put them all together, and it was a life of great love. That was how it was done. I thought of Dan, and his offer to get me ginger ale. I was in love with him. That was never the question.

The previously empty sidewalk was now jammed with people shuffling to their next literary event. I held Larissa as they streamed by.

Chapter 13

DEREK

Age:	28
Height:	5'8"
Weight:	160–190 lbs, maybe?
Occupation:	Telecommunications muckety-muck
About me:	TBD
About you:	TBD
Biggest turn-on:	TBD
Biggest turnoff:	TBD
Five things I can't live without:	TBD
Most embarrassing moment:	TBD

Derek Cartwright was his name, telecom was his game.
Derek didn't actually say that, of course. But within five minutes of meeting him, that refrain was in my head. Driving a BMW, living a block away from Danielle Steele in Pacific Heights, wearing an expensive suit. And those shoes. I didn't even want to think what his shoes had cost, and that he probably had another pair in brown. When I'd arrived, he'd actually handed me his card. Why did I need his card? This would be our only meeting, and I already had his cell phone number. It was just part of the presentation. It was just part of his Derek-ness.

I loathed him.

It was probably just a fluke that up until this moment, I'd basically liked all my clients. But I had to admit, some of my liking for them was their tendency to meet me slightly hat in hand, embarrassed at having sought my services. They generally deferred to my authority, which was unique in my professional life. It was kind of how I imagined it went when decent men met prostitutes for the first time: shy, uncertain, abashed, needing some hand-holding before they got down to it. A weird analogy, I know, but bear with me.

Derek, in contrast, seemed like someone who had the phone numbers of several high-end escort services programmed into his cell phone. I could picture him waiting in the swankiest hotel room in San Francisco, and when the knock came, he'd answer it buck naked. He'd smack his open palms against his abs a few times with evident self-satisfaction and say, "Yeah, you get *all this*."

I had cause for this suspicion. I mean, I was meeting him in this absurdly upscale hotel bar. A hotel bar! In a neighborhood replete with local bars. I passed no fewer than four while walking the two blocks from the parking deck (where it cost me $14 an hour to park, I might add. I'd never done an expense report for any other clients, but I was thinking it over).

"You want a Cosmo?" he asked when the waiter came by. "An appletini, maybe?"

"Root beer," I said. "I'm on the clock."

I wanted him to wince at that, to wonder what the waiter would make of a statement like that in a hotel bar, but Derek didn't miss a beat. He held up his ice-filled glass, shook it slightly, and said, "Another."

"Of course, sir," the waiter said. He practically did a little bow before departing.

"So as I was saying," Derek said smoothly, "I just haven't had the time to write one of these profiles myself. But I'm twenty-eight now, and I'm tired of the sex toys and the gold diggers." He cast me a slow smile. I stared back blankly. "I'm ready for some-thing real. I'm ready for some*one* real. I travel a lot for my work, and I come home to an empty apartment. I'm ready for that to change. I'm ready to get some home fires burning, if you know what I'm saying."

"So I'd be writing your profile from scratch. You have nothing written." I tried to keep my tone as bland as possible.

"Nada."

"Okay." I thought a moment, then decided to price myself out of the market. "That'd cost you a thousand dollars."

"Done. The best is worth paying for, right?"

My stomach churned at the deal we'd just brokered. On the one hand, I was thrilled to be making a thousand dollars. On the other hand, I'd have to make it by spending enough time with Derek to write him a profile. I pitied his prostitute.

"One of the important rules is that you want to know your au-dience," I said. I planned to be a cold pedant throughout the evening. There was no indication that Derek was even remotely attracted to me; he probably considered me way below his league, which made my blood boil. But for the sake of my pride, I planned to convey to him that I was a professional, that he was on my turf, and that there'd be no hanky-panky—hotel bar or not. "The key is to think about what you want in a woman, and what traits that woman would be looking—"

"Yeah, yeah." He did a dismissive arm wave. His staple ges-ture, no doubt. "I don't need the philosophy." Then he gave me what he clearly thought was his killer grin. He bore a certain resemblance to Tom Cruise. I detest Tom Cruise. "I'm just looking for results. I'm a big-picture guy."

"Well, that's good to know." I doodled a picture of a big-screen TV on my notepad, and next to it, a gun. "What kind of woman do you see yourself with?"

"One who likes the fine things in life, but isn't obsessed with money. Or, more specifically, isn't obsessed with my money."

"So you want a woman who's committed to her own career?"

He appeared to consider this. "She should *have* a career, but it should be one that gets her home before me. I don't want her to be more into her career than into me, right?"

I had to ask. "And will you be 'more into your career' than into her?"

"I have to be. I can't let up now."

"So how much time do you actually have to devote to a relationship?" I added, "For the profile. I want to give an accurate impression of what a woman will be getting if she decides to be with you."

"Accuracy? Your ad said your approach is about the marketing."

"Marketing is a big part of it." It occurred to me that if I didn't win his approval, he could withdraw the money. Then I would have subjected myself to him for nothing. "But I want to make sure you end up with something that'll last. If you put something in your profile that isn't true, or creates an impression that you can't back up in person, then you'll end up with nothing."

"Oh, I'll end up with something. It's a numbers game."

I realized with horror that I had used that phrase more than a few times myself. With much greater delicacy and nuance, of course, but still.

"Look, I don't want you to lie. And there's no reason you'd

have to." That grin again. Ech. "But as you said, we're creating an impression here. It's not facts that move people; it's impressions."

"So what impression do you want to give a woman?"

"The impression of availability. I mean, I'll be around enough." *More than enough, I'm sure.* "I don't think she needs to know up front that I travel a lot for business. I do think she needs to know up front that I'm successful in business."

"I thought you were trying to avoid gold diggers."

"I can smell a gold digger a mile away. Your job is just to do volume for me." Grin.

I consulted my pad. "So far, I have down that you want a woman who has a career, but puts her relationship first. What else?" I kept my eyes fixed on the paper. If I could do that 70 percent of the time, I'd make it through this.

"She needs to look good, of course. She should wear Prada; Prada shouldn't wear her, right?" From that flashing grin of his, I was starting to wonder if the man had Tourette's. Maybe all this bravado was just to compensate for a disabling tic disorder. "Good in bed, but you can't say that right out. You need to finesse it a little." He paused to think. "She should like cats. I've got a cat." I looked at him in surprise. He shrugged. "My exgirlfriend left me the cat. He's purebred. What else, what else. A good sense of humor. Someone who can get along with my friends. Someone who doesn't get seasick. Or carsick. That one would be a deal breaker. I like to drive switchbacks a little faster than advisable." He looked at me. "Do you need more?"

"No, that'll do it." I continued to scribble for a minute while thinking of my next question. "Five things you can't live without?"

"BMW 650i convertible. The open road to drive her on." He stopped, momentarily stumped. "Five, right?" I nodded. "Sleep.

Food. Sex." He ticked them off on his fingers. "It would be kind of funny to take the question really literally, right? No one can live without sleep, food, and sex."

I nodded approvingly as I wrote his answers down. The good thing was he would be warding the ladies off all on his own.

A half hour later, he counted ten $100 bills into my hand and we called it a night. I told him that I'd e-mail the finished product to him in the next couple of days, and that was it. It was the quickest profile meeting I'd had, and by far the most profitable. I'd never held $1,000 in cash before, and clutched my purse tightly as I walked to the garage. Then I loosened my grip, figuring that I should stop looking like a woman with $1,000 in cash in her purse.

When I got home, Dan was out and the apartment was silent. I immediately turned on the desk lamp at my drafting table and started working on the profile. I wanted it done as soon as possible. I'd been trying to muster a feeling of satisfaction that I'd taken Derek by charging so much for so little, but I felt the opposite. I just felt dirty. I shouldn't have taken Derek's money, I should have walked out on behalf of womankind. I should have shown Derek that women couldn't be bought. Instead, I'd confirmed his obvious belief that it was all a matter of price. Though honestly, Derek probably didn't think he'd bought me, because he wasn't thinking about me at all, the same way he would barely think about whatever woman he would net with his profile.

I should donate this money to the women's movement. Was there still a women's movement? I mean, feminism was the default mode for women under forty, so no one needed to carry a card anymore. I could donate it to the National Organization for Women, or the League of Women Voters. To People for the Ethical Treatment of Women. To the Self-Respecting Women of America.

But I looked at the pile of hundreds, and I really, really wanted them. I had earned them. I *was* a self-respecting woman. It wasn't like I worked for a tobacco company. I was just a woman trying to run a business. Gloria Steinem would understand. If not, Helen Gurley Brown would.

In writing the profile, I put in every asinine thing he'd said. I dressed it up prettily enough that he wouldn't suspect I was trying to sabotage him. In the final version, there were more than enough clues that he was shallow and self-involved. The depressing part was that I knew he'd get plenty of responses anyway.

After e-mailing the profile to Derek, I found myself roaming the apartment, pent-up and antsy. I turned the TV on for a while, scanned through all hundred channels twice, then turned it off. I did the same thing with the pages of a magazine. I wished Dan were home to talk me down. Finally I took a sleeping pill and went to bed.

• • • •

When I woke up the next morning, Dan had already gone to work. I was disappointed; I'd been planning to surprise him by initiating morning sex. Since the literary festival the week before and the Dustin/Larissa debacle, I'd been trying to make at least one gesture of love a day. There'd been a tender voice mail left for him at work, a back rub, and lots of praise for a new drink he'd concocted with fig liqueur. I didn't complain that he used the last of the milk without telling me or buying more. I'd watched an entire baseball game with him, and even worn the baseball cap he'd bought me months before, the one that he thought was cute and I knew made me look like a rodent.

So morning sex would have to be tomorrow's gesture. I wasn't sure how long I was supposed to keep this up, with Dan taking it all in stride. Except for the back rub. He was really appreciative of that, and he even reciprocated with his own, much less thorough rub. Obviously, I'd have to go bigger. That night, I decided to surprise him with a four-course gourmet meal.

I spent much of the morning poring over recipes that involved ingredients like enoki mushrooms, fruity green olive oil, and ruby chard. As I made the shopping list, I was filled with good humor. *It's so nice to do things for someone you love,* I thought, captivated by my own beneficence.

That is, until I actually started having to do things. There, the plan unraveled. I'd assumed I could find everything in one place, but instead, I ended up going to three different outrageously expensive markets. As I pushed my cart through each of their narrow aisles, I was struck by just how ill-conceived this was. I don't like cooking. Neither Dan nor I have a particularly refined palate. And Dan probably wouldn't even know how much money or energy I'd spent, unless I told him. He'd know there were more courses than usual, but beyond that, I'd have to point it out. Which just seemed tacky and pathetic. But if he didn't notice, I knew I'd sit there stewing through all four courses. I was supposed to be doing this with the spirit of kindness, buoyed by my love for Dan. Instead, I was standing in my third line, fuming.

I was also silently tallying my purchases, with rising horror. Sure, I'd known that dinner would be expensive, but "expensive" is such an abstract notion. I started to seriously consider abandoning my cart full of groceries and going back to the other two grocery stores to return the rest of the ingredients. But how to do it? I could wait until it was my turn at the register, and then explain that I'd changed my mind. Of course that would inconvenience the staff and draw disgust from the other shoppers. I could walk down an unoccupied aisle and ditch the cart. If an employee caught me, could he force me to return to my cart? It didn't seem likely—though there could be some measure of public shaming. The final option was that I could replace everything myself, but I'd have to pull produce back out of the plastic bags, which would get me even more dirty looks. The customers who shopped at a market carrying seventeen varieties of mushrooms cared about sanitation. They probably already thought I was the riffraff.

The problem was that all the plans risked humiliation. On another day, I could withstand the ire of the staff and the other patrons. But I was suddenly feeling very fragile. I was getting exhausted just thinking about potential ways to dispose of my groceries, and besides, the woman in front of me was already paying and the man behind me was genially pointing to the conveyor belt, maybe thinking I was from another country and didn't realize I was supposed to unload my own cart. My window of opportunity was rapidly closing. Which was fine, because I was also realizing that I didn't want to tell Dan that my day had been spent planning and shopping for an aborted dinner. It looked like I was going to have to suck it up and carry on. I would have to cook.

Once I got home with the groceries, it became clear that the plan hadn't just been ill-conceived; it had been completely insane. That morning, I'd come up with what I'd thought was an image of myself cooking, but now I realized it was actually an image of me smiling while I garnished some impossibly beautiful dish. It certainly wasn't an image of me sitting with a pad of paper for a half hour trying to get the timing of the different recipes down. How I would simultaneously cook the goat cheese tart and the charred tomatoes when they required ovens a hundred degrees apart, I still didn't know.

At two o'clock that afternoon, I officially started cooking. The salad alone took forty minutes to assemble (ever so lightly steaming asparagus, chopping mint leaves, shredding three kinds of lettuce). Everything took longer and looked sloppier than it should have. I was running back and forth from one dish to another, consulting my itinerary, rereading the recipes, and trying to clean up some of the two thousand pots, pans, bowls, and kitchen implements that I was sullying in the process. It was four hours of frenzy and fury, and when Dan walked in, I was tussling with a goose—yes, a goose—and upon seeing him, I burst into tears.

Dan gently pried my fingers from the goose and looked into my face with great concern. Not the expression I had pictured when I set out that morning. "Sweetie," he said, "what happened?"

"You're looking at it," I sputtered.

"Is it"—he searched for just the right word—"dinner?"

"Yes, it's dinner!" I exploded. "It was supposed to be a four-course gourmet dinner made from scratch to show how much I love you. And look at it! This can't bode well."

"What do you mean, 'bode well'?" He narrowed his eyes, almost imperceptibly.

"For us. Look around. This can't be good."

"You think *this* says something about *us*?" He pulled away from me abruptly and angrily strode around the kitchen. "You think the fact that you're a lousy cook trying to attempt something way out of your depth says something about us?" I stared at the floor like a naughty child. "Do you?" he demanded.

"Well, I don't know," I nearly wailed.

"Well, I know. And what this kitchen says is that you are bored with your freelancing and you need to get a job like a normal person."

"That's not true," I protested. Or at least, I wasn't yet sure if it was true. I was feeling like Lucy to his Ricky Ricardo, and I didn't like it.

"You're not bored with your job?" He stared at me, pointedly waiting for my answer.

"I don't know what I am! But you accusing me isn't helping."

"What did I accuse you of?" He looked exasperated.

"Of being a bad cook and being bored."

"Are you not a bad cook and are you not bored?"

"I can't answer all your double negatives," I said sulkily.

Dan took a deep breath and was visibly trying to collect himself. "Are you a bad cook?" he asked, prepared to break the complicated ideas down into their component parts. I wasn't used to him condescending to me; even when he talked me out of my meta-life, he never made me feel small.

"I'm not a good cook. But that's the whole point. That's why it was supposed to be a nice surprise for you." Through my hurt, I felt the barest trace of pleasure at having found a way to be the aggrieved party.

He took a moment to consider. "I'm sorry I got so angry. You were trying to do something nice. But Nora, you're bored. I don't care about your cooking. It's not about cooking or about us. You know that, don't you?"

"No."

He moved in closer. "You're not happy doing the freelancing anymore. I wish you would just admit that."

"Admit it and then what? Then what would you have me do?" I said challengingly. The egg timer went off, and I went to remove the tomatoes from the oven. Was that really how they were supposed to look? Dammit, there was probably one more step after the charring that I hadn't factored in. But it was all ruined anyway. Everything was ruined.

"I'd have you admit it, and then together we can come up with a plan—"

"You mean I should settle, like you have."

"I'm fine with my life."

"Because you're not like me."

"Nora, you're just like everyone else. And there's nothing wrong with you being a freelancer. If you could accept that's what you are, maybe you'd be happier. And if you were happier, I'd support it one hundred percent. Even if you never made a dime more, I'd support you in that. But this"—he gestured around the kitchen—"is a sign of some trouble with you. Not with us. With you."

I don't remember us saying anything more, though I can't think how we managed to extricate ourselves from the stalemate. I guess we just stared at each other until one of us walked away. I know that we did eventually eat the dinner in silence. I had no appetite, but surprisingly, with the exception of the tomatoes (which I threw out rather than look at the recipe again), the food tasted fine. Not disastrous, just fine. I guess I was more comfortable with the extremes than with the ordinary. I would have preferred disastrous. This was anticlimactic food.

"I'll do the dishes," Dan said when we had eaten our fill. He gave me a wan smile and pushed away from the table.

"Thanks," I said. I did appreciate the offer. There were a lot of dishes.

I took a long, hot shower, put on my pajamas, and cloistered myself in the bedroom. Dan took the living room. We stayed away from each other the rest of the night. When I passed by the living room, he looked up at me with the same smile he'd given me at the end of dinner. No, we weren't angry anymore, just separate.

I lay in bed much of the night thinking. The truth was, the profile business was over for me. I wasn't having much fun meeting people anymore, I was saying the same things over and over again. I had nothing to tell Dan when I came home at night. It took me longer to get out of bed every morning and I stayed in my pajamas until the last possible minute.

Then it came to me: I was depressed.

It probably seems strange that this was such a revelation. In part, it was that there was nothing in my life worthy of inducing depression. I'd always thought of depression as something big and dramatic, a thick velvet curtain falling down. Instead, it was more like a gauzy veil. Colors were muted instead of vibrant. Lately there had been highs, but now that I thought about them, they weren't nearly as high as they'd been just a few months before. When Dan and I had taken our coastal drive that past weekend, we'd stopped at a deserted beach and while I knew that it was beautiful and said so, somehow I didn't feel it. But I didn't want to let on. I wanted it to go on record as having been a great day for us. We needed a great day.

I took another sleeping pill, and when I woke up at six the next morning, I tiptoed from the bed, where Dan was still sleeping soundly. I shut the door as gently as I could and moved into the kitchen to call Kathy. I had never been so grateful for a three-hour time difference.

"Hello?"

"Kathy, it's me," I whispered.

"Nora?"

"Yes."

"Speak up, okay?"

I raised my voice slightly. "Dan's still sleeping and I don't want him to hear."

"What's going on?"

"I just realized I'm depressed."

"You just realized it?"

"Last night. I put all the pieces together and it turns out I'm depressed." I glanced at the bedroom door to make sure it was still closed.

"I'm not sure what to say to that."

"Say 'go on.'"

"Go on."

"I'm not as excited about anything as I used to be. I'm still walking around doing everything; it just doesn't make me happy like it should."

"I guess if you want to call that depression, then it is."

"What do you think it is, then?"

"I'm just saying that there might be other explanations, that's all."

"What's the difference what I call it? I need some help."

"You're right," she said, conciliatory. "Like a therapist? That kind of help?"

"Maybe." I poured myself some orange juice. "Or maybe I need to shake things up."

"Do you have anything in mind?"

"Not yet. I just realized it last night. I thought you could help me come up with a new direction, something instead of the profiles. You're good at that."

"Nora, that's too much pressure. You know I want you to be happy, but I just don't know that finding you another career right now is the key."

"I've tried the profile business for a while. It's been fine. I actually made a thousand bucks the other night. For three hours' work."

"Wow, that's great, Nora."

"But it wasn't." I lifted one finger like a sleuth explaining how she's cracked a case. "It wasn't great. The guy was a real asshole. And that's the thing, this is a service profession. So if I want to make money, I've got to work with whatever client comes my way."

"No, you don't. I turn projects down."

"I'm not in a position to turn clients down. I don't see how I'll ever be in a position like that." I took a long swig. "I think we should get back to basics. This profile thing, like I said, it's fine. But I want to be a writer. Remember? Let's brainstorm how I can be a writer."

"Have you had anything to eat this morning?"

"I'm drinking juice right now. You're not going to get me on that one twice."

"Okay, okay. I'll play along. What do you want to write?"

"Maybe I could be a ghostwriter. I was pretty good at meeting people and getting them to open up to me."

"It's a pretty tight market for ghostwriters."

"But you'd help me navigate it. You could show me the ropes." I waited for her reply, but she stayed quiet. "You'd help me, wouldn't you?"

"Of course I'd help you. I just think you should slow down and really think this through. Maybe you're not done in the profile business. Maybe you just need to take it to the next step."

"Which is?"

"I don't know. We can come up with it together." Kathy let her last statement hang there; then she said gently, "I'm worried about you. Everything takes time. Especially with writing. It's all a really slow build, and you're showing signs of burning out right at the beginning. Do you know what I mean?"

Her voice was so full of concern and love that it stopped me in my tracks. I felt myself sag. "I know. I'm good at beginnings and endings, but I suck at middles."

"And if you suck at the middle, then the ending could be coming way too soon. You know?"

"Dan thinks I'm just bored. He thinks I should settle."

"Is that what he said?"

"Not exactly."

"You know what this reminds me of? The immigrant experience. I read this article about how immigrants get depressed the second year. That first year, they're just so thrilled to be out of their old country and so hopeful about what'll happen for them in the new one that it keeps them going. But then that second year, they crash."

"So what are the second-year immigrants supposed to do?" I asked.

"Adjust their expectations, I think. Make some realistic plans. Get some counseling. All the obvious stuff." She was quiet, and when she next spoke, her voice had brightened. "I have an idea. Why don't you come visit me next week? I'm sending a book off for proofreading, so next week, I'll have a break between projects. You buy your ticket; everything else is my treat." I was about to leap at the invitation when she added coyly, "And you could meet Matt."

"Is he new?" I asked, startled.

"I met him last week. We were e-mailing for about a week before that. He's amazing. I'm completely smitten."

"And he is, too?"

"He is." I could hear Kathy's smile.

"Well, I wouldn't want to pass up the chance to meet Matt."

"We'd have a great time. A trip always helps pull me out of a funk, gives me a little perspective."

"A little perspective sounds perfect." I was smiling; then I thought of something. "I should probably visit my family. My mother would lose it if I came to the East Coast and didn't see her."

"She'd get over it."

"No. She wouldn't." I continued to sift the idea of a trip in my mind. "It'd be nice to see Casey."

"So you'll come?" Kathy asked excitedly.

"As long as I can find a plane ticket for under a thousand bucks, I'm there."

Like so many immigrants before me, I was going to New York, in search of a new life.

Chapter 14

MATT

Age:	38
Height:	6'3"
Weight:	200 lbs
Occupation:	Baker
Hometown:	Small town, Maine
About me:	I love food, but I hate food snobs. The best French toast I ever had was at a roadside diner in Tuscaloosa. I can re-create practically any restaurant dish in my kitchen, but somehow, ranch dressing eludes me. If I could spend half my life in the city, half by the sea, I swear I'd never want for anything.
About you:	Anything I write here can only narrow the field. I like a broad field.
Last book I read:	A biography of Frank Gehry
Biggest turn-on:	Statuesque women who never slouch
Biggest turnoff:	Timidity
Most embarrassing moment:	At a party, accidentally critiquing a book I'd just read to the author of the book. Only in New York.
Five things I can't live without:	Seasons, the beach in winter, revival houses, companionship, desirability

Smoke:	Sometimes
Alcohol:	Sometimes
Drugs:	Never
Wants kids:	Yes

The cabbie pulled up in front of the address I'd given him, a five-story brick building in Brooklyn Heights. I looked around admiringly. It was almost dusk, and there was a park down the street with children engrossed in their last game of the day. It was a scene out of a neighborhood association brochure: the happy, multiethnic children playing, oblivious to the spectacular view of the Brooklyn Bridge and downtown Manhattan.

I'd braced myself for the cab ride to cost a fortune, and it had. I counted out the money, Derek's money, glad to purge myself, bit by bit.

I pressed the buzzer, and Kathy's voice rang out. "Nora?"

"Yes!!!!" The dampening effect of a day of travel yielded to the excitement of arriving. I couldn't wait to see Kathy. She had the most impressive effect on my meta-life. It tended to cower in her presence.

"I'll be right down."

As I waited, I read the names next to the various buzzers. Rodriguez, Stanton, Williams, Aurelia. And Pecoe. Even when she'd been married, she'd stayed Kathy Pecoe.

Kathy burst through the stairwell door. "I didn't want to wait for the elevator!" she said, grabbing me in a hug. "I can't believe you're actually here!"

"I can't believe it, either," I said.

"Are you tired?"

"I was, but now I'm feeling pretty energized."

"Do you want to meet Matt?" she asked, her voice full of anticipatory delight.

I was surprised that she would suggest meeting Matt the first night I was in town, but I figured that I had four more. "Sure."

"Are you hungry?"

"Famished. I always forget that they don't feed you on the plane anymore. Well, they do, but you have to pay twelve dollars for reheated ham. It's disgusting."

"We could meet Matt for dinner, then." She pushed the button for the elevator.

I thought of saying that I'd rather have dinner with just her and then meet Matt for a drink later, but I reminded myself that there was plenty of time for us to catch up. As hungry as I was for dinner, I felt hungrier for Kathy's company. Now that I was standing beside her, I realized how profoundly I had missed her. I put my arm around her and squeezed.

"This was the best idea," she said, beaming. "I mean, I know it was my idea, so maybe I'm not supposed to say that, but I've been beside myself all day waiting for you."

"I'm really happy, too."

We rode up in the elevator. Kathy's apartment was on the third floor, and it was perfect. The rugs, the furniture, the art, the view. I rushed to her window to take in the Manhattan skyline.

"Yep, it's the Chrysler Building," she said, with evident satisfaction.

"My God, Kathy. This is incredible."

"I know. I've never loved a place this much. I'm hoping it'll go condo so I can buy it. Otherwise, to buy something, I might have to move."

"Wow. You're actually thinking of buying real estate?"

She nodded. "I don't know anything about the market, though. I don't even know what people mean when they say it's 'soft,' but I just feel like for me, it's getting to be time. Matt and I were just talking about this the other day." She flopped on her couch. It was an orange sectional, which sounds frightening but looked great. Kathy had always had an eye. I loved the abstract painting above it, and the skylights in the kitchen, and the hardwood floors. I missed hardwood floors. "He was saying that he's getting ready to buy, and he doesn't know if he'll do it in the city or here in Brooklyn. Who knows, maybe we'll be doing it together."

My ears pricked up. A week together and talking about buying real estate. Well, even thirty-year-olds could fantasize in the throes of a new infatuation, I told myself. It didn't sound like she was actually making plans. Given Kathy's history, though, the situation merited watching.

"I'm going to call him." Kathy crossed the room to the phone. She had put on a little weight, but it seemed to have mostly gone to her chest. She looked wonderful, her trademark hair just as wild and curly and black as ever. As she dialed, I salivated over her kitchen. Gleaming granite countertops, exposed brick in the eating area. "Hey, babe . . . yes, Nora's here. How did your meeting go?" She waited for his response, then let out a peal of laughter. "I know, right? Well, she's up for dinner. What time can you get out here? . . . Are you serious? . . . Come on over then . . . You too. See you soon."

I sincerely hoped that the "You too" was not a truncated "I love you, too."

She returned to the couch, her face aglow. "He's actually on the train right now. He knew you'd be hungry after your flight and he didn't want us to have to wait too long, so he figured he'd head out this way. If we weren't up for dinner, he'd just turn around and go home. Isn't that so thoughtful?"

I thought it was most likely manipulative and definitely intrusive. I mean, if he'd called when he got to Brooklyn, would we really send him home? No, obviously we'd let him join us for dinner, even if we'd wanted to be on our own. Just as obviously, I couldn't say anything. I just nodded and tried not to let my concern show. "So you met him online?"

She nodded. "He wrote to me. I loved his e-mail, I loved his profile, I just felt this real kinship with him even before we met. And you know me. I don't go wild for many people. It's pretty hard to get through to me."

That was true. Kathy does an incredible amount of nitpicky rejection. The problem was, once she "went wild" for a guy, he basically got a free pass. There could be a million clues to his unfitness, but she saw none of them. She ignored every unpleasant attribute, rationalized every awful moment that passed between them. There had only been two such men in her thirty years, but each relationship had ended in utter devastation. I've theorized that something primal and/or chemical must pass between Kathy and these men for them to fixate on one another so intensely and at such personal cost. It always reminded me of something I'd read about birds. Apparently, birds form this deep connection to their mother the moment they first see her by a process called imprinting. It's like Kathy and this particular species of man imprinted on each other, and released only when threatened with true extinction.

"What does Matt do for a living?" I figured I'd try to ground Kathy in specifics.

"He makes wedding cakes."

"What kind of meetings does he have then?"

"With suppliers. With his backers. I don't know." Kathy's apathy for this line of questioning was obvious. It was not impossible that this man was lying to her, and my brilliant Kathy would not pick it up because she'd already stopped thinking. Now was not the time to lose her meta-life. It occurred to me that nearly the only time a meta-life could be a true asset was in the first month of a relationship. "He just designs the cakes. Someone else makes them. Maybe he had to meet with the bakers."

A cake architect. Who knew? "So he's successful."

"He seems to be. We don't really talk about money. We talk about . . . other things." She smiled to herself.

I wondered how much talking they actually did. "Is the sex really great?"

Her smile widened. "Phenomenal. There ought to be a new word for it, it's so celestial. It's like, hours pass in minutes."

I beat back the twinge of envy. I knew that I didn't really want what she and Matt had; that is, I wouldn't want all the suffering that was certain to come. But what if the pain never came? What if Kathy had found herself a successful wedding cake architect and she spent the rest of her life humping him on a cloud? *Then you'd be happy for her. This isn't about you and Dan.* "Time always has a different quality in the beginning."

Kathy shook her head. "I'm telling you, there's something—mystical about it." Her voice resumed its normal tone as she said, "I'm not going to get into all that 'he's the one' crap. But I will say that he's blowing my mind. But tell me about you. What's been happening?"

That was a tough act to follow. "I've been doing pretty well."

"Well, what happened after we talked?" She was looking at me, her eyes bright and encouraging.

"After we talked, I put all decisions on hold. I'm not making a move until after this trip. And knowing that made the days a lot easier. I did one more profile, but I haven't scheduled anything else. A couple of people e-mailed, but I wrote them to say I'd be in touch soon. I took my ad down." I resettled myself on the couch with my feet tucked under me. "I think a little hiatus will be good for me."

"It can't hurt," Kathy agreed. We talked until we were interrupted by the buzzer, at which point Kathy practically ran to the intercom. "Matt?" At his affirmative reply, she pushed the button to let him in, then waited by the door for his knock. She was awash in pleasure.

I wanted to be happy for her, but as you've gathered, my reaction was mixed. The good-friend part of me was concerned because of her past, but also wanted to remain open to the possibility that this time around, she was falling for a good person and would have a better outcome. The bad friend in me was jealous of her sex life, and didn't want to believe that it could continue to exist within the confines of a healthy relationship. I wanted to think that the road Dan and I were currently traveling was the one where all other roads converged. The synthesis of the good/bad friend was a hope that Kathy and Matt were a great match and that they would remain happy, coupled with a belief that their sex life would become just like everyone else's, i.e., like mine.

That's where I was as I stood watching Matt and Kathy embracing. He was tall with dark hair and blue eyes, and he would have been a little too handsome if not for a somewhat pronounced overbite. He was stylish without looking effete. When he realized how long he had been holding on to Kathy before greeting me, he had the decency to look a tad embarrassed. And when he reached out to shake my hand, he seemed sweetly nervous and a little overenthusiastic. So far, so good.

"Kathy's told me a lot about you," he said.

"She's been telling me about you, too," I answered.

He looked at her. "All good," she assured him, and we all laughed in that way you have to for a first meeting.

"What are you in the mood for?" he asked, looking from Kathy to me and back again.

"We haven't even talked restaurants. I'm thinking someplace without too much of a wait?" Kathy looked over at me.

"That would be good. I am pretty starved," I said.

"And Kathy's told me how you get when you're starved." Matt was smiling as he said it, but at Kathy, not at me. I didn't appreciate the idea that my blood sugar crises had become an in-joke between them, but I told myself to stop being so sensitive.

"There's that Italian place, the one with the checkered tablecloths. It's big, and you can always get a table." Kathy was trained on Matt as she spoke.

"It's nothing fancy," he explained to me.

"Quick seating and not too fancy. That sounds perfect," I said.

Kathy and Matt headed for the door, arm in arm. I grabbed my jacket and trailed behind.

Dinner isn't worth recounting. We split a carafe of wine, Kathy and Matt seemed to be groping each other under the table, and we talked about nothing. I mean, words were exchanged, but they were all frothy and meaningless. Everything was just an opportunity for Kathy and Matt to feign detailed knowledge of one another, or to express amazement at some new facet that had just been revealed. It was depressingly like tagging along with your friend and her high-school boyfriend. A few times Matt looked ever so slightly askance at something Kathy said, and she didn't seem to notice. But I noticed, and it was always when she'd just said something that showed she had a life outside of him, and that she liked that life. Maybe I was just being hypersensitive, but those moments gave me an eerie sense of déjà vu.

• • • •

I never really got to know the first man Kathy was in love with, but what I saw between her and Stephen terrified me. Kathy met Stephen when we both lived in Boston. He was a struggling musician who supported himself as the super of Kathy's building. She was twenty-two, and he said he was twenty-seven, though it later turned out he was much older than that. He lied about all matter of things—large and small—but Kathy was addicted to him from the first. He was tall and semiemaciated, but he had a beautiful face and Kathy certainly wasn't alone in finding him sexy. He'd been working his way through the women in Kathy's building, but when he got to Kathy, he said he never wanted to be anywhere else. His flip-flop between bad boy and over-the-top romantic seemed designed to keep Kathy completely wrapped up in him. When things were good, she had never felt so extravagantly and perfectly loved; when they were bad, she was destroyed. He didn't think she should need anyone else but him, that he should be everything to her. And while he never told her outright what she should and shouldn't do, he made his disapproval felt. She broke up with him every time he cheated or lied or shouted about how worthless she was, but she also took him back every time he made another grand gesture of love.

Family and friends tried repeatedly to help her break free of him, but it would have taken nothing short of deprogramming or rehab. I saw how she distanced herself from all of them in the face of their criticism, so I tried to be circumspect. That was why, when she married him, I was their only witness. I was sobbing in the bathroom twenty minutes before, wondering if I could even go through with that. But I cleaned myself up, picked up my bouquet, and suffered. Kathy looked so happy; she was convinced that marriage would change him. It was nearly inconceivable to me that Kathy would believe something so retrograde, but she believed it totally.

The marriage lasted less than two years, and it only changed Stephen for the worse. He had believed in the redemptive power of marriage, too, and when he saw that he was still just who he was, the despair enveloped them both. They felt trapped together, and their moments of torment far outweighed their moments of ecstasy. Finally, one day, Kathy found she couldn't get out of bed. I don't mean she just felt tired, or that she just felt depressed. She describes it as a physical paralysis. Psychosomatic, a therapist declared later. As she lay there, she decided, "If I can get up, if I'm lucky enough to get back up, I'm leaving." And she did. But it took her a long, long time to recover fully. She moved home to live with her parents, went to therapy three times a week, and worked as much as she could to get her mind off Stephen. She told me she temporarily needed a substitute addiction, and work was it.

It had been years since Kathy laid eyes on Stephen, and in that time, she'd done more therapy than Larissa, and she's no longer a work junkie. But watching her with Matt still alarmed me. I'd suffered vicarious trauma throughout the Stephen period and didn't want to see that happen to her ever again. *Give her more credit. This time she'll know she's being broken down and she'll get out.* But I couldn't help thinking about the resilience of our patterns, and as I lay there on the couch trying to sleep, about the resilience of my own pattern. Matt was in the bedroom with Kathy, and through the closed door, I heard the occasional loud moan escape one of them, then the sound of the other shushing. The sounds of their quieted ecstasy were disconcerting, but I didn't know if that was because of my fears for Kathy or for me.

• • • •

The next day, Kathy and I decided to walk the Brooklyn Bridge and then the extra mile or so to Little Italy. She was in a great mood; mine was more subdued.

I'd walked the Golden Gate Bridge in San Francisco a number of times, and it had a remarkably different feel. The Golden Gate felt less rugged somehow, in the way that San Francisco often did when compared to New York. The Golden Gate was orange, in part so that it could be seen through the fog that routinely descended on the city, while the Brooklyn Bridge was simple stone masonry. The view from Golden Gate was lush in contrast to the urban majesty of Manhattan. I was taken with New York, but it intimidated me. It felt tougher than I was. I realized I probably fit better in the Bay Area, but I admired people who fit best in New York.

As we walked, my mood improved. For one thing, Kathy was so obviously thrilled to have me there. For another, she wasn't talking about Matt. When I started talking about the experiential contrast between the Golden Gate and the Brooklyn Bridge, Kathy chimed in her agreement.

"You know," she said, "there might be a magazine article in this. I know tons of people who've tried San Francisco and moved back to New York, because even though San Francisco might be prettier and the weather is better and California's gorgeous, New York is just more them. And I bet you know people who've felt the reverse."

"I do. I also know the people you're talking about, people I knew when I first moved to San Francisco who don't live there anymore. There's that 'grass is greener' syndrome, too, and those people who boomerang between the Coasts every few years and never really settle anywhere."

"I'd never thought about how interesting the word 'settle' is," Kathy mused. "When you think about our ancestors and settling and how virtuous that seemed, and about what it means to settle now . . . I don't know quite what I mean, but like I said, it's interesting."

"I've never tried writing articles, but that might be fun." I stopped walking to gaze into the distance. I thought about my own ancestors coming through Ellis Island all those years ago, about the nobility of settling. I started to feel excited about working on an article that integrated all those disparate ideas. Then I caught myself doing it, and turned back to Kathy. "See, this is the thing. This is what I did with the profile writing. I seize on it, and I think, 'Yes! Now I have it.' But it turns out I don't."

"Maybe all of those things together are it, and you just give up on each one too quickly." She turned to face me fully. "I'm not saying that profile writing is it for you; I'm just saying that you shouldn't rule it out yet. Over the years, I've found that the best thing about the freelancing life is that you can have your finger in a lot of different pots. For a commitment-phobe, it's the perfect career choice."

"You might be right," I allowed.

"Just think it over. I'd be happy to help you figure out markets for your article. And if you wanted editing assignments, I could help you get started with that, too. Instead of being wholly dependent on the profiles, they could just be one source of income.

You might even like getting out and meeting people after you've been cooped up half the day working on an article. Trust me."

I didn't feel elation; I felt a measured calm. That was better. I looked at Kathy as a feeling of immense gratitude spread through me. "Do you know how much I appreciate the way you look after me? It's like you save me from myself."

"Don't think I've forgotten how hard you tried to save me from myself back in the Stephen era." I was surprised to hear her say it so casually. We almost never referred to Stephen. It was like how people never mention a past suicide attempt to a survivor. "I don't think I could ever repay that debt."

"Good thing it's not a debt, then."

"I have to confess, that wasn't really a spontaneous pitch I just made," she said. I noticed how quickly she steered us back to the original subject. She still didn't like dwelling on Stephen long; she said once that that chapter of her life seemed like it had been lived by someone else and that she'd spent all that time in therapy to exorcise whoever the hell it was. "I've been thinking about things since we talked, and about what might be the most Nora of all careers. And I thought, 'Being in everything at once might be the most you.' "

"Bouncing back and forth between the Coasts rather than settling?" I asked, smiling.

"You've settled a little bit. I mean, you've got Dan."

I groaned.

"I didn't mean you settled *for* Dan; I meant you've settled *in* with him. For the most part, recent fight excluded. I mean, every couple fights." She cast me a sidelong glance. "How have things been since then?"

"We only had a few days together before I flew out here. I

guess everything seemed back to normal. Dan said his piece, and now he feels fine again." I threw up my hands in exasperation. "What can I say? We're your perfectly average, basically loving couple—except for my dissection of everything. I mean, we're still affectionate, I still adore him, but everything's gotten routine."

"When you say everything's gotten routine . . . ?"

"Yes. The sex too."

"So spice it up."

"That's what people always say. Why should we need to work so hard? If we're right for each other, it seems like the spice should happen naturally. Just thinking about working at something like that depresses me."

"I think that in the beginning, the endorphins and the pheromones and all those chemicals buzzing around do all the work. You're horny all the time. Then a bit of time passes, you're not as new to each other, and you've got to take over where biology leaves off. The only relationships I've had where the sex didn't cool down over time were the ones where we were so crazy together that our chemicals just stayed buzzing. Like with Stephen, the adrenaline never stopped. But in a decent relationship, at some point, they will. It's inevitable. And that's where the work comes in."

"You don't find that depressing?"

"No!" She shook her head emphatically. "That's the part you can control. What I don't want anymore is a passion that's out of control."

"Controlled passion seems like an oxymoron."

"No." She shook her head again. I was relieved to see she'd given so much thought to this. It was a theory that let me know I didn't have to worry so much about her and Matt. "I want to know that I can get things moving again whenever I'm willing to try. I think that's a really powerful thought."

"I've never had any success with getting the passion going again," I said.

"Because you spend so much time beating yourself up, instead of seeing it as a normal part of the relationship and working at it. It sounds trite, but we all just need to find someone great, and make it work. I know from everything you've told me that Dan is great. I don't know yet if Matt is, but if it turns out that he is, that's what I'm going to do."

"So what do you think I should do? How do I start to work on things?"

"Well, an article I read said that the way to jumpstart passion is to do new things together. It can actually get the chemicals moving in a way that simulates the beginning of the relationship. You and Dan could try . . . skydiving. I hear that's pure adrenaline."

"Have you met me before?" We both laughed. "No way."

"Some sort of lessons," Kathy suggested. "Like dance lessons. Salsa. Or flamenco. Something sexy."

I laughed, picturing Dan wearing all black with a rose in his teeth. "I don't know if he'd go for it."

"Then he can come up with something else. But it has to be something you wouldn't normally do, right? Otherwise, it won't stimulate the chemicals."

After we'd traversed the bridge, Kathy and I walked through the narrow, cobblestone streets of Little Italy for what seemed like hours. I told her my fears about Matt; she told me her fears about her own discernment. It felt good to be so honest, and to know that Kathy was looking after herself this time around.

There was a sudden downpour, so we ducked into the first café we saw for cappuccinos. Laughing, we took off our damp jackets and Kathy blotted her wet hair with a napkin. Then she reached over and blotted mine. I didn't want to be anywhere else in the world. That's when I realized my meta-life had gone dead silent.

Chapter 15

NORA

Age:	29
Height:	5'6"
Weight:	130 lbs
Occupation:	Internet dating consultant/writer
About me:	Under construction
About you:	Under construction
Last book I read:	*The Big Love*
Biggest turn-on:	A man who knows when to play and when to take you over a bar
Biggest turnoff:	Under construction
Five things I can't live without:	A little of this, a little of that. (Does that count as two?) Whatever. It should all add up to at least $3,000 a month.
Most embarrassing moment:	The gourmet-dinner incident

The visit with Kathy had been just what I needed. We settled all the big questions on our second day, so for the rest of my time in New York, I felt more relaxed and hopeful than I'd felt in ages. But as the train pulled into the station just outside Baltimore, a familiar knot developed in my stomach. How old did I have to be before a visit to my parents' house would be knot-free?

I wasn't technically visiting my parents. I hadn't seen my biological father since I was six. I was visiting my mother and my stepfather, Ed. Ed's been around for the past fifteen years, and he's a pretty easygoing guy. When he picked me up at the train station alone, the relief I felt was immediate and palpable.

We had a pleasant, small-talky ride back to the new house. It's the third time they've moved in the past ten years. Ed's successful in real estate, and their houses keep getting bigger. As we pulled up, I tried to quell my distaste. The house was a Greek Revival-style behemoth; it actually had a portico supported by columns. I half-expected it to be topped by a statue of Zeus in full repose. Not only was it absurd to have transplanted such a home to suburban Baltimore, but there was no reason for three people to inhabit a space that large, except to show others that they could.

Ed let us in the front door. I was slightly disappointed that Casey wasn't waiting nearby to hurtle herself into my arms. But it had been almost a year since I'd seen her and the difference between twelve and thirteen was sizable, at least in the head of the thirteen-year-old. Ed was telling me during the car ride that Casey's exasperated response to everything now was "I'm *thirteen*!" He said she seemed to be really embracing the worldliness of being thirteen, which amused him. Casey was luckier than she knew to have a dad like Ed.

He shouted my arrival, and my mother came from what I presumed to be the direction of the kitchen. Her short black hair was shot through with more silver than the last time I'd seen her, and she'd dressed up for my arrival, wearing a bright silk scarf and matching silver jewelry. I was company.

She took my face in her hands and smiled. "You look beautiful," she said.

I was thrown off by that opening gambit. "Thanks," I stammered.

When she released me, I watched Casey descend the staircase. The house I'd grown up with just had steps, but this one had an actual entrance hall and a curving staircase. Casey looked taller and had a smattering of pimples on her forehead but other than that, she was just Casey: a girl with bad posture who didn't realize how cute she could be. I noticed she wasn't wearing her glasses anymore; she'd told me on the phone that she'd gotten contact lenses. And while they did make her eyes burn, she thought they were the best thing that had ever happened to her.

"Hi, Nora," Casey said, a little shyly.

"Come here," I said, smiling. I hugged her thin frame. "It's so good to see you."

"I'm glad you're here," Casey answered, hugging back.

"We're glad to have you, even if it is only for two nights." My mother smiled. "Would you like to freshen up, or should we have dinner?"

I opted for dinner, and she led me into the dining room. "You've never been here before, have you?" she asked.

"No." I gaped at the dining room. It was huge. The mahogany table was set for four, but could seat twelve. "Do you entertain a lot?"

"Never," my mother said.

I sat down and Casey sat next to me. Ed helped my mother bring the food in from the kitchen. "You look great," I told Casey.

"Really?" She self-consciously pushed her hair back.

"Yes, really. You must be getting used to your contact lenses. Your eyes don't look red at all."

"I think I am used to them." She smiled.

"I wish I could have been here for your birthday."

"It was really nice." She reached for her hair again, though it hadn't moved since she last pushed it back. "I invited a lot of people, and most of them showed up. Dad gave me these earrings. I wear them practically every day." She jutted her ear out so I could see.

"They're beautiful."

"Yeah. I really like them."

"Don't say 'yeah,' " my mother corrected as she sat down.

We got quiet except for saying, "Could you please pass the . . . ?" and "Thank you" while we filled our plates. The spread looked wonderful, but true to form, the chicken was rubbery and flavorless and the vegetables were slightly overcooked. My mother didn't care much for food; she cared more for appearances. I thought that someday she should take it to the next level and just put replicas of an attractive meal on the table while we all secretly ate microwaved food in the kitchen.

"We were hoping to meet Dan this trip," my mother said. It had taken some time, but once she'd finally accepted my freelancing job, she'd forgiven Dan for not keeping me chained in the bedroom for my own safety.

"He would have liked that, too. It just didn't work out this time." I sawed my knife back and forth over the chicken until it yielded.

"So you live together now. That must be nice," Ed said benignly.

"It's going well." I kept my tone light.

"I never even saw your last apartment." My mother dabbed at her mouth. I noticed that her lipstick was cracking at the corners.

"I didn't live there that long."

"Will you live in this one very long?" she asked.

"What are you saying, Mom?" I put my fork down and stared at her.

"I'm saying, how long can you keep living in apartments? You're almost thirty. Don't you want a house?"

"San Francisco isn't like Baltimore. Houses are way more expensive." *Stay calm. Talk to Casey. Talk to Ed. Don't let her control every interaction.*

"You don't live in San Francisco."

"We've been over this, Mom. Oakland is expensive, too. Unless you're living in a bad part of town. Do you want me to live next to a crack house?"

Casey laughed. My mother glared at me, presumably for corrupting Casey. If my mother could, she'd have a five-second delay at dinner like they have at the Grammy Awards so she could bleep out any comments that she didn't want Casey to hear.

"Real estate's a good investment," Ed said, always a smooth mediator. "And maybe you could buy something with a lot less money down than you think. I could help you figure that kind of thing out."

"Thanks, Ed," I said. "I'm not there yet."

"Meaning, you and Dan aren't there yet?" my mother asked.

"No, we're not. We haven't even been together a year."

"Which didn't stop you from living with him," she said out of the corner of her mouth, as if as an aside for the studio audience.

"Things are coming along fine," I said tersely. "When anything changes, you'll be the first to know, don't you worry."

There was silence at the table for several minutes. Casey started biting her nails, and my mother stared at her until she stopped.

My mother finally broke the stalemate with a sigh. "We just really want him to be the one. The one who'll take care of you."

I sighed, too. I knew she was just worried, that she was always just worried. I hated that I had inherited her need to know, her inability to sit with uncertainty. It was the very reason I had forced the issue with Dan by living with him so early. It saddened me to realize how often my mother and I shared the same intention and impulse, while I generally chose the precise opposite course of action.

"I know, Mom. I wish I could answer that for you."

Casey piped up. "But he's really cute. I got the pictures you sent."

"He does seem very attractive," my mother said, with a smile.

"He is very attractive." I smiled to myself, imagining him. I thought how if Dan was there right now, he'd be holding my hand under the table and running interference with my mother. I thought how funny he would be later when we were alone, recounting little gestures and nuances I'd missed. He had an eye for humorous character details, and he never sounded snide or mean when he pointed them out.

"He's just my type!" Ed joked, and we all laughed eagerly. Then Ed teased Casey about the boy she liked, and she claimed she didn't like anyone—and no one would ever like her—and we all protested that that wasn't true. We three adults were content then to make the rest of the dinner Casey-centric.

After dinner, we played board games and drank hot chocolate. I noticed that my mother and Ed seemed much more at ease together than I'd ever seen them, and Casey didn't have any crying jags at all. I thought maybe I would bring Dan for my next visit, and it was not inconceivable that he would enjoy himself some of the time.

· · · ·

The next day, Casey and I went to the mall. She needed new shoes and wanted my opinion. I was momentarily flattered, though Casey was a pretty unfashionable kid. I kept trying not to think of her as a kid, to remember that she was *thirteen*, but it was nearly impossible.

"What do you think of those?" Casey pointed to a chunky mule.

"Would you be able to walk in them?" I asked.

"Okay. Forget it," she said immediately.

"If you don't know how to walk in them now, you could learn."

"Yeah, right." She was studying a pair of hideous ballet flats.

"You could! Why don't you try the other shoes on?"

"I didn't really like them anyway."

"What size are you? I'm going to find a salesperson and get them for you." I figured I should have a take-charge big-sister moment. And what could be better bonding than me teaching Casey how to walk in heels?

"Nora, I really don't want them." She seemed on the verge of tears.

"Okay. Well, let's keep looking around." It was sad, knowing she was still this sensitive. As late as last year, she sometimes cried in class when she couldn't do a math problem. I hoped that she'd outgrown that, at least. "What about these?" I picked up a pair of shoes with a heel in between the flats and the mules.

She cocked her head while she considered.

"Casey, it won't hurt my feelings if you say no."

"No," she said. She laughed, and I laughed with her.

"But what do you think about that size heel? I figure you could gradually get used to walking in higher heels."

"Okay." She started looking for heels of precisely that height, studying a series of shoes with intense concentration. Finally she held one up triumphantly. "What do you think?"

"I like them," I answered honestly.

"Great. I'll try them on." She seemed relieved. I felt a twinge of annoyance that my mother had sculpted her to be someone who was constantly swinging between tension and relief.

As we sat waiting for the salesman to bring the shoes in her size, I asked her about things at home.

"They're fine. The same as always," she said, tugging at her gum with her fingers. On top of everything else, my mother had made her orally fixated.

My mother had been overinvolved through my elementary-school years, but it was nothing compared to how she acted once I got into junior high. She was obsessed with my safety and convinced any bad choice would have dire consequences. I occasionally caught her eavesdropping on my phone conversations, and she tagged nearly every friend as being a "bad influence." That was her favorite expression until I turned eighteen. What she didn't realize was that she didn't actually prevent much of what she considered bad behavior; she just drove it out of the house. Well, she succeeded in making me completely anxious while I did it, which was why, for example, I needed to smoke pot before having sex.

"Is Mom freaking out about you being thirteen?" I asked.

"She's been giving me a lot of lectures lately," Casey said.

"Yep."

"And she asks questions constantly."

"She would have made a good private investigator."

Casey laughed.

"Just remember that the world isn't always the scary place she makes it out to be. And you can be trusted, even if she acts like you can't. Do you know what I mean?" I asked.

"Not exactly."

"Mom has a tendency to treat the people she loves—meaning, the people she's worried about—like criminals. And when she treats you like that, you probably start to doubt yourself. And you figure that the world must be really scary for her to be so worried. You end up doubting that you can handle things, and thinking that you're better off not trying. But you're better off thinking less and trying more." Feeling a little self-conscious about my speech, I added, "At least, that's my opinion."

We were interrupted by the arrival of the shoes. The salesman helped Casey slip them on and she walked toward the mirror, hesitantly at first and then more confidently. "I like them," she said.

I realized she hadn't asked my opinion first, and that made me smile. "Then let's buy them."

• • • •

That night, by force of habit, I made sure my mother wasn't listening on another extension before calling Dan.

I told him in detail about how much better the visit was going than I'd expected. "I actually wish I lived closer so I could be a big sister more of the time," I said wistfully. "Maybe I should visit more often."

"We could have Casey come out and stay with us," Dan said. "I think it'd be fun having your sister around."

I closed my eyes and pictured the expression on Dan's face when he said that. I'd been missing him all day. I'd been missing the sound of him and the sturdiness of him. Just hearing his voice, I felt held by him. And then I felt a pleasant tingling. *No, you are not having phone sex in your mother's house.* But I liked that I wanted to.

"Things have been off with us for a little while," I said. "I know it's my fault, but I'm ready to really work on things."

He didn't speak for a minute. "I've never told you my theory about coasting, have I?"

"No."

"In general—remember, this is just in general—men are better at coasting than women."

"What do you mean by 'coasting'?" I asked, intrigued.

"Coasting is just going along and presuming everything's okay. You're not gearing up for anything, you're just coasting. It's like figuring that if there's no noise under the hood and the car's running, there's no problem. I think women listen a lot harder for noises, and even if they don't hear them, they think there's still something going on."

"So you think I'm listening too hard," I said. I was smiling.

"You might be." I could almost hear him shrugging. And smiling. I knew he was smiling.

"I'm coming home tomorrow." I just wanted to hear it out loud. My smile widened.

"Oh, I know."

• • • •

The next morning, I said good-bye to Ed and Casey and packed my luggage into my mother's Lexus. *I should always do shot glass visits*, I thought, settling into the front seat and waving at Casey as my mother backed out of the driveway.

"This has been a good visit," I said, smiling at my mother.

Surprise flashed across her face, then a nanosecond of evaluation (Is Nora being sarcastic? she wondered), and then a return smile. "I wish you'd come more often. Or even better, invite us out to visit you. We haven't been to San Francisco in years." She started humming "Do You Know the Way to San Jose."

"That's San Jose, Mom, not San Francisco."

"I know. I'm just in a good mood. I don't get to see you often."

My mother spent nearly half the time in my presence commenting on how little she got to see me. It often seemed that the idea of me was far more satisfying than the reality.

I scanned the radio to find the classical station. Classical music has always calmed her nerves. For that reason, classical music tends to remind me of just how high-strung my mother is, and by extension, of my own inherited temperament, so it has the inverse effect on me. One time I went to the symphony on a date and almost had a panic attack during the first movement of Shostakovich. But right then, with my visit just minutes from its completion, I decided that it was best to keep my mother calm and contained.

"Hey, Mom, you just missed the exit," I said, pointing.

"That's not our exit." She had a Cheshire grin that chilled my blood.

"What do you mean? That's the exit for the train station." Oh, no. Anything but that. Not one of her surprises. When I was growing up, she made terrifying dinners, food that was surpassed in its awful taste only by its inexplicable texture. She made huge portions because she liked to freeze the leftovers, often in single-serving containers that she wouldn't label. Then she'd microwave an individual container for each of us, and I wasn't told of the contents, and once she'd given me one, she would never trade. She called this abusive practice "Surprise dinners!" She always said it just that way, too, with her voice shooting up an octave with feigned excitement.

"I wanted to surprise you," she said. "I'm going to drive you back to JFK. You can help me navigate. I put the road atlas under your seat."

Don't react yet, just breathe. Calm and contained. Okay. On the one hand, as far as she understood herself, she was doing this to spend more time with her daughter. On the other hand, she had to know that her daughter would not want to spend four hours in the car with her, hence the surprise. It was a surprise assault, was what it was. It was blitzkrieg. But as angry as I was fast becoming, I couldn't tell her I would never voluntarily submit to a four-hour car ride with her. Though she obviously did know that, in the same way she knew I didn't really want to eat her leftovers. "Surprise," in my mother's vocabulary, was an underhanded way to get what she wanted. Still, her aims were always fundamentally sound: she wanted to spend time with her family, or take care of them.

I wasn't just angry that she was essentially kidnapping me. I was also angry that she was placing me in the same bind she always did: she worried and she manipulated, which drove me away and drove me crazy, and she did it because she loved me. I never questioned my mother's love for me, but it was such a sticky love that I tried to think about it and engage with it as little as possible.

Now I was trapped in a car with her for four hours. Four hours! And that's if we didn't hit traffic. This could be a five-, even a six-hour odyssey.

"You really should have checked with me first," I said. If I stayed calm, I could convince her to turn around. It was best to treat this like a delicate hostage negotiation. "On the train, I know just how long the trip is going to take. But in the car, it could take another hour. It could take another three hours, who knows."

"I did a practice run of the route at just this time of day," my mother said. "We've got plenty of time."

"Then why would I need to look at the atlas, if you already know the route?" I asked triumphantly. I finally had her, the slippery old broad.

"I said you could help me navigate, I didn't say I needed your help. I thought it might be fun for you, like when you were a little girl and you'd try to read the maps."

"Mom! I'm not a little girl!" I fumed. "I want you to turn this car around. I want to take the train!"

"If you're not a little girl," my mother said smoothly, "why are you acting like one? We're just taking a little trip."

So there'd be no negotiation with terrorists. "This is sick. No, this is a felony. I am a grown woman. If plans are going to be changed, I should be consulted. And right now, I'm so angry at you that there's no way I'm driving with you to New York." I almost crossed my arms over my chest, but realized how petulant it would look.

My mother kept driving; then she actually started humming "Do You Know the Way to San Jose" again. Did she think this was a joke? I was livid.

"Mom, turn this car around. I'm not kidding."

"Nora, please. Calm down. A ride back in a Lexus is much better than sitting on a crowded train. We could even stop and get some lunch, if we're making good time. Or maybe I could get something to eat with you at the airport." She seemed completely unfazed by my reaction. I narrowed my eyes at her. She was unfazed, because she expected it.

"If you wanted us to spend more time together this trip, you should have said something. But this is total bullshit!" She hated when I cursed. At least I got the pleasure of seeing her flinch.

"If I'd asked if I could drive you back to the airport, what would you have said?" she asked.

"I'd have said yes," I lied.

"Nora." She said it in that despicable I-know-you-better-than-you-know-yourself tone. "You would have come up with some excuse, the same way you come up with excuses to get off the phone with me."

At this point, it was obvious that I wasn't going to catch my train. My mother had planned this, and she was committed to it. Now I just needed to figure out how I was going to get through it as painlessly as possible. I took a deep breath before responding. "I don't want to talk about that," I said. "You have succeeded in making me miss my train. You have succeeded in making me feel like a powerless child. You can drive me to JFK, but you can't make me talk to you."

She pressed her lips together tightly. Now she was mad. "That's fine. If that's how you want to pass this time—this limited time that we have together—we'll just do that." She reached over and shut the radio off. I smiled privately, thinking that she was the one who'd suffer from that little maneuver.

Five minutes later, she started talking again. "I'll tell you what's bullcrap, Nora. It's the fact that you have no use for me, and when I try to be a part of your life, you shut me out. That's the bullcrap."

I gritted my teeth and said nothing. This was my power, right here. My power was silence.

Another five minutes, and then she said, "You think I don't know that you screen my calls? You haven't picked up a phone in two years. I know you're not that popular. Every time we talk, it's like pulling teeth. All I wanted was a nice car ride with my daughter. I wanted us to talk like people. Like regular people.

And you're sitting there staring out the window, acting like I'm not even here!" I wasn't looking at her, but I knew she was tearing up as she said, "I don't understand why we can't just talk. I'm not so hard to talk to."

It was a combination of her tears (which made me sad) and her absurd contention that she wasn't hard to talk to (which annoyed the hell out of me) that weakened my resolve. I finally spoke. "Yes, you are. You're impossible to talk to."

Maybe it was her relief at finally hearing me speak that caused her to actually consider what I'd said. "I *can* be difficult," she amended.

"You're always difficult! You call and you ask me the same questions every time, like you think I'm hiding how badly I'm doing. Then I ask you questions, and you clam up. You're the one who acts like you're hiding something."

"You don't need a girlfriend, Nora. You need a mother."

"And what do you think that means?" It was such an antiquated notion that I found myself curious despite myself.

"You need someone to look ahead for you. You need someone who won't just pretend everything you do is wonderful."

"Well, then, you're a great mother."

That stung her. I was actually thinking of backtracking when she said, "I guess you got the mother you deserved then."

After that exchange, we both withdrew for the next hour. Part of me wanted this to be an opportunity for reconciliation, but the rest of me knew how preposterous that was. My mother and I had practically never had a conversation that didn't leave me feeling like a suspect or a lunatic, and I couldn't imagine that we were going to start now. I wondered what she had hoped to accomplish during the ride, and at first I thought she just wanted to ask me the usual questions while glancing at my profile to gauge my truthfulness. But she had known I would be angry, and she had clearly prepared herself for it. That made this particular surprise an unusual addition to her oeuvre.

"Why did you do this?" I finally asked.

She looked at me quickly, then returned her eyes to the road. "I don't know," she said. She sounded tired and sad.

"I mean, what did you want to talk to me about?"

She shrugged, as if in defeat. "The usual things, I guess. You're right. I'm no fun to talk to. I understand why you don't want to take my calls."

It didn't seem to be a ploy. She just looked too demoralized for that. And even though I might have implied otherwise, my mother is not a liar, except to herself.

"Well, you could be more fun," I conceded. "If you'd stop acting like the Grand Inquisitor and tell me some things about your life, I wouldn't screen my calls so much." The second I said that, I wanted to take it back. It sounded too much like a promise.

"I can try," she said, sounding more hopeful. "I really hate being screened."

"I'm still going to screen you sometimes. I have a live-in boyfriend, you know."

"Oh, Nora!" A look of distaste passed across her face, which made me laugh.

"I'm an adult. I have sex with the man I live with."

"Now you're just being mean," she said, but she smiled a little bit. "So what do you want to talk about?"

"How are you and Ed doing?" I asked mischievously.

"We're the same. We're old. Nothing new happens."

"Mom, you need to try. We're turning over a new leaf here." I made a show of patience, waiting for her answer.

"Well, we're in the new house."

"Seriously, Mom, what's with the new houses every few years?"

"It's not me. It's Ed. I wouldn't care if we stayed in the same house for five years." She said it like five years was an epoch.

"Don't you get tired of moving? I hate moving."

"You know I like a project. It must be why I like motherhood. It's like a lifelong project."

There it was, in black-and-white. The one story my mother told over and over again was how all she'd ever wanted was to be a mother, and that marrying Ed was a gift because she got to quit her job and be a mother full-time. That passion for motherhood had been invoked as a defense for her meddling in every aspect of my life. I remembered when my mother told me she was getting engaged to Ed, and my first thought was: "Please, just let her keep her job." The last thing my mother needed—well, that I needed—was more free time for snooping and prying and painting the world dark.

"You're good at projects, too, Nora. That's why you were so good at that animal job."

I hadn't expected that. "How do you know I was good at that job?"

"I've read your little paragraphs, you know, the ones about the dogs and cats. You did a nice job with those. They were very— succinct. When you read them, you really had a sense of each animal's personality."

I found myself on the verge of tears. I'd never known that she read my bios. "I always thought you should keep trying to be a writer. That one year just wasn't long enough, I think," she said.

There it was, the criticism. I should have known. "The year I tried to be a writer, you told me constantly that I should get into advertising. 'Something that pays,' that's what you kept saying. Oh, and you also said, 'It's one in a million, getting published, and I love you, but you're not one in a million.' Do you remember saying that?" My cheeks burned at the memory.

She shook her head, and the sadness was back. "No, I don't remember saying that."

"You're really critical, do you know that?"

"I get worried, and then I get critical. But you need to stick with something. Even if I criticize it, you just need to stick with something. It's just not healthy for you, all the switching around. You don't want to be someone who can never really apply yourself to anything. Some dilettante. That's the worst thing to be."

I didn't even know my mother knew that word. "You always said the worst thing is to be a penniless failure."

My mother considered and then said, "You're right. That's worse."

Chapter 16

PETER

Age:	31
Height:	I don't answer those sorts of questions.
Weight:	Ditto
Occupation:	Self-employed
About me:	Personally and professionally motivated. Interested in all things unexpected. I've been studying Tantric sex; I figure if Sting can do it . . .
About you:	I'm a Virgo, so I'm fascinated by the salacious and the sordid. Tell me a great story, and I'm yours.
Biggest turn-on:	Try me.
Biggest turnoff:	Trying to force chemistry
Five things I can't live without:	I'll only tell in private.
Most embarrassing moment:	Ditto

I actually dated that guy. Briefly. He's lying about his age. He was thirty-three when I knew him. I didn't even think men lied like that, given that there's no shelf life on their reproductive organs. It's just pure vanity. Peter was one vain son of a bitch.

But he sure could fuck. That's all it was between Peter and me.

We didn't even get together until at least eleven at night, which circumvented the pesky problem of having to talk to each other. Our tryst/dalliance/affair/whatever it was ended right after Christmas. I'd decided not to go back East for the holidays, none of my local friends were around, and I figured it was better to be with him on Christmas than to be alone. At the very least, I'd get good sex. But I didn't even get that. On Christmas Day, we'd decided to make Cornish game hens, and thoroughly sloshed, we got into a fight about how to tie their little legs together. He was so verbally savage that I ended up calling Kathy, sobbing, from his bathroom. After listening for a while, she said sagely, "You know, it's not really about the game hens," which made us laugh forever after.

When I came across Peter's profile, I had been back from my New York trip for about a week. I didn't go looking for Peter. Thinking I might be rusty after my hiatus, I'd innocently gone online to read some profiles and there he was.

My response to seeing him was complicated. On the one hand, I felt embarrassed that I'd ever known such a person, let alone had sex with him (a lot). He was proof that I did not want to be back out in the dating world, trawling infested waters. I had Dan, and my trip had confirmed that was where I wanted to stay. But remembering how voracious I'd been with Peter—well, like I said, it was complicated.

I should make clear, however, that my homecoming with Dan couldn't have been better. We were thrilled to see each other, we devoured each other the minute we got in the front door, and he even called in sick on Monday to spend the day with me. But within the week, we were back to our old selves, with our old routines. *All* of our old routines.

"We have to talk," I said, sitting down next to Dan on the couch.

He lowered his book. "I'm in the middle of a chapter. Can you wait until I get to the end of it?"

"How about until you get to a section break?"

"Fine." He exhaled loudly. Several minutes later, he set the book aside. "Fire away."

"I know you think we've been coasting, but I think our car might be in a ditch." I meant it to be funny, but Dan could not have been less amused. "What I mean is, we need to pull out of our rut."

"How did it go from coasting to a rut?" he asked, with thinly veiled annoyance.

"In a way, we're saying the same thing. It's just different terminology."

"No. We're saying entirely different things. You're saying we're stuck; I'm saying we're in neutral, but we're still moving. We're still rolling forward." He did a hand gesture to illustrate the downhill progress of our car. "We're coasting."

"Well, if one person thinks things are fine, and the other person thinks they're not, you kind of have to yield to the person who says they're not, right?"

"No."

"No?" I repeated, surprised by the matter-of-factness of his response.

"No."

"Aren't we in this relationship together?"

"We are, but that doesn't mean we need to see things your way. We have a lot of good times together. There's nothing wrong with our relationship. You're just getting stuck in your head again." He stopped looking at me and stared obstinately ahead.

I was sorry to find us in such polarized positions: me wanting things to either go back to the way they had been in the beginning or to go forward toward something deeper, Dan insisting we were fine as we were. It was true; I was a bad coaster. But this time, I had a plan. I tried again. "What I was really trying to say is, we should take salsa lessons."

At that, he stared directly at me. "Salsa lessons?" he repeated incredulously.

"Maybe I should have led with the salsa lessons. Let me start over," I said, holding the bright yellow flyer up in the air. "Salsa lessons! It'll be fun!"

"You think we're in trouble, and your answer is salsa lessons."

"No, I didn't say trouble. I said we were in a rut, and salsa lessons would be a fun way to start pulling out of it." I put a conciliatory hand on his leg. "I'm sorry this conversation has gone so badly. I really just wanted us to try something new and fun together. The first class is this Monday." I paused, waiting for him to say something. "Please? We could just go to one class, and if you hate it, we don't have to go back."

He took the flyer and read it with a furrowed brow. "If I try the one class and hate it, you can't try to convince me to go back. That's the end."

"I promise." I held up two fingers in what I thought was a gesture of Scout's honor. I knew that if Dan went once, he'd be determined to master it. There was no way he'd allow himself to be thwarted by salsa dancing. It was the safest deal I could make.

"You've got that all wrong," he said, starting to smile as he repositioned my fingers. "Now I've got your word."

• • • •

On Monday night, we showed up for our first salsa class. I'd been expecting an intimate space and maybe ten other couples who—in my fantasy—were the same general age, proficiency, and comfort level as us. Instead, the class was being held in a room nearly the size of a gymnasium, but with the hardwood floors and mirrored walls of a dance studio, and we were surrounded by what appeared to be about sixty college students. There were no other couples except for Dan and me. It hadn't even occurred to me until I saw them that the class was in a Y across the street from a college; we had apparently stumbled into a university mating ritual.

"What do you want to do?" I asked Dan as I surveyed the scene. "We only paid for the one class. I guess we could leave."

"We should at least give it a try," he said. He was scanning the crowd, too. I couldn't help noticing that there were significantly more women in the room than men. Even though Dan didn't seem to be looking at any of them in particular, I felt a little self-conscious being in a room full of nubile eighteen-to-twenty-one-year-olds, many in spaghetti straps. I wished I'd worn something other than an old T-shirt and yoga pants.

"We can find another class. This was just the one closest to the house."

He rubbed my shoulder. "Relax. We haven't even started yet."

Just then, Roxy trotted to the center of the room. She was wearing a headset with a microphone so that we could all hear her. She was a trim Latina woman of about forty, wearing jeans. The jeans surprised me. I'd pictured some sort of leotard, or a skirt that fanned. Her partner was an Asian man named Thiep, which was also unexpected. She introduced herself and him, but he wasn't miked, so it was clear who ran the show. She arranged us into five long horizontal lines, and she faced us while we faced the mirror.

"We're going to start with the basic step," she said. She illustrated it while counting off the beats.

Dan and I smiled encouragingly at each other before following along: back on the right foot, hold a beat, feet together, left foot forward, feet together. When we were both able to successfully execute the most straightforward dance step in history, we smiled at each other again, this time in congratulation. So far, so good. Roxy had us do it four more times.

"That's the follower's basic step. So that would usually be the woman," Roxy explained with a smile. "But not necessarily in San Francisco." People tittered at her canned joke. Dan rolled his eyes at me. That was the one good thing about a class this size: we could have honest reactions without getting caught. "Now here's the leader's step, usually the man." She showed us the same step with reverse footwork, and we practiced that one four times.

For the next twenty minutes, we did variations on that theme. We progressed from the basic step, to the side basic. She showed us what she called "hairbrushes," where we took one arm and moved it around our heads like a halo. Dan and I exchanged sheepish glances in the mirror during our hairbrushes.

"Don't put the hip in it!" Roxy cautioned. "Right now, we just want everything to be smooth. We go forward, we go backward. We go side to side. Don't get sexy." She did an imitation of a gringo getting too enthusiastic, and all the undergrads laughed. I couldn't fault her; she knew what her audience liked. But because I had been trying to throw my hips into it, I felt a little foolish.

"I liked when you got sexy," Dan whispered to me.

"It's time for partner work!" Roxy sang out. "I need a row of leaders facing a row of followers. That means men facing the mirror, women facing the men. I see there are some extra women here tonight, so those of you who are comfortable can be leaders."

There were murmurs and laughter as people scrambled for their places. Dan and I took our positions facing each other.

"Now we're going to learn closed position," Roxy said. Thiep, who had been off to one side, now came front and center. Thiep took hold of Roxy in what seemed a fairly traditional couples-dance pose. Then he released her. "That was closed position. I'd like you all to try it."

Dan and I got into closed position. "This isn't so bad, right?" I asked.

"I'm not commenting until it's all over," he said, but he smiled.

"Now we're going to do our basics. That is, the follower will be starting with her right foot moving backward, and the leader will be moving his left foot forward. Watch." She and Thiep demonstrated. "Now it's your turn. When I get to five, you'll begin." She clapped her hands and counted off.

On five, Dan and I did our basic. Or rather, we both did the follower step. When Dan realized it was his mistake, he seemed embarrassed and muttered, "Sorry."

"It's all for fun," I said.

He nodded, looking slightly preoccupied.

Our next two attempts went better, and then Roxy explained the twist. We were going to switch partners. That is, the follower was going to move down the row to the next partner. Undoubtedly, this was to give our classmates ample chance to hit on each other.

"Well, I guess I'm off," I said, and dutifully moved down to the next leader.

"Hi, I'm Marty," he said, thrusting his hand out to shake. He looked all of nineteen.

"Nora." I smiled as he pumped my hand enthusiastically.

"Closed position!" Roxy trilled. "And on the five, go into your basic!"

I moved backward, Marty moved forward, and it seemed interminable. I didn't know how much eye contact to maintain with this clammy-handed child.

"Now rotate!" Roxy said, indicating the switch to the new partner.

It continued that way for the rest of the class: Roxy's command, introductions, closed position, clear signal of disinterest from me, basic step. Mostly I didn't need to bother with the signal, though it seemed that one of the boys liked the idea that I was an older woman who'd come to debauch him. He kept trying to catch my eye and made suggestive small talk. A few men were substantially older, and they seemed more uncomfortable than I did, though they might just have been disappointed that I wasn't one of the coeds they'd come to hunt. Or maybe they'd really come just for the lesson. Who knew?

It was still so strange to realize that forty-year-old men were in my dating pool. Sometimes I forgot I was almost thirty, since I didn't know half the things I'd expected to know, and I wasn't half as settled as I'd expected to be. Sometimes when I was riding the train, a man of about forty or forty-five would obviously be looking at me, and I'd instinctively think, "Pervert," having forgotten my age completely and reacting as I would have when I was in high school.

I glanced down the row and saw Dan in midbasic. He didn't seem to be having the eye contact problem at all. In fact, he looked pretty animated. His partner was laughing in what seemed an overly coquettish way, though I couldn't fault her for that. She didn't know he'd come there with his girlfriend; she probably thought it was a free-for-all.

I tried to see Dan through her eyes. I imagined that in a room full of old perverts and nervous boys, Dan was a fantastic catch. I mean, he was always a good catch, as far as I was concerned, but in this company, he was a shining star. I was painfully aware that the same could not be said for me.

Finally class ended. Dan immediately looked for me and we moved toward each other. His smile was definitely bigger than mine.

"Hey, you," he said.

"Hey."

"What did you think?" he asked.

"No. You first. You're the vote that matters." Even though a substantial part of me wanted to leave and never return, my pride wouldn't let me say that. Dan would have to be the one to veto the idea.

Before he could answer, I felt a light hand on my arm. I turned, and it was Roxy.

"I just wanted to see how you liked the class," she said, with a friendly smile.

"It was good." I wondered if I sounded convincing.

"It was really good," Dan echoed, seeming sincere.

"You might have noticed that I don't get a lot of couples in this class. The one I teach in the city, there are a lot more couples."

"I did notice that," I said.

"I just wanted to let you know that it's okay for you to stay together. If you'd like to," she added hastily.

"We'd like to stay together," I said quickly. I glanced at Dan to see if he was in agreement. His face was inscrutable.

"Then next week, when I say rotate," Roxy said, "instead of moving on to the next partner, you'll stay together."

"Okay. Well, thanks!" I said, pleased. "I guess we'll see you next week."

"I hope so. Thank you for coming." Roxy smiled at both of us and moved away to talk to others who had lingered behind.

As we walked toward the car, Dan was quiet. I thought of telling him my impressions about being a follower with a bunch of strangers as my leader, but I wasn't sure he wanted to hear them.

"Is anything wrong?" I finally asked.

He didn't answer right away. "You just talked over me in there. With Roxy."

"I didn't realize that. I'm sorry."

"I hadn't told you that I even wanted to go back, and you committed us with Roxy."

I waved a hand. "That's not a commitment. If you don't want to go back, we won't go back."

"I didn't say that I didn't want to go back. I just wanted the room to say what I wanted."

"I said I was sorry." I felt wounded by his interpretation of what had just happened. "I just spoke up because I assumed you wanted to be my partner. The whole point of the class was for us to be together."

"I thought the point of the class was for us to have a new experience. We wouldn't need to be partners for that." We had reached the car. He unlocked the passenger side for me, and once I was inside, I scurried over to unlock the driver's door.

I waited for him to say something else, but once he'd gotten into the car, he just started the engine and drove. After a few minutes, I burst out, "Are you actually mad at me?"

"It's not about me being mad. It's just about me noticing something."

"What did you notice?" I asked, a little fearfully.

"You're not a very good follower. I don't mean that you're a bad dancer. You were pretty good at the basic, and I thought that hip swivel was nice." I expected him to smile when he said that, but he just went on. "But you're not a good follower. You know how Roxy said that the leader is supposed to let the follower know when the dance is starting by moving his body forward just a little? Well, you didn't wait for the cue. You just started."

"Because I knew which beat we were starting on."

"That's not the point."

"I'm sorry that I talked over you, and I'm sorry that I didn't follow you the way you wanted me to. If you want to quit the class, we can quit. If you want to keep going, I'll try to do better next week." There was something in Dan's steady way that made me feel worse than when other men attacked me directly. "Okay?"

Dan's mood seemed to change then. He reached for my hand, and I gave it to him gratefully. "Nora, will you be my salsa partner next Monday?"

"I will," I said. There was no other answer I could give.

· · · ·

That night I got an e-mail from Candace, my first client. She'd gotten engaged. She said she was sure I had other success stories, but she thought I'd like to know about hers. She hoped it wouldn't be too weird to invite me to the wedding, and she wanted me to bring my own success story with me. It took me a minute to realize she meant Dan. I'd forgotten my white lie about meeting Dan over the Internet. I'd stopped telling clients that story a long time ago.

It was strange how far away that meeting with Candace seemed. It had only been a few months. And soon Dan and I would be celebrating our one-year anniversary, if we were lucky.

Chapter 17

NORA

Age:	29
Height:	5'6"
Weight:	130 lbs
Occupation:	Writer?

About me: I haven't tried my hand at one of these for a while. My own profile, I mean. The last time I wrote one for real was when I was hoping to meet someone like Dan. I wrote it honestly, in that there were no untruths. But it didn't really say who I was. It was just a collection of cute anecdotes, moments, and factoids, like that I try to watch the National Spelling Bee every year. But since I'm writing this as an exercise in clarity (and with the hope that I'll never have to post one of these again), it'll read a little differently.

The plain truth of it is, I'm scared a lot. I'm afraid of losing what I have, of wasting my life, of not appreciating anything enough, of never getting anywhere, of being left behind. In my relationships, I've always eventually reached a place where I looked around and said, Is that it? Is that all there is? Once I said yes, it could only be the end. I don't want that to happen anymore. I don't want to keep losing, but I don't know how to win.

About you: This is where so many profiles read the same. Who doesn't want their mate to have a good sense of humor? Or to be intelligent? Or kind? I guess I'm lucky, because I can say without hesitation, Dan is all three.

He also has my favorite hair of any man I've ever been with. It's thick and black and would be perfect except for one cowlick, and that's actually what makes it perfect. And he smells great. Not like cologne; like Dan. He smells like autumn, and I love that.

The sensory is an important part of a relationship. You especially realize that when over time, you touch so much less and things fester so much more. In the beginning, you might feel annoyed and then sex gives you a completely clean slate. Or you're so lifted up by your sexual connection that little annoyances can't even reach you. Good sex can give you immunity.

I also love that Dan is solid and a straight talker. Even a few days ago, when he got upset with me at salsa class, he told me so right away and then it was over. By the time we were home, he was fine. I mean, I'm no fool. I realize that his follower comment is about how I am all the time, not just in salsa class, but he doesn't walk around resenting me. I've had that happen before, and it's awful, and Dan just isn't like that. He doesn't let his feelings percolate for days. He just takes a long minute to collect himself and he speaks up. That's a pretty rare quality in a lot of ways. Most people don't have Dan's willingness to take a minute; it requires self-confidence and discipline. It would be easier to either go off half-cocked or say nothing. And the bigger part of that is that Dan knows himself. I bet he could write his profile in about ten minutes, and when he re-read it, he wouldn't make a single change.

But I sometimes wonder how well Dan knows me. For example, he thinks the fact that I have too much free time is to blame for my meta-life. What he doesn't seem to realize is that my meta-life doesn't take additional time at all; it's the soundtrack that plays while I'm doing other things. And he seems to think if I just took certain steps, I could exorcise my meta-life for good. But the fact is, as much as I like to pretend otherwise, my meta-life *is* me. Love me, love my meta-life. I'm not sure he does. Then again, I'm not sure he should.

Fuck it, I'm going on to the next question.

Five things I can't live without:

1) Love. Obviously love. If you're writing honestly, what else could claim the top spot?

2) Sex/Passion

If I never had sex again, that would be undeniably bad. The problem for me is that in monogamous relationships, my desire for sex can drop so low that it seems like I actually could live without it completely. Like, if I didn't know I was supposed to want sex, it would be perfectly fine to never have it again.

But when I remember the early days with Dan, what stands out most to me isn't the sex itself. It's the fact that whole days seemed like foreplay. Walking in a park and brushing against him and feeling the tingle of arousal, a pang that wouldn't be satisfied for hours. By the time we got in bed, we'd been aching for each other all day. Now sex seems so abrupt. We're still affectionate with each other during the day, but something has changed. Sex is no longer an inevitability. It seems so optional.

And salsa class isn't helping any. I thought proximity plus rhythm would have us panting for each other, but it's not working out that way. I had this image of us smelling each other's sweat and getting animalistic, but we never do anything long enough to get sweaty. Try something twice, and then we've got Roxy shouting at us to rotate. If I never heard that word again, I'd be a happy woman. We've gone to three classes now and we haven't had sex after any of them. We're both just trying so hard not to mess up, and there's nothing sexy about that. We might as well be taking couples' calculus for all the charge we're getting out of it. Instead of breaking us out of our routine, now Monday-night salsa class is the routine.

3) Knowing I'm consistently loved and desired. Being grounded by love. Compatibility. Stability. These things matter.

Maybe all of this should actually fall under #1. If I assume that "love" as listed at #1 is the love that I want, it encompasses these other things. Why is so much of my list about love anyway?

Because the right love leads to kids. And I know kids are on the wish list. If only I could put them on layaway, get on a five-year plan like Dan with his book-bar, know that they'll definitely be there someday when I'm ready . . .

Dan would be a great dad. He'd be kind and unflappable and playful. He comes from a good family, a family where they like each other. I can already see him barbecuing with kids running barefoot through the yard. I just can't tell if I'm in the picture.

But I'm only twenty-nine. There's time. I'm sure there's time. There has to be.

3) So, final answer: kids (someday).

4) Something more significant than a job, more flexible than a career

5) A sense of forward momentum, even if it's only an illusion

I was supposed to meet Hunter, my next dating profile, at 7:30, but he called to say he'd have to change it to 8:30 PM or reschedule for another day. After a whole day of inconclusive self-exploration, I needed the reprieve of diving into someone else's life, so I agreed to meet him at a café around the corner from his apartment at the reappointed time.

I'd never met a Hunter before. I didn't know if I found the name appealing or affected. I was much clearer about the man himself.

When the man who was definitely Hunter came through the door, my jaw nearly dropped. He inspired immediate attraction. It sounds ridiculous, but it was something in the way he scanned the crowd. It didn't hurt that he bore some physical similarity to Jude Law: dark blond tousled hair, blue eyes, and a long lean body in a T-shirt, blazer, and jeans. It was crowded and loud in the café. One of the baristas greeted Hunter by name, and he shouted something friendly back, then resumed his search for me.

His search for me. I couldn't believe what my stomach was doing in response to the notion that Hunter was looking for me. *He's looking for you so that you can help him look for other women. And you're with Dan. You belong with Dan.*

I waved and Hunter made his way over. He maintained a wide smile during the trip. "I can't believe you got a table!" he said.

"I got here early. I've been reading."

"What are you reading?" he asked, leaning in curiously.

I lifted it up so he could see the cover.

"That's a good one," he said. He rapped his knuckles against the table. "What can I get you?"

"I'm set." I pointed to the empty espresso cup in front of me.

"Wow. You're tough. It's a strong pour here." He remained standing. "Would you mind if I grabbed something? I actually haven't had a chance to eat today."

"All day?"

"Well, not for a long time," he amended, with a smile as if I'd caught him in a lie.

I smiled back, transfixed. I looked down at my book to break the moment.

"I'll be right back," he said, energetically loping into the line.

I watched him for another second, then tried to return to my book. I was a little shaken by the encounter, and by the visceral response I was having to Hunter. Since Dan and I had been together, I hadn't really been attracted to anyone but him. I wasn't the type to fantasize about other people during sex with Dan; I was more the type to just want Dan less. I was a serial monogamist, true, but the monogamist part was always in the foreground.

I took deep breaths to steady myself. The line was moving slowly. Hunter glanced back at me occasionally with an apologetic expression. I waved my hand to let him know it was okay.

Being attracted to other people is completely normal. Being so freaked out by it is what's abnormal. I had largely convinced myself of this and even gotten a few pages of reading done when Hunter returned to the table with a bagel, a muffin, and a cup of coffee.

"I know. I'm the picture of good health," he said, taking his seat opposite me. He started opening packets of sugar and dumping them into the coffee. "I get engrossed in a project and I lose track of time, space, biological urges. It's a terrible quality. Don't put it in there." He pointed at the notebook I'd just removed from my bag.

I laughed. "I'm not so sure it's a terrible quality. What do you do?"

"I'm a software engineer."

I almost said, *You're kidding.* Same as Dan. "And you're really into it, huh?"

"I love it." He started to peel the paper bottom from his muffin. "I like to eat backward. Always dessert first."

"Really?"

He shook his head no. "For some reason, I just really wanted to get at this muffin. I hope it doesn't seem too impolite that I'm eating?"

"Not at all."

"So how did you get into this line of work? Being a profiler?" He said "profiler" with a devilish narrowing of his eyebrows.

"I just stumbled into it, I guess." It was surprising how few people tried to make small talk with me during these sessions. I realized it was probably my demeanor. I was always shooting for pleasant professionalism. I didn't necessarily succeed, but at the very least, I created enough of a boundary that people almost never asked me personal questions.

"It seems like such a fascinating service to offer. You can dig around in people's hopes and idiosyncrasies and then craft those into something other people will want to date. Fascinating."

"Are you British?" It came out more suddenly than I'd intended.

"No. You're not alone in asking me that, though. I don't have a British accent at all. It's my diction." He was devouring the muffin at an alarming rate.

"Oh. Because being British would have increased your market value."

"So we're on to business. Just like that." He gave me a mischievous smile. "That's fine. I just thought we'd start in earnest when I was done eating. But let the profiling begin!"

"No. I didn't mean that. Let's wait until you're finished." My face flushed.

"You live in San Francisco?" he asked, without missing a beat.

"No. Oakland."

"I love Oakland."

"What do you love about it?" I gave him a slightly bemused look that I realized a second late was flirtatious.

"The bars. They're more—rugged." He was moving on to the bagel. "I'm a big fan of blues and R and B. Go on, laugh. Everyone finds that hard to believe, but it's true." He leaned in and said in a low voice, "You know you want to laugh."

He was right. I did want to laugh. I couldn't picture Hunter in that scene at all. "I can't laugh when you're telling me to laugh. It's like someone shouting, 'Be spontaneous!' You just can't do it."

"Well put." He struggled to spread one of those too-frozen pats of butter on his bagel. "Let this bagel be my lesson not to get too caught up in my work. But back to you. You live in Oakland, you help people find love. That sounds satisfying."

He didn't seem to be making fun of me. In fact, he had very

benevolent, very beautiful eyes that were fixed on me. "It's not a bad life," I said.

"Have you helped people find love? I mean, do you know your track record? I'm not asking that because the answer would bear on our business here; I'm just curious."

"I actually got an e-mail recently from a former client who's engaged. She wants me to go to her wedding." His attention was turning me on, and I was sure he must be able to tell. I wanted him to stop looking at me and let us get on to business, and I also wanted to be pinned there in his spotlight for all eternity. I knew I should get this profile done and go home as soon as possible. There would be nothing at all wrong with whetting my appetite with Hunter and feasting on Dan. Even Dan wouldn't think so. Not that I'd tell him. "Can I ask you something?"

"Of course." He took a large bite of his bagel and chewed it for what seemed like a hundred times.

"Why did you call me? I mean, why do you need my services?"

He looked at me quizzically. "That's an unusual question."

He was right. I hadn't asked that of any other client. But they weren't like Hunter. "You don't need to answer. It's really not relevant." I looked down at my pad.

"I've lived in San Francisco for about a year, and I spend the vast majority of my time working. I'd place an ad without your help, but I'm an appalling writer." He spread his hands. "That's it."

"I didn't mean to put you on the spot."

"It's what we're here for, right? For me to be on the spot. It's not where I'm most comfortable, which is why I've been peppering you awkwardly with questions. So I'm the one who should apologize."

"Not at all." I almost reached out to touch his arm, but with great effort, I stopped myself. "I'm the one who was awkward. It was just a role reversal for me, and I didn't adjust very gracefully. You'd be surprised how few people I meet have any curiosity about me at all."

"I am surprised by that."

"Clients, I mean." My blush deepened.

"That's surprising, too."

We smiled at each other; then I said, "Well, I guess we should start working."

"I think what you'll find is that I'm naturally more of a listener than a talker, so I hope this won't be too boring for you." He drained his coffee cup. "Your move."

I did find that Hunter was more of a listener than a talker, but he was the most charismatic listener I'd ever seen. It was like how Bill Clinton in his prime used to listen to people: he listened with his entire being. I asked questions and Hunter always answered them, but somehow, I was talking more and more. Unlike any other client I'd worked with, Hunter inspired equal disclosure. He showed me his, I showed him mine. We'd traveled to some of the same places, and realized we'd both lived in Boston at the same time and frequented some of the same bars and restaurants. Neither of us spoke Spanish well, and both of us wanted to improve. We'd both had roommates with fat cats (though Goliath could have eaten Romano). No big revelations, nothing earth-shattering, just two people laughing and chatting in a café until closing time. Just two people out on what looked like a really great date, except that occasionally the woman jotted down something in her notepad.

Hunter helped me into my coat. "There's a bar around the corner."

"I should really get home," I said.

He looked at his watch. "It's only eleven."

I bit my lip. I really wanted to spend more time with him, which was exactly why I shouldn't. But I hadn't felt sexual energy coursing through me this strongly in a while, and it affected my judgment. "Okay," I said impulsively.

We went to a dark bar around the corner. It was the kind of place that seemed like it would disintegrate if direct sunlight ever penetrated the interior. There was a long bar, and velvet couches scattered throughout. There seemed to be lots of nooks and corners with their own small love seats or couches. On two of them, couples looked like they'd been making out for hours.

You can't do this. You need to go home.

I ordered Absolut Mandrin straight up. Hunter laughed—I guessed at the boldness of my choice—and ordered a gin and tonic. Holding our glasses, we wandered through the bar, checking out the available real estate until we chose a corner couch. I downed my drink quickly. I wanted my inhibitions lowered and my meta-life turned off. I wanted Hunter, and the only way I could have him was blind drunk. I considered ordering another, but was self-conscious about the kind of impression that would make.

He was sipping his drink slowly. "So how do you think the profile will turn out?"

"Good. You're an easy sell." Why was he talking business now? Because that's what this was. A business meeting. *You met him to transact business, that's all. You did not come here to*—I wouldn't allow myself to finish the thought.

"It occurs to me that if this goes badly"—he gestured from himself to me and back again—"it could also go badly for my profile."

I fixed him with what I hoped was a sexy/challenging stare. "I'm a woman who can separate business from pleasure." I'm really not. But playing the femme fatale was getting me even more turned on. I was feeling the vodka.

He met my eyes directly. "You have a boyfriend, don't you?"

I didn't answer, but my act dropped away in an instant.

"The way you keep pushing me away and pulling me in, I can tell. You don't know what you want."

But I did know what I wanted; I just didn't want to want it. I didn't want to want Hunter. And I wanted him bad. Emboldened by the vodka, I said it. "I want you to kiss me."

"Well, why don't you kiss me then?" He watched me, his lips slightly parted.

I didn't move. I wanted him, but I wanted him and the alcohol to be responsible. Here he was, calling my bluff. Could I actually do this?

I must have waited too long. "Maybe you should go home." He said it matter-of-factly, then took another sip.

"I probably should." But I couldn't move then, either. I was throbbing for Hunter, but now I had a picture of Dan in my head. I could still kiss Hunter. I could still make this happen.

No, I couldn't. Not unless I drank a whole bottle of vodka. That was the only way I'd get Dan out of my head now.

I gathered my coat. "I'm sorry."

"Don't be sorry," he said. He was smiling. "It's been a pleasure, Nora."

"I'll have the profile to you in a few days."

He lifted his glass to me. "I'll be interested to see how it turns out."

Chapter 18

HUNTER

Age:	32
Height:	5'11"
Weight:	160 lbs
Occupation:	Software engineer
About me:	I'm more listener than talker, and I'm inclined toward fascination. I've been mistaken for British, without actually having a British accent. Intriguing, eh? I intend to have a dog and improve my Spanish. I should have stayed longer in Chile. I work too hard, which means I don't read as much as I should, and I pledge to work on all these vices for the right woman.
About you:	I'll show you around the blues clubs in Oakland, and introduce you to all the baristas at my favorite café. Around me, you'll realize just how captivating you are.
Five things I can't live without:	A vivid fantasy life, my passport, my work, my future love, my future dog
Last book I read:	*The Book of Laughter and Forgetting*
Biggest turn-on:	Not knowing where the time's gone
Biggest turnoff:	Weak coffee

I crept in the apartment past midnight. I'd had a breath mint and was sure I didn't smell like vodka, but I suspected I smelled like something. Like longing for someone else. Like longing unfulfilled. Like regret about walking away from Hunter. Like guilt about feeling regret.

Maybe I smelled like that.

Dan was in the bathroom in his underwear, his hair askew, brushing his teeth. Watching him, I felt the strangest sadness, like nostalgia. I stood behind him for a long moment, wanting to touch him, to smooth his unsmoothable cowlick, but I feared that somehow that would tell him everything.

He swished water around in his mouth and spit. "How was your night?" he asked, his eyes meeting mine in the bathroom mirror.

"It was a job," I said. "I'm really tired." I left the bathroom and sat down heavily on the bed. I could still see into the bathroom from there. Now he was flossing. My sweet Dan. How rare it was to find a man who actually flossed, and used a tongue scraper so that his breath would be fresh.

On the car ride home, I'd tried to decide if I should tell Dan. It wasn't that much of a story, really: I was attracted to someone else; I didn't act on it; I drove home; nothing had changed. I still wanted to be with Dan, and I was always questioning. Same old story. But did he deserve to know? Did he deserve to know that I intentionally had placed myself in a compromising position so that Hunter would kiss me, and then I chickened out? Because if Hunter had kissed me, I don't know what would have happened. The odds were good that I would have kissed him, at the very least. I didn't think I would have gone so far as to sleep with Hunter, but I would have wanted to. Did Dan need to know that

I'd had those thoughts and feelings? Would he deserve to know if Hunter and I had actually made out? If I had stopped it before we had sex? If we had sex?

I rode that slippery slope the whole way home, and I was nowhere near a decision. There'd be no harm in waiting a few days to clear my head and then telling Dan. As much as I hated keeping secrets, as tempting as it was to confess to Dan, I said nothing. In bed that night, when he ran his hand up my thigh, I yielded. It seemed the easiest thing to do.

• • • •

The next night, I was relieved to be meeting Larissa and Sonya for dinner, even if Sonya's mood was markedly different from mine. Her cheeks were rosy with happiness. Palance was almost ten months old, and this was only her third time out without him.

"Driving the bridge to get here, I thought, 'This must be what it feels like to make a successful jailbreak.'" She bit into a piece of bread. "It's crazy. All my sensations are heightened. And you know what I keep thinking?" She didn't wait for a response; she was too giddy. "There's not a baby in this restaurant. Just pleasant, adult conversation. We don't go out to restaurants much anymore, but when we do, they're all baby friendly. So if your baby's not crying, someone else's baby is. And we're all very sweet and tolerant about it, because we want the same treatment. Well, if someone in here attaches a human being to her boob, I'm going to march up and say, 'Put that thing away!'" She looked around, but there were no exposed boobs to be found. She smiled at us joyously.

I tried to return her enthusiasm, but couldn't. I had been antsy all day waiting for this dinner. I didn't want to talk about anything other than my situation with Dan, because once I got their opinions, I could finally either take some action or forget about it. I'd been out of my head all day, wondering if Dan really did suspect and he'd just been playing it cool; then thinking that if he didn't suspect, that made it all the worse. In the latter scenario, Dan became a baby deer that didn't know there was a Hunter nearby.

Oh, God. I was punning. In my distress, I was resorting to the lowest form of humor. Or were limericks lower? I'd never heard a black pun before, but if ever there was one, mine was it.

So here was Sonya, up in the clouds, and then there was Larissa. She just looked, well, perplexingly serene. Looking back and forth between them, I couldn't hang on another minute.

"I'm freaking out here," I said. "I didn't want to just jump into it. I wanted to wait and observe normal social graces, but I can't."

Neither Larissa nor Sonya looked particularly surprised. Concerned, yes. Surprised, no.

"It's real this time. It's not in my head. I almost cheated on Dan." As I said that, I realized that the crisis was still in my head, because I hadn't cheated. And I hadn't cheated because when Hunter put the ball in my court, I stepped out of my body and back into my head. I was too much of a head case to even cheat properly!

Now Sonya and Larissa were surprised. "That doesn't sound like you," Sonya said, with what sounded like reproof.

"Well, the 'almost' doing it sounds like her," Larissa said. "She has a commitment problem."

Now it was my turn to look surprised. Since when did Larissa make concise diagnoses of her friends, then calmly butter her bread? "What's happening here?" I demanded, indicating Larissa's countenance.

She seemed to understand just what I meant. "I made a break-through in therapy, and things have been much clearer since."

Sonya clasped her hands together. "That is so great, Larissa!"

"It is. It is great." Larissa took a swallow of water.

"What was the breakthrough?" Sonya looked at Larissa eagerly. While I was desperate to get back to my own situation, I did want to know when Larissa had been replaced by a pod.

"I quit therapy." Larissa could see that we were waiting for more. "That was the breakthrough. I quit. I've felt worlds better since. I decided life is not about self-awareness. It's about being decent and honest and saying, I need what I need and I'm not going to question those needs. So I haven't been. I need a man. I know how anti-feminist that is. And I don't care. I am a far happier person with a man than without one, and I'm not going to pretend otherwise." Larissa was getting more and more animated as she went on. "I *love* watching poker tournaments on TV. Why do I act like watching TV is for losers? Why judge myself for that? No one but me ever gave a shit about my TV-viewing habits, but I'd be sitting alone in my apartment beating myself up. It didn't change the fact that I was watching TV; it just made my experience way less pleasurable. And therapy was definitely making my life less pleasurable, so I quit." Her eyes danced with ebullient defiance.

Now I was stuck with two of them. "Well, my life's not pleasurable and I'm not in therapy," I said.

"Because you're doing therapy on yourself all the time. The analysis. The assumption that all the struggle should add up to something." Larissa's condescension was seriously starting to grate. "It's like I said, you have a commitment problem. You're always thinking yourself right out of everything. Like the way you thought yourself out of cheating on Dan."

"You thought she should cheat on Dan?" Sonya asked.

"I was just using it as an example."

"You don't even know the story yet," I said, offended.

"Tell us the story," Sonya mollified.

"It's not much of a story," I admitted. "I met this client named Hunter last night, and he was really, really sexy. I was literally weak in the knees from the moment I saw him. We were getting along really well, and he suggested we get a drink."

"What an asshole," Sonya said.

"What an operator," Larissa echoed.

I shook my head. "He didn't know about Dan. I hadn't told him. I mean, obviously I knew I should say no, but I really wanted to go." This was the part where I started to squirm. "And I basically did a shot the minute we got to the bar."

"You were setting it up," Sonya said. "We've all been there."

I nodded miserably. "I was sitting there hoping he'd kiss me, knowing I shouldn't be doing this, which made me want to do it more." They nodded in solidarity. "And he calls me on it! He asks if I have a boyfriend, says he could tell by the way I've been acting, and says that I should be the one to kiss him."

"Again, what an asshole." Sonya looked disgusted.

"But he didn't do it like an asshole. He was putting me in the position to decide what I really wanted."

"And you didn't really want him," Sonya said, relieved.

"It's not that simple. I did really want him. I wanted him from the minute he sat down with me at the café. But I couldn't make the move."

"Because you love Dan, right?" Sonya prompted.

"I don't know. I mean, I know I love Dan. I just don't know what really stopped me. And I don't know whether I should tell him or not."

"You should tell him," Sonya said.

"You shouldn't tell him," Larissa disagreed, with equal certainty.

I looked back and forth between them, waiting for them to make their respective cases.

"You should tell him because he has a right to know," Sonya said. "It's not a matter of whether you went through with it. You seriously considered being with this other guy, and he should know that."

"I've been thinking that, too," I said. "I guess he has the right to decide whether he wants to stay with a person like me."

Larissa shook her head emphatically. "No. Think about it. If you had slept with someone else, that would be new information for Dan. But there's no new information here. Like I said before, this is just another example of your commitment problem. It's not some indictment of your character."

I didn't know whether Larissa had just insulted me, or defended my honor. "But is it that I can't commit, or that something is wrong with Dan and me?"

Larissa shook her head again, continuing her reign of condescension. "You're a serial monogamist, Nora. That's when it comes to jobs, boyfriends, cities, you name it. Not when it comes to friends, though. There you're true-blue." She paused to smile at me before continuing. "But the other stuff—a lot of the time you're in it, you're agonizing about whether you should stay. I'm not trying to hurt your feelings. I just think you make your life so much harder than it needs to be."

"You always have, too!" I said to Larissa passionately. With her sudden shift, I felt bereft. It was like losing a sister.

"It's not like it's the worst thing in the world, being a serial monogamist. I mean, look at the divorce rate. It's an epidemic." She deflected my comment expertly, like the lawyer she was.

"It's true," Sonya said. "Serial monogamy is the new philandering."

"What does that mean?" I asked her.

"It means that for people who have problems with commitment, it's easier to be a serial monogamist than to be alone or to keep cheating."

"So you think it's my problem with commitment, too?"

"Well," Sonya hesitated, "there might be some evidence to suggest it."

Our food arrived, and we started eating silently. Larissa and Sonya seemed tentative. They probably thought they'd been too hard on me. I wasn't sure if they had or not. I only knew that I didn't want to talk anymore, and that I was no closer to an answer.

* * * *

The most prudent course, at least for the time being, was not to tell Dan. Larissa was right. There was no new information in it. Dan knew my ambivalence already. It was my job to figure out what the Hunter situation really meant.

But it wasn't easy looking Dan in the eye when I got home. I still didn't feel right touching him, and positioned myself at the opposite end of the couch. We made awkward small talk: I told him about Larissa's transformation, and about Sonya's excitement at being sprung from her house. The conversation plodded along, and he listened attentively. I felt awful. I now understood those magazine articles that said people who confessed their affairs weren't doing a kindness to the other person, they just couldn't take the guilt.

Soon we'd exhausted our conversational reserves. Maybe sensing that I needed some levity, Dan suddenly went into monkey paroxysms. He whooped and beat his chest. He pretended to juggle. He added a few pratfalls. All he wanted was to make me smile, and the display was depressing the hell out of me.

I didn't feel like playing Mrs. Pimmbottom just then, but I made a halfhearted attempt. Seeing that my heart wasn't in it, Dan finally fell back on the couch. He was actually out of breath. It was one of his most acrobatic Rodney performances yet. I wondered if it was wounding to him that after all that, I hadn't fully played along.

We were all out of talk, Rodney and Mrs. Pimmbottom hadn't worked, and I realized, with great sadness, that we didn't know what to do with each other just then. It dawned on me that Rodney and Mrs. Pimmbottom had become our default mode of interaction when we couldn't be bothered to be us. I remembered when the characters were a sign of how close, safe, and intimate we were. Playing together was a kind of intimacy, but the more we lived out our silliness, the less we were available for adult intimacy. Because while Dan found me funny as Mrs. Pimmbottom, he surely didn't want to fuck Mrs. Pimmbottom. See, it wasn't just me that was getting lost in this relationship; it was us.

Suddenly it seemed imperative to tell Dan what had almost happened between Hunter and me, to get him to finally see that we weren't just coasting, we were stalling.

"Dan, I have something to tell you." He looked at me expectantly. "Last night I went out for a drink with my client and I almost kissed him. I didn't, but I wanted to."

I waited nervously for his reaction. His face belied nothing. Five minutes passed. Even for Dan, that was a long time.

"Do you have any questions for me?" I finally said, when I couldn't bear the silence a second longer.

"Is that how this is supposed to go?" I'd never seen Dan's face so cold. "You tell me you almost cheated, and I pump you for the details?"

"I don't know how this is supposed to go. I haven't been in this situation before."

He stood up. "I'm going to spend the night at Fara's."

"Don't you think we should talk about this?" I asked helplessly.

"No. I don't."

"Why Fara's?" Bart had moved out of Fara's apartment, and I knew she'd always had a thing for Dan. I could picture her settling him in the guest room (my old room!) and then finding her way in there in the middle of the night. The image made me feel sick. Was that his point?

"Because she's my friend, and she has an extra room."

No, that hadn't been his point. Because no matter what Fara did, Dan would stay faithful. Dan knew how to make a commitment, the bastard. I loved and hated him profoundly in that moment.

"I'll be back on Monday to pick you up for salsa class." Had he actually just said that? I stared up at him in shock. Then I realized: We'd made a commitment to Roxy. Now he was making his point.

"Can I call you?"

He sighed. I saw what an effort it had taken him to be so contained for the past few minutes. "No. You can't."

He left the room and I could hear him pulling luggage from the top of the closet. I collapsed against the couch, terrified and numb.

Chapter 19

DAN

Age:	34
Height:	6'
Weight:	175 lbs
Occupation:	Network engineer
About me:	Honest. Decent. Too good for Nora Bishop.
About you:	You're not Nora. Be nothing like Nora.
Biggest turn-on:	Truthful women. Women who can be trusted. Women who can get out of their head once in a while to appreciate what's right in front of them.
Biggest turnoff:	Nora Bishop
Five things I can't live without:	Fidelity. Trust. Reliability. Dependability. Sanity.
Most embarrassing moment:	Letting Nora move into my apartment

Dan didn't say another word to me. He wouldn't even look at me.

Once he was gone (*once he was gone, oh, God*), I wandered through the apartment, dazed. He had to come back, right? I mean, this was his apartment. That was his bar. He might leave me, but he couldn't leave the bar for good.

No, he could just kick me out. I could soon be homeless. How would I get another apartment? I hadn't been saving very much each month; my whole standard of living had been predicated on my cheap rent with Dan. I'd spent my Derek windfall. I didn't have the first month's rent, last month's rent, and security deposit I'd need to get an apartment of my own. Even if I humiliated myself by borrowing the money from my mother (*oh, God, talking to my mother*), I wouldn't be able to pay my own rent and bills each month on what I was currently making. I'd have to answer an ad for another Fara. I could have just sent myself back to my pre-Dan life: a roommate I hated, a cat that waddled, despair over ever finding someone as wonderful as Dan.

What had I been thinking, telling him that? Oh, God. I hadn't been thinking. My meta-life had crapped out on me at the most inopportune time, when I had a secret to keep. The one thing my meta-life usually provided me with was a sense of caution. The more I thought about it, the more insane it seemed. I had just thrown away my relationship because Dan tried to make me laugh by acting like a monkey.

Why hadn't I thought through the ramifications? Why had I acted so rashly? I mean, the first and most obvious ramification was that instead of changing our dynamic, Dan would never want to see me again. Once he got some time away from me, he might realize that I was more trouble than I was worth. Me and my meta-life. Me and my self-doubt. Why should he put up with a woman who couldn't just be happy and secure in what she had?

I was too distressed to cry. I couldn't seem to activate any sort of release valve. I just kept thinking: *you lost him, you lost him, you lost him,* on a continuous loop. Finally I couldn't take it anymore. I took two sleeping pills, and when that didn't work, I took a third. This was not a suicide attempt; it was a desperate measure to stop the barrage in my head. It worked. I slept.

The next day was one of the worst of my life. I woke up groggy and instinctively reached for Dan. It flooded back to me, what I had done and the possible consequences, and that's when the tears started. I cried for hours, pummeling myself mercilessly. *You, with your juvenile need for excitement. You, with your ridiculous expectations. You and your fear of commitment. You and your inability to coast. Why couldn't you just coast? You stupid, stupid bitch, why didn't you just coast?*

I wanted to call Dan every minute. I wanted him to call me every second. I carried the phone into the bathroom with me just in case he called while I was in there. He never called. Of course he never called.

I wondered what he was doing just then, if he could focus at work, if his calm had given way to rage, if he had just shut off his love for me like a faucet. I believed he could do that. He had that kind of emotional control. I, on the other hand, had none.

I can say that those first twenty-four hours afforded me a clarity of thought, feeling, and purpose I'd never experienced before. All I wanted was for Dan to come home. Every last fiber of me was in agreement. I ached for him, 100 percent. I missed him to the *nth* degree.

"I'm dying here," I moaned to Kathy on Thursday night, exactly twenty-four hours since Dan had left. I had barely left the bed except to sniff Dan's clothing and to microwave bowls of oatmeal that I couldn't eat. I had my laptop next to me, and had been logged on to my e-mail all day. Just about every five minutes, I'd been clicking the "refresh" button to see if anything from Dan had appeared. It never did. I thought it never would, but I couldn't stop. Recrimination, then "refresh;" more recriminations, then "refresh." It was the most soothing self-flagellation.

"I know what you mean," Kathy said. I knew that she, of all people, really did get it. I had not fully appreciated her suffering when it came to Stephen before this moment. "But it's the uncertainty that's killing you. You don't know whether to hope or to grieve. But by Monday, you'll know."

"I can't do it! I can't make it until then!" I wailed.

"What option do you have?"

"To call him and tell him I can't take it."

"No. That is the one thing you can't do. You can't force his hand. Remember when you were a kid, and you'd nag your mother for an answer, and she'd say, 'If you need an answer right now, your answer is no'? It's the same principle here. You push for certainty, and you'll get certainty, and you'll be sorry."

I sobbed openly then.

"Oh, Nora," Kathy said softly.

"I want him to come back. Why won't he just come back?" I gurgled through my tears. "I need him to come back . . ."

"I know you feel that way now, and I know that you love Dan. But you've nursed me through some dark hours, so know that I'm saying this because I truly love you. You made the choice to tell Dan. You were that desperate for something to change. You were that desperate to never hear Dan make another monkey noise. I know it hurts now, but you need to maintain some perspective."

"No! I made a mistake! It was a mistake, and I need to call Dan and tell him that. I need to take back what I said."

"Listen to me. You know I hate hearing you suffer, and I'd do anything I could to make this hurt less. But you have to suffer on your own. You can't ask Dan to relieve you of it. I'm telling you, if you don't respect his decision not to talk to you right now, you will lose him."

I couldn't answer; I was still crying too hard. But I knew she was right. Whatever strategies I came up with to make it until Monday, they couldn't include calling Dan. "Could I e-mail him?" I whimpered.

"NO!" Kathy took a deep breath, then said in a deliberately hopeful voice, "He's still willing to salsa dance with you. That must say something."

"It says he honors his commitments. We told Roxy we'd be there. See the symbolism? *He* honors his commitments."

"You honored your commitment. You had a guy who looked like Jude Law—Jude Law!—just waiting for you to plant one on him and you went home to Dan. You had a perfectly ordinary moment of weakness, and if Dan can't forgive you for that, he doesn't deserve you."

"Thank you," I choked out. "Though now that I think about it, he didn't look that much like Jude Law."

"So you've got about four days until you see Dan. During that time, there is nothing you can do to change the outcome, right? So you can spend it abusing yourself, or you can spend it doing something productive. Have you started writing your article?"

"What are you thinking, asking me that? I'm in pain here."

"Some of the best writing comes out of pain," Kathy said helpfully.

"I can't think straight, let alone write." I balled up a tissue and threw it across the room. It landed softly among its fellow wads.

"When you can't think straight, that's the perfect time to start writing. Do something you can lose yourself in."

"Why are you suddenly on a mission to make me write?"

"Because your life is more than Dan. I just think you should recognize that."

"I don't think I have much to say about bridges right now."

"Then write something else," Kathy said. "Do *not* spend the next four days crying and moaning. I beg of you, do not do it. When Dan comes to pick you up, let him see that you're a strong, worthwhile person, not a quivering mess."

"And how are you?" I asked abruptly, in a feeble attempt to emerge from my self-absorption. "How's Matt?"

"We're fine. We're good," she said. "Now go write."

I considered her advice. Then I clicked "refresh" and took sleeping pills. The next day, I woke to insistent knocking on the door. After a few groggy seconds, I bolted upright. Dan! I looked down at my nightgown and touched my tangled hair. I didn't want him to see me like this, but I wanted nothing more than to see him. I practically ran to the door, and that's when I heard the baby crying. My disappointment was so acute that there were tears in my eyes when I opened the door.

"Nora," Sonya said. There were probably few more pathetic sights than me, and her eyes were filled with sympathy. I was so pathetic, in fact, that she didn't even seem to be paying attention to Palance's screams. Her maternal instinct had a greater target for the moment.

"Hi, Sonya," I said. I was ashamed of my current state, and more ashamed to have brought it on myself.

"Could we come in?" she asked.

"Sure. Of course. Yeah." I moved aside self-consciously and she walked in.

"This is nice," she said, and I remembered she had never been here before. "Masculine, but nice." She surveyed the living room. "That bar is—"

"Yeah, I know, it's beautiful," I cut her off.

Now she looked a little embarrassed. "I'm sorry, I guess you don't want to hear me talk about the apartment."

"No, it's not that. I'm just—I'm going crazy here." I gestured toward myself. I wanted her to know that I knew. I mean, I was starting to smell. I had a knot in my hair that I'd probably have to cut out with scissors someday. "As if you can't tell, right?"

"Is it okay if I put Palance down and let him explore a little?" she asked.

"Sure. Yeah. You can do whatever you want." I sank down on the couch, and she put Palance on the floor before sitting down beside him.

"I should have called first, I know. I just thought you might not answer the phone, and I was kind of worried about you. From what Larissa said—"

"I was kind of a basket case when I talked to Larissa." I laughed in spite of myself. "As you can see, I've come a long way."

Sonya laughed, too; then we looked at each other for a long minute. "I wanted to tell you I'm sorry for the bad advice."

"What?" I asked, confused.

"For saying you should tell Dan. I feel kind of responsible for what happened here. I mean, obviously you really love Dan and want to be with him and that's the important thing. I talked to Chris about it, and—"

"Sonya, you've got nothing to be sorry for. I made the decision on my own to tell Dan. A split-second decision that's mine to regret, not yours. And I do regret it. I've been doing nothing but regretting it." I was about to cry again. "I fuck everything up, Sonya. Why do I fuck everything up?"

She moved to the couch beside me and put her arm around me. I leaned into her gratefully and wept. It felt good to be touched; it seemed to suggest that I would be touched again someday, whatever my current situation was, however momentarily repugnant I was. After a few minutes, I stopped crying. That's when I noticed that Palance was crawling toward us, his own eyes dry and bright. The boy was pure possibility.

"God, Sonya, he's magical, isn't he?" I said.

"Sometimes I really think so," she said as we both watched his progress.

Chapter 20

While I showered, Sonya went through the cupboards and refrigerator to find something for me to eat. It felt good to be clean and wearing a bra, but there was a certain disorientation to it, too; I imagine it was a little like the first day out of the sanitarium. I wasn't sure I was fully out yet, but I had an afternoon pass.

Sonya offered to make grilled cheese, which she knew was comfort food for me, and I took her up on it while I sat holding Palance. Dan never left my thoughts, but he receded a bit.

Sonya stayed the whole afternoon. We watched bad television, and spoke whatever came to mind. Finally she said she should get back home, but she said it regretfully. We hugged tightly at the door.

"I've really missed you, you know?" she said.

I hadn't known. I'd thought her life was full, with Palance and all those Mommy & Me friends. "I've really missed you, too."

"You're going to be okay. He's coming back, or someone better is coming along. I swear, that's how it works."

I nodded, and we smiled at each other. I leaned in to nuzzle Palance. "Thank you so much for coming here."

"We were glad to do it, weren't we, Palance?" His hands were entwined in my hair, and she extricated them gently. She obviously expected him to protest, and when he didn't, she jiggled him up and down happily. "Did you see that? He didn't even cry."

"Another milestone."

I watched her walk down the hall, my smile fading. One day down, three more to go.

. . . .

Alone again, I plunged back into fear and sadness. Despite Sonya's optimistic theory that either it would be Dan or someone better, I was sure there was no one better, and that Dan's very goodness was the reason he was likely to never be with me again. Dan would leave me, and I'd burn in the hell of my own making.

These sorts of thoughts dogged me into the next day. I knew I actually needed to do something, take some sort of action, and I had resigned myself to the fact that it would not involve contacting Dan. I had also resigned myself to the fact that he wouldn't be contacting me before Monday, which meant I only checked my e-mail every half hour. I tried to follow Kathy's advice and lose myself in writing, but it was no use. My mind was a minefield that I couldn't escape. Then it came to me, on a whim, and it seemed so obviously, thoroughly right that I couldn't believe it hadn't come to me sooner. I'd find Sonora Watson, someone who knew the meaning of life.

The perfection of my plan was confirmed by how easy it was to locate her. Just a quick Internet search, and I had her phone number and address in Napa. I dialed with only the vaguest idea of how to introduce myself ("I'm a big fan!" might smack too much of Kathy Bates holding James Caan hostage), but I figured my very earnestness would speak volumes. Sonora had been a therapist and would probably want to help someone like me, and as a writer, she'd like knowing she had touched someone so deeply. Good for her soul, good for her ego. It seemed foolproof.

But the line was busy for the next hour. With my tolerance for delayed gratification at an all-time low, I finally decided just to get in the car and drive. Napa was only an hour away, and a jaunt through wine country could be just the thing. I decided to hurry, since she was clearly home right then (hence the busy signal), but if I waited too long, she might leave and I'd miss my chance. If she didn't want to talk to me, I wouldn't make a fuss or a scene; I'd just apologize and leave. In my gut, though, I felt she would want to talk to me, that she'd relish the chance to share whatever it was that she knew and that I needed to learn. Then I could tell Dan and he wouldn't want to leave someone who was prepared to love him so well and so completely.

The day was gray and misty, but that's how Napa looks best. I drove past lush vineyards in the foreground, verdant hills in the background, thunderclouds threatening overhead, and I wished Dan and I had taken that weekend trip we'd once talked about. But we would. We would take the trip someday soon. I would make sure of it. I wouldn't lose him.

The directions took me to a modest suburban neighborhood. Somehow I'd pictured her in a more rural part of Napa, tending to her horses when she wasn't writing. But no matter. I peered out at the numbers, identified a small ranch-style house as hers, and parked across from it. There was a car in the driveway, which was promising.

I crossed the street and rang the bell. After a minute, I tried the brass knocker. After a longer pause, I tried both at once. And again. Then I stood for a long time, accepting that she either wasn't home or wasn't answering the door. It seemed I'd need a new game plan.

I got back in my car and tried calling her from my cell phone, thinking that maybe I could leave a message, explain who I was and what I wanted, as succinctly and sanely as possible. The line was busy. Did that mean she was inside and not answering the door because she was still on a call? It seemed like an awfully long call. And who in this day and age didn't have call-waiting? Well, she wasn't of my day or age, which was the whole point of coming out to talk to her, so she could be forgiven for that. Should I let a little time lapse, and then knock again? Or call again? Or both?

The longer I sat, the less appropriate my behavior seemed. The more it seemed a bit—unhinged. And Sonora had spent her life working with the mentally ill. Maybe she was burned out. What if I wasn't the first mentally ill person to show up on her doorstep? Maybe that was why she'd stopped answering her door and her phone.

Here I was, staring at an ordinary house, in an ordinary neighborhood, that belonged to an ordinary woman—not the keeper of love's mysteries, not salvation itself. What was I doing? This was the act of a woman who had come untethered. There was not one area in my life that was secure, sturdy, beyond reproach. Perhaps that was the slot I'd wanted Dan to fit into, and now he was gone. Dan was gone, and I was a stalker. And I wasn't even stalking Dan; I was stalking a stranger because I was too afraid to stalk Dan.

After crying piteously into my steering wheel, I realized I had nothing left to lose. Dan wasn't e-mailing, he wasn't calling. He was obviously through with me. There was no reason to hold anything back. He couldn't be more lost to me than he already was.

I dialed his number and reached his voice mail. I knew I should hang up, save myself, but I couldn't. Through tears, I said, "Hi, Dan. I know you didn't want me calling you, and I understand why you're not picking up. You probably screened me. Or maybe you're out somewhere, doing something. I tried to go out today and track down this short-story writer who I thought had the secret to love. Isn't that crazy? I think I'm going utterly crazy. I can't even tell you how lost I am right now, and how much I love you, and how much I . . . Oh, fuck. I'm so sorry, Dan. I'm so sorry for almost kissing that guy, and for telling you about it in such a stupid way. I'm sorry for being the kind of person who does those kind of things. Because I want to be better for you. I want to be as good for you as you are for me. I'm rambling like this, because I can't take not knowing if I ruined everything for good . . .

"But what just occurred to me is that I have to take it. I can't ask you to make things easy on me. That's how I got into this mess in the first place. Our relationship had gotten hard, and I never know how to handle it when things are hard, and I fill up my head with bullshit thoughts, and I fill up your voice mail with my bullshit ramblings, because I can't fucking stand to face myself. I can't fucking stand it . . . But I'm going to leave you alone, and I'm going to find a way to stand it, because that's how much I love you. I love you enough to face my shit this time around, and I'm not running away, okay? I'm not. I'm going to give you the space you asked for. Even though I want you to call back so much and distract me, I need to be in this until Monday. I need to do that for us, and I hope you know I'm sincere. I want to be better. And I hope we come out the other side on this, but if we don't— well, okay. I'm going to hang up now. Don't call me back, please. I love you."

I was breathing deeply, trying to return to my body, when I was startled by a knock on my window. I peered out, and it was a man of about sixty, with a concerned look on his face. I rolled down the window.

"Are you okay, ma'am?" he asked.

I wiped at my face, though the tears had already dried. "I'm fine."

"You've been sitting out here awhile, and I just wanted to make sure you were all right."

"Yes, thank you." I tried to smile at him. "But actually, could I ask you something?" He nodded. "I'm an old friend of Sonora Watson's. Do you know her?"

He tilted his head. "You mean the woman who lives there?" He pointed at Sonora's house. "Grim-faced? Witchy hair?"

"Well, I've never seen her grim."

"I'm sorry. I don't mean to speak bad of her. I don't know her. No one around here does. We're a friendly block, for the most part, but she really keeps to herself."

"Maybe she's been sad." I thought of telling him about Sonora losing her husband, but I didn't want to invade her privacy any further. Besides, maybe the story wasn't true. Maybe it was just the fantasy life of a grim-faced woman.

The man nodded politely.

"Well, I should get going. I don't know what time she's getting back. I just thought I'd surprise her."

"I don't think she goes out much. That's her car." He gestured toward the driveway.

"Oh." I looked at the house, thought of the busy signal. "I guess she doesn't want to be disturbed."

"You'll be okay to drive? I mean, you're sure you're okay?"

"I'll be fine."

"Have a good day, now. A better day." He smiled in at me.

"Thank you. You too."

I was glad he approached me. That brief talk had anchored me somehow, reminded me that I was in the world, and that it could be kind. I started up the engine, thinking that maybe I'd write

Sonora a letter. I wouldn't say I'd ever been here. I'd try to send her a dispatch like the one I'd just had, let her know it was safe to come back out now.

• • • •

My message to Dan had been a promise: a promise not to let myself off the hook too easily, and not to indulge in any of my usual mental tricks to avoid true self-investigation. I needed to understand how—despite the faux self-awareness of my meta-life—I had landed here again.

Self-excavation is a daunting task. It would have been a lot easier to let myself keep crying, or to keep beating myself up for my failures. Looking at my past and my present with cold, clear eyes—that was the most brutal of all. But I was determined to do it, and to stay in it no matter how hard it got.

The next two days were excruciating. I wrote harder than I ever had, in every sense of the word. I didn't know where to start, so I just started. Then I kept going. And somehow through the pain—through my disappointment and anger and sometimes even self-hatred—I also felt prouder of myself than I'd ever been. I was pushing myself further than I'd ever gone, and whatever the outcome, I'd have that.

But I wanted to have Dan. Even though I told him not to call or e-mail, I was still hoping for some smoke signal. Finally, on Monday morning, he sent an e-mail confirming that he'd pick me up for salsa class at 6:30 PM, and that we could talk afterward. That was all. No mention of the message I'd left, or even a statement that he was looking forward to seeing me . . . Was he really so cold? Had he stopped loving me so completely?

Well, in a matter of hours, I would know. Until then, I could fall apart in my fears, or I could choose to keep writing. Dan could choose me, or not. Either way, I needed to make sure I wouldn't end up back here again, not at my own hands. So I kept writing.

It was fast approaching six-thirty, and I wasn't done, but I'd gotten somewhere. I had a sense of what I'd tell Dan later that night, but no idea how he'd respond. He'd given me no clues about what he was thinking, and I was suddenly terrified.

Right at six-thirty, he knocked on the door. I guess I should have figured that he wouldn't use his key, but I still felt a jolt of sadness. I stood up, so nervous that it was actually hard to walk. My hand shook slightly as I reached for the doorknob.

I ached, seeing him there. There was a long moment where neither of us knew what to do with the other, and it was agonizing. We didn't move, we didn't speak. Until, finally, Dan said, "Hi."

"Hi."

"Are you ready to go?"

Give me something. Anything. Was he a sadist? Did he want me to suffer? Would it be wrong if he did? I wanted to tell him, I've already been stewing in it. Stewing in me. I've never put myself through anything like the past few days, ever. "Let's go."

We drove to class in silence. I needed to let him handle this his way. I needed to let him lead, much as it killed me.

Class started predictably, with everyone in horizontal lines, practicing their basic step. I watched Dan in the mirror; he didn't seem to be watching me. My body was on autopilot, my mind jumbled. I had so much to tell him, and I didn't know if I'd get the chance, if he'd even want to listen to me. I'd started to figure myself out, at least a little, and he was the one I wanted to tell all my discoveries.

Finally, mercifully, Roxy directed the leaders to form their line facing the mirror, and followers to form their line facing the leaders. I wanted to believe that once Dan had his arms around me again, he'd have to relent. Until I knew otherwise, I'd believe that.

When Roxy gave the order, I leaped into closed position. He held me stiffly, and we smiled at each other with painful awkwardness. I made sure that I waited for his signal before starting to move, even though his signal came a few beats late.

"Now rotate!" Roxy said.

The ponytailed woman to my right came up smiling, expecting me to move on. Four weeks and these co-eds still thought Dan was up for grabs. Only now, was he? I turned to Dan, my heart thumping. *Please say it. Please.*

"We're staying together," Dan finally said.

I smiled at Dan with relief, wanting to believe that something had been settled. He smiled back uneasily, as if nothing had. I tried to think what to say as Roxy and Thiep took center stage.

"We're going to learn the cross step now," she said. "Watch closely; then I'll break it down for you." She and Thiep did a combination that ended with Roxy facing the opposite direction. But I didn't know what else had happened. I couldn't concentrate; I just wanted to step closer and breathe Dan in. "Now watch again," she instructed, and she and Thiep repeated the maneuver, slower this time. She explained what she was doing on each beat. They broke apart, and Thiep demonstrated the leader's part; then Roxy demonstrated the follower's part.

"Okay, now everyone start in closed position. Try doing a full basic before moving on." Roxy lifted her hands, about to start clapping.

Dan took me in his arms, and I noticed the preoccupation on

his face. It occurred to me that he didn't want to make a fool out of himself in front of me anymore, that the intimate space between us had closed that completely.

I blinked back tears as we started to move. Dan didn't do the full basic before going into the new sequence. I followed him without saying anything. But it was clear his footwork was wrong and he was using too much force to help me cross over. I felt like a rag doll being yanked around.

He stopped moving. "Sorry," he said, avoiding eye contact.

"It's okay," I replied softly.

"Rotate!"

I waited for Dan to say the magic words—I desperately wanted to hear them again—but he didn't seem to notice another follower had come to claim her place. "We're staying together," I finally told her. She actually looked to Dan for confirmation, which made me want to wring her scrawny little neck. He nodded, and she went around us.

We were partners for the rest of class, but not like I wanted us to be. We alternated mistakes: One of us messed up nearly every time and apologized, and the other absolved politely, and all that courtesy served to underscore the distance between us, even as we held each other. There was no laughter. There was no ease.

As we walked back to the car, Dan said, "So we'll go back to the apartment and talk?" There wasn't much of a question in it, just grim recognition that there was nowhere left to go, nothing to divert us from the inevitability of what was to come.

"Yes."

After what had just transpired between us, I thought there was only one possible outcome. The car ride was the equivalent of a gangplank. But I fought to remain hopeful, to recognize the artificiality—fuck, the actual insanity—of the situation we'd just been in. When Dan and I made it out of this, we'd laugh about it. *Salsa class?* I'd say, poking him. *Next time we're contemplating a breakup, let's enter a shuffleboard tournament.*

I was the one to unlock the front door; he was still playing the visitor. He followed me into the apartment, and we took our places on the couch as if prearranged. He was sitting against one arm of the couch, I was flattened against the other. It was the furthest apart we could be and still be on the same piece of furniture.

"I guess I should start," Dan said. He rubbed his hand across his face, and I could see how exhausted he was. That felt like the most he'd let me in all week, and there was hope in that.

"Please."

"I got your message. Christ, that was a long message." He didn't smile. "I listened to it twice. The first time—it was intense. I was so mad at you, dumping all your feelings in my lap, but I also hated hearing you hurt like that. My first reaction was that it was you being selfish again, same as always. It's always about your meta-life, and your feelings. You've got more feelings than—" He shook his head. "But then I listened again a day later, and I thought, 'Shit. If this girl actually does what she says she's going to do, that would be the fucking bravest thing. Whatever happens, I'd be proud of her, you know?'" At that, he teared up, and so did I. But I didn't talk. I needed to let him finish. "I don't have an answer for you. I know what I want, and that's to be with you. But I don't know if I can anymore."

I broke down into sobs. Without looking at him, I knew he wanted to reach for me. He wanted to help me. And I knew, also without looking at him, that he was still sitting right where he had been. Finally I gathered myself. I had to tell him what I'd been realizing about myself, the whole truth of it, even though it was just as likely to make him go as it was to make him stay.

"Thanks for saying that. That it was brave, I mean. I've been writing for days. Practically nonstop. It's been crazy, but it's been good. I just picked a place to start, and at some point, I could see my own logic. I could see my own downfall. And I wanted to stop, because it was awful, but it was kind of weirdly exhilarating. It was like I was a safecracker, but I was also the safe, you know?" I looked at him, and he nodded. "When I left you that message, I was sitting outside this stranger's house. I'd gone there with the idea that somehow, she was going to help me find a way out of this mess, out of myself. And it turns out, she might be this total fucking depressive hermit. Which isn't the point, really. The point is that I went looking for her because I thought she'd be the magic bullet, just like I thought salsa class would be the magic bullet, and then maybe I thought leaving you that message would be the magic bullet, and halfway through, I finally got it. There's no magic bullet.

"We both know I've got a lousy track record when it comes to working on things. When things get hard, I decide it's because I'm doing the wrong thing. I'm in the wrong relationship, or the wrong job, and so if I go on to a new one, I'll be happy. I say it's that I don't want to waste my time on something that's not right, but I think what I'm really afraid to do is admit that something can be right and still not last forever; I don't want to commit to something or someone all the way, and lose someday, in some way that's completely out of my control. I always want to be the one choosing, and I always want a definite answer, and what I'm starting to realize is that the only way you ever get a definite answer is when it's a no. Because if I say yes, someday it might turn into a no—a yes can always turn into a no, but a no stays a no, if you know what I mean." Again he nodded intently. "I came up with this image while I was writing today about how I've always been someone who'd amputate her arm sooner than live with arthritis. I'd rather cut the thing off than accept that sometimes on rainy days—or worse, for no reason at all—it's just going to ache. And I'd never realized that before, not in those terms."

He was still just watching me, so I continued. "So my whole life, I've been asking whether whatever I'm doing, whoever I'm with, is right or wrong for me. And the irony is, the question is what's wrong. Everything's going to be wrong at least some of the time. Relationships are boring sometimes, and they can be tedious, and you wonder who the hell you are and who the hell he is. The question is: Can I live with that inevitability? Can I have strength and faith that someday, if I want it enough, I can turn it around?"

Being Dan, he waited me out. Fucker. "And the answer is, I don't know. I've never really done it before. I've always acted like a victim of my thoughts and feelings, like there was nothing I could do once the love started to fade. But the thing is, I'm onto me now. I started to see through my shit this weekend. Like, after you left, I was overcome by emotion. I just loved you so much, it was overwhelming. I didn't leave the bed for two days, I loved you so much. And what I now realize is, I created a whole drama to get the old feeling back again, to make things intense again, to amp everything up. But if you come back, that's not how things will stay. Everything can't stay heightened; soon we'll be normal again. I don't want to spend my time finding ways to make our relationship artificially high, avoiding us. I feel like I'm seeing you, and us, clearly, and I know I want to be with you. You said you don't know if you want to be with me and I can understand that, but you should know that I do want to be with you."

I was done. I kept my eyes steady on his and finally he said, "I do want to be with you. I just don't know if I can." He shifted his gaze away from me, then back. "Sometimes you really put me through it, you know? This was the worst, but in some ways, it's also more of the same. I need to be able to count on you."

"I want you to be able to count on me. I want to be able to count on me."

"How do I know you won't give up on us again?"

"Because I didn't give up on us. I got to the edge, and I stared over, and I came back. All I can do is tell you that I want to do this, and that I'm determined to try. I'm not going to expect you to pull me back from the edge anymore; you don't need to talk me down. That's not your job. It's mine. I get that."

He sighed. "Maybe I'm just looking for guarantees here. And like you said, there aren't any."

"No. There aren't."

"Nora," he said, his voice suddenly suffused with pain, "you hurt me. Do you get that? Do you get how much you hurt me?"

Truthfully, until he said that, I hadn't. I hadn't seen it in him the night he left, and I hadn't known what to make of him tonight. I hadn't wanted to assume anything about what he felt. "I didn't really get it. But I'm sorry. I'm really, really sorry."

We were both crying. I wanted to reach across the couch to him, but it still felt like crossing the Delaware. All this self-confession, and we were still so far away.

"I realized some things, too," he said. "These past few days, I realized that I'm not always the easiest person, either. I can be stubborn and sometimes I've put you in a bad position by acting like everything in our relationship was fine, and that you were crazy if you couldn't see it. I turned your doubts into a character flaw. And I don't always let you know how much is going on inside me. I mean, I've been breaking apart this past week and you didn't have any idea. I just retreated." He paused. "So we've both got work to do. The question is, do we do it together or not?"

"You're the one who's not sure."

He laughed. "Well, that's new."

I laughed, too. "I guess it is."

"So, no guarantees."

"No guarantees."

He reached for my hand, almost experimentally.

Chapter 21

NORA

Age:	29
Height:	5'6"
Weight:	130 lbs
Occupation:	Writer/reviser
About me:	A work in progress. Currently learning to: tolerate uncertainty; salsa dance; balance play and passion; enjoy middles.
About you:	You are the much sought-after triad of intelligent, funny, and kind. You have great hair. You smell like autumn. You're a straight talker and you don't hold a grudge. You mix killer cocktails. You're confident enough to take a minute before you speak. You know it's not just you and it's not just me; it's us, and we're worth the work.
Last book I read:	*Writing Down the Bones*
Biggest turn-on:	Not being afraid to let ourselves be changed, especially for the better.
Biggest turnoff:	Rigidity (not to be confused with routine)
Five things I can't live without:	Love. The ability to jump-start passion when it lags. Struggle. Contentment (not to be confused with stasis). Kids (someday).

Most embarrassing moment: Almost losing a relationship because of a
                               monkey impersonation

We were in our single-file rows facing the mirror, practicing the leader's basic, then the follower's. I was enjoying being part of the chorus line. We did it long enough that I could put more hip action into it and fancy myself a salsa queen. Dan and I smiled at each other's reflection as we went back and forth, back and forth.

Then we moved into partners work. Dan and I faced each other and dutifully got into closed position. During the review of last week's steps, somehow, magically, we were able to get it right the first time. But Roxy picked up the pace that day.

"Focus, people, focus," she exhorted as she taught us three new combinations in rapid succession. She and Thiep executed the first, and she didn't even break it down before she had us trying it. When she wasn't demonstrating, Roxy was tapping what looked like a wooden cane against the floor instead of just clapping and counting off. I thought of it as her "get serious stick." I'd had a course in college with a professor everyone knew to be a drunk; when he sobered up on week four and realized how much material he'd missed on the syllabus, suddenly it was triple time. Roxy didn't seem to be a drunk, but something had lit a fire under her.

Dan and I couldn't keep up. We hadn't fully mastered the first set of combinations before it was time to go on to the next. We tried to stay upbeat, but we felt like complete clods, which wasn't either of our idea of a good time. In that class, I definitely saw the benefit of being a follower; it seemed like our success or failure was more dependent on him than on me. "It's okay, it's okay," he said every time we faltered, but he was talking more to himself than to me. When your boyfriend turns into Rain Man, you know dance class has gone awry.

We weren't the only ones messing up. Roxy finally slowed down, did another demonstration, then had us practice it three times in a row. Each time, Dan and I couldn't seem to get past the second step of the combination. "You need to step back on that beat," I finally diagnosed, trying to camouflage my rising frustration.

On our next time through, when the screwup came predictably on the second step, we stopped dancing completely, while the rest of the class twirled around us. Of course, they were all twirling completely out of sync with one another; it was impossible even to tell which was the right beat by looking at that class. But we were the only ones to stop moving.

"I'm trying," Dan said, his face tight.

"I know. I'm just trying to help. Let's do it again." I offered myself up in closed position.

"Let me think a minute." He raked a hand through his hair and looked around, trying to figure out exactly where the error was coming from. Again it was nearly impossible to tell by looking at everyone else.

Roxy appeared at our side. "Show me what you're doing," she said, clipped but not impatient.

We started dancing awkwardly, self-conscious at her attention. Once again, we were off on the second step.

"You're going too early. You're going on the four instead of the five." Roxy was indicating me. "Let me show you." I stepped back, and she stepped into Dan's arms. "Now lead."

And he could lead. Maybe Roxy was just making him look

good, but they executed the combination on the first try. I watched, embarrassed. So it had been my problem.

Roxy said brusquely to Dan, "You need to lead more strongly." She addressed me. "And you. You need to follow more. No pushing. It doesn't work in salsa. You need to take what comes." I nodded, chastened. "Now try again."

"Let's do this thing," Dan said, smiling.

This time, we made it through. Our form was probably terrible, but we'd finally hit all the marks. We shared an exultant glance.

"Very good," Roxy said. She raised her voice, "Everyone, again!"

· · · ·

The bar around the corner was crowded with college kids. No one was even checking IDs (not that we would have gotten carded). I spied a table, and said I would grab it while he ordered my drink at the bar.

"Rum and Coke?" he asked.

"That sounds great."

I claimed the table just before another couple could. I smiled at them apologetically, and they turned away without acknowledgment. Ah, the social graces of youth.

When Dan came to the table, he had a beer for him and a glass of wine for me. "No hard liquor," he said apologetically. "Just beer and wine."

"Once we're regulars, you'll need to carry a flask."

"I'm on it." Dan slurped the foam from his Guinness and surveyed the room with bemusement.

"Remember being this young?" I asked. "I can't believe I just said that, but look at them." At the pool table, a girl who couldn't be more than eighteen had arranged herself into a position of near obscenity. She was presumably making a shot, but she held the pose for so long that it was clear what she really wanted was to bend across a table with impunity.

"Not that well, actually." I was pleased to see that Dan's eyes were grazing the room and didn't land on the girl at the pool table.

"Really? When I'm someplace like this, it all comes back to me. How great and how awful it was at the same time. It's a blessing and a curse to have so many possibilities. You know what I mean?"

"I think so." He reached across the table for my hand. "Our anniversary is next week."

"I know. We made it." I leaned in for him to kiss me. It was fun to be in this bar full of kids, tonguing each other at the table. We broke it up sooner than we would have if we were actually their age. As he drew back, I asked, in true eighteen-year-old style, "What are you thinking right now?"

"Remember in class when we stopped dancing?" he answered slowly. He didn't seem to realize that I had been teasing him. "Well, I was just thinking how easy it was for everyone else to keep dancing because they don't know each other. They don't show each other their frustration like we do, because they don't have any history. They're polite, and they want to make an impression. In some ways, it's easier for two strangers to keep dancing."

"That's probably true."

"And because they keep moving, you can't tell exactly what's wrong with them. Like, Roxy came over to us because we'd stopped dancing, but if we just kept going like everyone else, she wouldn't have."

"But then we wouldn't have learned that I was going too early." I said it lightly, but I still felt a little embarrassed about my arrogance in telling Dan what to do.

"It was a good thing she came over because we were getting

kind of tense, but next time, I think we should just keep moving and we'll figure it out ourselves."

"We could practice at home, too. That could be fun."

"Sure."

"Maybe we could go salsa dancing on our anniversary. Go public."

He laughed and shook his head. "Some things need to stay under wraps."

. . . .

"Tonight it's club soda only," Larissa said. "I want to stay sharp." Her eyes roamed over the scene, which wasn't promising. They'd lowered the lights, but we all still knew we were on the tenth floor of an office building. The office building that housed a Jewish singles service, to be more precise. Larissa adjusted her name badge and smiled around generically.

"I still can't believe you got me to come to this with you," I said.

"I needed to make sure I'd have someone to talk to. You're my sure thing, in case there's no one interesting."

"There's no one interesting." The women outnumbered the men two to one. Most of the men seemed socially inept and those who had even a modicum of charm were cutting a wide swath through the women.

"I see a few I wouldn't mind talking to."

"The same few all the other women want to talk to?"

"I didn't say I had great odds." Larissa realized she was leaning against the wall in a way that was less than inviting. She straightened up and took a sip of her drink. "Friendly and available, that's what I'm going for here." She glanced at me, almost coyly. "So when are you going to help me revise my profile?"

"I was starting to think you'd never ask."

"Yeah, well. I had to maintain some pride."

"Pick a night next week and it's yours."

"Thanks. I mean, there's got to be a trick I'm missing. Look at this . . ." She gestured toward the room, trailing off dispiritedly. Then she smiled at me and said, "You know, it's okay. We can leave whenever you're ready."

Larissa had continued to make strides since breaking it off with her therapist. Lucky for me, the serene goddess act had slipped away. But she was still at peace with doing things like watching poker tournaments while eating gummy worms and drinking tequila sunrises. (I never asked how she stumbled upon that particular winning formula.) Most important, she didn't beat herself up for feeling like she needed a man. Sometimes she got depressed about not having anybody; sometimes she worried that it would never happen for her. But mostly, she was prepared to do what it took to get what she wanted, even when it led her to places like this. I had to respect that.

"Let's stay a little longer," I said. "This is my first mixer. Don't you want to show me a good time?"

"Stop calling it a mixer."

"I think it's a funny word. This whole thing feels so 1955 to me."

"You're right, it is." She was looking at one specific man, who was failing to make eye contact with her. "So what's going on with you?"

"On Sunday, Dan and I will have been together a year." I announced it proudly, then realized it was a somewhat dubious accomplishment for someone my age.

"That's right! That's so great. Mazel tov!" Larissa exclaimed, loudly enough for people nearby to glance over. "The first year's the hardest," she added. "That's when you make a map of the territory."

"What does that mean?"

"By the end of the first year, the blinders are off and you see what you're really dealing with. You've done your scouting, and now you've got a map of the territory: all your faults, all his faults, what you like about you as a couple, what you don't. So at the end of that first year, once you've got the map, you have to decide whether you actually want to go forward and explore. It's like, you know you're going to have to work at things, but you've decided the discoveries are worth it."

I nodded, smiling to myself. "I like that. Dan and I have our map now."

"I've got to say, I was worried about you for a while. I didn't want you to lose a good thing."

"I'm glad I didn't lose him, too."

She smiled at me. "So that's it, then. You're sticking." I looked at her blankly.

"Blackjack terminology. You like your hand and you don't need any more cards. You're sticking with what you've got." She laughed. "I, on the other hand, could use a hit."

"You'll get one. But not here."

"You're right. Let's go." Larissa smiled at me, and arm in arm, we headed for the door.

· · · ·

When I pushed open the front door, Dan sat up, blinking rapidly. He'd fallen asleep on the couch and now he had the startled, unkempt look of a hatchling.

I perched beside him and tousled his already-tousled hair. I liked him like this, uncomposed and childlike. "So I guess I know what you did with your night."

He glanced at the clock. "Just a quick catnap. But how was yours?"

"It was an awful scene, just like we knew it would be."

"Why does Larissa go to those things?"

"She likes to have them on the calendar. Something to look forward to."

He nodded and yawned.

"I'm tired, too. We could go to bed early." I snuggled beside him on the couch, still wearing my coat.

"First, we have to dance." Dan forced himself alert through a split-second act of will.

"Now?" I whined.

"Remember, we agreed to practice." He got to his feet.

"Hey, that was my idea. It's not fair to use it against me." I tried to burrow more deeply into the couch, but he started pulling me up. I continued to protest, mostly in jest.

"I bought us some music." He ran to get the CD player remote, and went through the selections until he got the one he wanted. Salsa music blared. "Sorry," he said, turning the volume down. He helped me out of my jacket, laying it on the arm of the sofa, and assumed his dance position.

"Is that what you did tonight? Shopped for salsa music?" I was still hanging back. The music seemed awfully fast, and my body felt leaden.

"Mostly I mixed drinks. None of them were quite right. I'm trying to come up with something really special for our anniversary."

"What are you calling it?"

"That part's not going so hot, either. I thought of combining our names: the Dora or the Nan."

"Ick."

"I know. I thought we could come up with the name together."

"How about Map of the Territory?" I suggested.

"That's a little long, isn't it? What does it mean anyway?"

"I'll tell you later. Right now, let's dance." I felt a renewed burst of energy, and stepped into his arms.

"Okay. Just give me a second to find the beat." He was bobbing his head just slightly. It was clear he didn't realize he was doing it, which made it all the more endearing. Finally he cued me to start my basic step.

We messed up within seconds, and then started over, laughing. "This music is really fast," I said.

"We've just never done it to music before. It's always been Roxy's syncopation."

"I hope she gets rid of that stick soon."

"And a one, and a two, and a one two three . . ."

We started again, with the same result. But Dan urged me, with his body, to keep going.

We tried out the various combinations from class, with frequent returns to basic. *Whatever happens, we'll always have basic.* But when Dan tried to lead me into the cross step, we botched it so thoroughly that we came to a halt.

"Let's just make up a few of our own," he said, lifting his arm for me to start twirling. As he led, I did my best to follow. We were lousy, and we were laughing.

"Just keep moving."

About the Author

Five Things I Can't Live Without was born when Miami mated with unemployment. If you've already finished the book, it might seem an unlikely spawn, so allow me to explain.

In early September 2005, I was headed for a cheap, end-of-summer vacation in Miami. The destination might seem strange, since I live in Berkeley (a bridge away from San Francisco) in California, state of legendarily beautiful beaches. But California beaches are something of a bait-and-switch: Undeniably gorgeous, but even as far south as San Diego, the ocean can chill your bones. Miami has no such handicap. What it does have is a hurricane season, starting right about Labor Day, which no one thought to mention. But I was thirty years old, and by that age, no one's obligated to tell you anything. Which is the best and the worst part about being thirty.

Well, I dodged a hurricane and the lasting impact of the Miami trip came in the unlikely form of beach reading. I'd never read chick lit before, but I wound up being delighted by my starter book. Sweet, vulnerable, winning, funny, insightful—all the things I'd want my writing to be, if I still wrote. But I hadn't written a creative word in years—I'd dropped my dream of being a writer to study marriage and family therapy—and I wasn't planning to. That's where unemployment comes in.

At that time, I was a social worker, a job that was intended to tide me over until I got to do therapy full-time. While I didn't have the grand epiphany in Miami that I couldn't stand my job, there is undoubtedly a relationship between getting away from my job and suddenly quitting it several weeks after my return. And there is undoubtedly a relationship between quitting my job and Nora quitting hers in the first chapter of the book. If nothing else, I knew where to begin. I knew a little something about the trifecta of liberation, fear, and hyperanalysis, and that thankfully, at least some of the time, it could be funny.

Chick lit came back to me with three weeks until my temp job started. I had some time to kill and a meta-life to occupy so I started working on the then-untitled *Five Things I Can't Live Without*. The more feverishly I wrote, the more I realized that chick lit was the perfect vehicle for exploring what had always been my primary interest and passion in life: relationships (with lovers, friends, colleagues, and most important, with ourselves). Turned into the best job I ever had. I'm just hoping it's not temp.

Holly Shumas

Five Things
I Can't Live Without

1 My computer. Fortunately, it's not just for googling anymore (though nothing beats a good google every now and again).

2 A mother who carries a printout of my book cover in her purse and shows it around like it's her grandchild. A father who, when I was sixteen, drove me to the office of a literary agent to personally deliver my (unsolicited) manuscript (and did a pretty good job of seeming surprised when it was rejected).

3 A CD player in my car. If I'm driving, I'm singing. Badly.

4 Love that's friendship, and friendship that's love.

5 At least five more spots on this list. It turns out I'm one of those shifty sorts who, if given three wishes, would wish for three more. But what about sugar/alcohol/guilty pleasures, my elliptical machine (to counteract my guilty pleasures), meandering conversations, a reach that exceeds my grasp, Trader Joe's . . .?

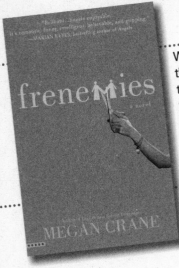
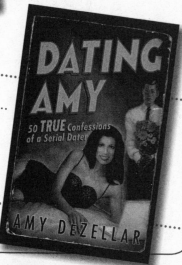